What They Are Saying About No Darkness

Well written, fast paced, wonderful characters, and the fascinating setting of a country in decline turned into a police state. There's much to like in this interesting hybrid of action, thriller and romance. **LaWrence – author of Skipping Stones Along The Kìchì Sibi**

No Darkness

by

Mark Morey

Mark Morey

http://markmorey.blogspot.com

Copyright ©

978-0-9944171-7-6

Published In Australia

March 2017

No Darkness

Mudiwa lay on his back in the grass. All was perfect in the world. He glanced to Rudo lying beside him. "Rudo…," he said, and then he remembered last night's conversation.

She looked at him and their eyes met.

"Rudo, kunaka chikomba wangu," Mudiwa said.

She smiled brightly. "Kunaka hanzwadzi wangu," she replied.

They lay on the grass in silence: Mudiwa's pretty lover, Rudo's handsome cousin.

"I like you," Rudo said quietly.

"I like you too," Mudiwa replied, and then he rolled onto his side to admire his beautiful companion.

"No!" Rudo said, moving to sit cross-legged. "I like you but I can't put it into words. I have such strange feelings. I crave you even though we're together like this. It's confusing and I don't like to be confused. But it's a beautiful feeling too, and I don't want to lose it." She punched his shoulder. "I hate you for what you've done to me. You've put me under a spell; you've done strange things to me."

"I have the same feelings, which is why I come to see you every night. Every day, all I can think of is being with you for the night."

"Are these nights enough?"

"Without these nights I don't know what I'd do."

"You didn't answer my question."

"No," he said quietly. "They're not enough."

"Why do we feel like this?" Rudo asked.

"I don't know."

"What can we do about these feelings?"

"Yesterday I suggested...."

"No, we can't do that."

"Perhaps there's a way."

An elephant trumpeted in the distance and Mudiwa shivered with the mournful noise.

"You should go," Rudo said.

"Can I see you tomorrow night?" Muidwa asked.

"Yes – no – I don't know."

"Please?"

"Just go."

Other Works by Mark Morey

The Red Sun will Come - June 2012

Souls in Darkness - August 2012

The Governess and the Stalker - July 2014

Maidens in the Night - September 2014

One Hundred Days - September 2015

The Last Great Race – April 2016

The Adulterous Bride – October 2016

Chapter One

The music was sharper; more rhythmic, more intense. Mudiwa sat with his back to the fire watching the girls dancing. No, watching one girl dancing with her eyes closed and far away. Dancing smoothly, fluidly, and even erotically. But it was more than her dance; she was the most beautiful young woman in the village.

The music continued but Mudiwa didn't hear it. The fire was hot but he didn't notice. The smoke and dust swirled about, but he didn't feel discomfort. He sat watching her.

She opened her eyes and smiled, and Mudiwa felt tightness in his chest. She saw him and she smiled! She continued her dance while keeping her eyes on Mudiwa.

She moved towards Mudiwa and danced a slow circle around him with her arms in the air. Mudiwa sat impassively while she passed close with her long legs almost grazing his shoulders.

She came close and took his hand. She straightened and he stood.

"Come with me," she said, and Mudiwa held her slim hand tightly. With the music still playing, she guided him towards the perimeter of the village. Mudiwa silently followed this girl to the grassland beyond the huts of Mufakose.

They crossed the plain, and in the half-moonlight Mudiwa saw a group of trees in the near distance. The girl strode quickly and yet gracefully towards a small clearing surrounded by five trees. She led Mudiwa between the trees with the grass long and soft against his bare feet. She stopped and let Mudiwa's hand go.

"I'm Rudo," she said.

Mudiwa's lips were dry and he licked them. "I'm Mudiwa," he replied.

"This is my favourite place," Rudo said as she knelt. "Come. Lie on the grass and I can show you."

Rudo lay on her back and Mudiwa lay beside her.

"Do you see what I mean?" she said. "Look at the stars; they're so close. It's like I can reach out and touch them. Can you see?"

"Yes," Mudiwa said.

Rudo sat up and loosened the tiny, beaded skirt wrapped tight around her slim hips, held in place by a leather strap over her shoulder. Mudiwa watched Rudo release it while easing the sash away at the same time. She was naked, except for leather thongs criss-crossed above her ankles. Mudiwa untied his knee-length leopard skin and let it fall to the ground. Again, Rudo lay on the soft grass and Mudiwa lay beside her. She took him in her arms and he responded, nuzzling against her neck. Mudiwa's heart raced, he felt short of breath, and at the same time he wondered why that was so.

Mudiwa held Rudo and she dug her fingernails into his back. She gripped him tight with her nails scratching and gouging.

"I want you," Rudo whispered in his ear. "Kuboora ndi zwinozwino."

And Mudiwa knew something special was about to happen.

* * *

Michael woke suddenly. Where was he? Ah, flying from Johannesburg to Harare. And the dream, what a strange dream, very intense. What did the girl say? How was it that he dreamt in another language?

Michael was in a British Airways Boeing, on a ninety minute flight to the capital of Zimbabwe. Cathy was asleep; resting against his shoulder and breathing gently. Michael looked around an aircraft with almost every seat taken. An aircraft filled with casually dressed African men and women: some African businessmen and businesswomen in suits, and a few whites like him. He checked his watch, a quarter past one, almost half-way. The hostesses were serving lunch: rolls, fruit and sealed plastic containers of juice. It was odd to be on the other side of the world in the midst of a strange and exotic culture, and yet be surrounded by things so familiar.

Cathy stirred and then she sat up with a start. Their eyes met.

"Tired?" Michael asked.

"No, not really," she replied.

8

"What does....?" Michael asked, remembering what the girl said in his dream.

"What does what?"

Michael suddenly felt silly. He shrugged his shoulders. "It's time to eat," he said.

She nodded and Michael lowered his table. The young hostess handed him a plastic tray and he put it aside. Michael looked out of the window and below was a wide, brown, meandering river in a broad valley. The Limpopo River: border between the two countries. The detail on the ground was very clear: dry grass baked by the sun and wanting for rain, with small stands of evergreen trees. Dirt roads, a dam, a cluster of buildings. He could have been flying above Australia, his homeland, except the river was much wider than any river in dry Australia. Even though it was late to be eating lunch, Michael wasn't hungry. He ignored the roll and ate his apple and drank the orange juice instead. Cathy did the same, leaving her roll.

Time dragged. The hostesses returned and Cathy handed their trays over. Michael gazed out of the window once more but the landscape hadn't changed. Then the noise of the engines eased. They were descending. In the far distance Michael spotted dark, Lake Kariba on the Zambezi River; the border with Zambia. Pressure on his ears with a dull ache. He took Cathy's hand.

"How do you feel?" he asked.

9

"I'm scared of how it may be."

Announcements for landing. The ground rushed to meet them with a gentle bump, followed by the final roar of the engines. There was a small, yellow-brown terminal ahead. Early post-war from the look of it. To the left was a construction site with the framework of a large, multi-storey building well under way. It looked like Harare was getting a new terminal, despite the lack of air traffic. Their aircraft taxied towards the old building and stopped, and moments later the passengers up forward stood. Michael grabbed his bag from under the seat in front and followed Cathy into the queue. They filed out of the aircraft and down an old-fashioned staircase onto the tarmac. The local air smelt strange: partly musty and partly heavy with diesel fumes. They walked along a pathway painted on concrete, with yellow lines guiding them. On their left, luggage was being unloaded by the ground crew working slowly and deliberately.

The airport terminal was eerie. Just the passengers from the recently arrived flight and a handful of uniformed security staff. Near the luggage carousels, soldiers in army green were armed with machine guns. Michael tried to ignore them while he grabbed his suitcase. He put it next to his girlfriend and waited. The purple-patterned case appeared and he lifted it from the belt. They simultaneously raised handles and locked them into place, and Michael led the way to the exit. No warm welcome for the new project manager and analyst, so they had to catch a taxi. They passed through automatic opening doors and the taxi rank was on the left.

The driver of the first car strode to them. His big hands took Cathy's heavy suitcase and hefted it into the boot of an old, white, diesel-powered Mercedes. The driver dealt with the second case while Michael climbed into the spacious back seat and settled into sun-cracked brown vinyl. Cathy joined him while the driver got behind the wheel.

"We're after the CBAC Bank on Samora Machel," Michael said.

The driver nodded and pulled onto a near deserted road, with buildings on the left and a large carpark on the right. They headed into the suburbs of Harare, with Michael pleasantly surprised by the tidy and well-maintained city. Wide roads in good repair, with traffic lights guarding major intersections. Cared-for houses with neat gardens: green grass and shady trees. Nearby, cars gathered around a shopping centre: a small supermarket, bakery and post office. On the left a park with more greenery. The driver turned on the radio and a simple song came on. Very simple in chiShona, with a repetitive, syncopated rhythm and a twangy lead guitar.

"What do you think of Harare?" Cathy asked.

"It's very pleasant," Michael said, and he meant it.

"Appearances can be deceptive."

"I know."

Michael pulled the memo from his bag and flicked through the pages. Washington Mabada was their contact, the Chief Information Officer. Beyond the politics there must be other reasons why Mabada was still CIO after the auditor's report. The auditors from Geneva: February 1999, ten months out from year 2000, and nothing had been done beyond installing interest calculation program updates supplied by Switzerland. That, and a half-hearted attempt to hire a project manager who was related to the branch manager. One month later and it was Michael's first day as project manager, working alongside a CIO who was out of his depth and probably hostile about having his power usurped. Michael's project was critical: all systems had to be upgraded and there were many branches. Twelve in Zimbabwe, ten in South Africa and five in nearby Mozambique. And more systems at the consumer finance subsidiary. Who knew what mess that was in? It was a complex task and the executive in Melbourne were expecting weekly reports. But Melbourne was a long way from Harare.

They closed on the city centre, with the road lined by shops and low-rise commercial buildings, and footpaths were crowded by pedestrians. But there was a country-town, main-street air about it, especially with cars parked diagonally at the kerb, something not often seen in capital cities. The driver turned right and parked in an empty space.

"Two hundred dollars sir," the taxi-driver said in a heavy accent, and Michael handed two of the almost-worthless notes. The driver climbed from the car and placed the two suitcases onto the footpath. "Goodbye sir," and the driver got into his car, leaving Michael and Cathy a short distance from the Southern African Regional Office of the CBAC Bank.

The pavement was busy with many walking by, but perhaps ambled was a better description. Like the taxi driver the men were not only tall but big in other ways: broad-shouldered, thick arms, big hands. Neat casual dress: long sleeved shirts, sports trousers, leather shoes. Very different to the jeans, runners, and t-shirt look of Australia, although Michael felt comfortable dressed in a suit, shirt and tie.

Older women in the crowd were generally shortish and sometimes plump, and mostly wore colourful dresses and equally colourful head scarves. Younger women were more like Cathy: generally taller and more Western-looking in slacks or jeans, although Cathy was dressed for work in a black suit and a white blouse. Michael suddenly felt threatened: his was the only white face in the street. He knew his history: those big men once fought a civil war against white minority rule. Those people had been segregated as much as South Africans were once segregated. They were second-class citizens in their own country. Even in 1999, the best land in Zimbabwe was held by white farmers. What did those people think of

13

whites now? They wouldn't know a visitor from an oppressor. Perhaps to them, all whites were the enemy.

Michael drew a deep breath and made his way towards the office. He held the door for Cathy and followed her inside, but it was awkward to hold the glass door and drag his case through the gap at the same time. A uniformed guard behind a reception counter came to his aid, and Michael was led into a spacious reception area.

"Michael Page and Cathy Shoko to see Washington Mabada," Michael said.

The guard in the blue uniform went to the desk and used the phone to talk in chiShona.

"Mr Mabada will be with you in a moment," the guard said to Michael.

"Thanks. Can you look after our cases please?"

"Certainly sir."

Michael and Cathy wheeled their cases behind the counter, and then Michael heard footsteps on the staircase. Washington Mabada. He was a big man, as all Zimbabwean men seemed to be big. And his dark skin was ageless: he could have been twenty; he could have been twice that age. Only his receding hairline gave it away. Thirty-five, nine years older than Michael. Dressed in a brown polyester suit with a white shirt and dark-brown tie. Brown was a terrible colour and the suit didn't fit: too tight around the middle, too short in the arms and legs. He reached the bottom step and stopped. Michael glanced out of the corner of his eyes at Cathy and he knew what had struck Mabada. After a moment Mabada regained composure, and strolled to his guests.

"Mr Page, Miss Shoko," Washington Mabada said while extended his hand for a sweaty handshake.

"Please call me Michael," Michael offered, not wanting formality between peers.

"If you wish," Washington Mabada replied before shaking Cathy's hand. "Did you have a pleasant flight?"

"Pleasant enough," Michael said. "Although yesterday was tiring."

"Yes, of course. If you are too tired…"

"No, we're fine."

"Do you want me to introduce you to the staff?"

"Please."

The foyer had a nineteen-seventies feel, from the timber-panelled reception desk to the staircase floating on a steel frame, complete with glass and timber handrails. They climbed rubber-tiled steps to the first floor and Washington Mabada opened a brown-painted door.

Michael and Cathy were led into a large open space surrounded on three sides by shabby, beige walls. The fourth wall had four offices separated from the main work area by floor to ceiling glass lined with curtains. Grubby cream netting blocking access to natural light. The central work area was divided by hip-high green partitions: cubicles formed out of steel frames and timber inlays: two desks, two chairs, two computers. So anonymous: it could have been any office anywhere in the world. Too anonymous: no personal belongings, no photos, nothing. A woman about Cathy's age, similarly dressed in a black jacket and matching black slacks, was studying a large flowchart, and was engrossed by what it was telling her. Washington Mabada led the way through a gap in the partitions and the woman must have noticed the presence behind her. She lifted her head but didn't turn her chair, which was strange.

"Alice Kanengoni, this is Mr Page and Miss Shoko."

Alice stood and faced her guests.

"Miss Kanengoni is our analyst," Washington Mabada explained.

"Pleased to meet you Alice," Michael said. "I'm Michael and this is Cathy."

"You are the manager from Australia?" Alice asked slowly and deliberately, quite different to Cathy's clear, British-sounding English.

"Yes I am."

"And you are the analyst who will work on the project, is that not so?" Alice Kanengoni asked.

"That's right," Cathy replied.

"You are...?"

16

"Manyika," Cathy said, and Michael wondered what she meant.

"If there is anything I can do to help."

"Um, yes." Michael said, before pausing to gather his thoughts. "We have a problem, but we don't know what it is, and I'm here to help find a solution for this unknown problem. So what we need more than anything else are good analytical skills. The rest follows from there."

"I see. So I take it that I will be helping you?"

"If Mr Mabada agrees."

"We can meet the others, if that is what you wish?" Mabada said.

Michael and Cathy were introduced the remainder of the information technology team, and one who registered was Thokozani Chipateni. Chipateni was a generalist and probably knew something about everything. It took more than an hour to be introduced and to get security passes. Cathy was given the desk next to Alice Kanengoni, and she had started her computer and was already at work. Michael and Washington Mabada were in the office overlooking the two girl's work areas. Michael's office: complete with desk, chair, filing cabinet and laptop computer. According to the clock on the wall it was half-past four. Michael sat on the edge of the solid timber desk with his eyes heavy. It was night in Australia and he needed coffee. He needed more than coffee, and there wasn't much that could be done that day in any case.

"Washington, who should I see about the car and house?" Michael asked.

"You are sharing the house and the car with Miss Shoko?" Mabada replied while staring deep into the newcomer's eyes.

Michael stared back. "That's right," he said.

"I have made arrangements as requested. I can show you now if you want."

"I'll get Cathy."

They went downstairs and the security guard at the front desk followed them outside with the two suitcases. Things *were* different in that country.

In the carpark behind the building, a shiny metallic blue Mercedes stood out from an assortment of old Nissans and old Toyotas. The badge on the boot said '320E'. Cathy stood stiffly beside Michael and showed no interest in their lovely car, which was strange for her.

"This is your car," Mabada said. "On the driver's seat there's a directory book of...."

"I used to live here," Cathy interrupted.

"Of course. I have pinned the address of your house to the directory book. These are the keys," and he handed a ring to Michael. "The maid has cleaned the house, and she will cook for you."

"Maid?"

"Do you not have maids in Australia?"

Michael shook his head. "No we don't."

"I see. Well, the maid will wash your dishes and clean the house and...."

"I know about maids," Cathy interrupted again.

"You've been very kind for arranging all of this." Michael said; ignoring Cathy's outburst. "What time do you start here?" he asked.

"Eight-thirty."

"Okay then, we'll see you tomorrow at eight-thirty."

Michael shook Mabada's hand and then he climbed into the leather seat. It was a gorgeous car, although very extravagant. Michael hoped they didn't find out in Melbourne.

Chapter Two

The house was in the suburb of Waterfalls, several kilometres
south of the city centre. It was a wealthy area with tree-lined
streets, large blocks of land, and every block was surrounded
by high walls and security gates. No social welfare in
Zimbabwe, so the wealthy protected their valuables. The
houses were uniformly large, and solid brick too. Their house
was functional rather than stylish. Starkly functional and
totally lacking style. Michael took his case to a bland
bedroom and unpacked his things. Cathy joined him and
worked at the opposite end of the built-in wardrobe. She was
in a strange mood.

"Are you okay darling?" he asked.

She looked up and smiled. "I'm feeling better now."

"What's the problem?"

"It was Mabada. Did you see the way he was looking
at me?"

Michael grinned with the memory.

"It's not funny!" she snapped.

He went to his girlfriend and hugged her. "I know
I've been here just a few hours, but I think you're the most
beautiful young lady in Harare."

She relaxed in his arms, and holding her reminded
him of just how much she'd entranced him. When they first
met he was almost overcome by her peaceful manner coupled

with her keen intelligence. She washed over him and enveloped him in a way he'd never experienced before. And she was beautiful. Beautiful and gentle Catherine, a woman like no other.

Cathy rested her head against Michael's arm. "You tell lies," she said playfully.

"I tell the truth."

Cathy turned around and put her hands on his shoulders. She looked at him eye to eye. In heels she was almost as tall as he. "Do you think we're doing the right thing?" she asked, as ever the practical young woman.

"If I didn't, we wouldn't be here."

"Can we make this work?"

"You know I can."

"No-one else could have convinced the Swiss to send the project manager and his girlfriend to do this together."

"There's no conflict because it's just a team of two. I can't show favouritism and the Zimbabweans will see that soon enough."

"If I didn't think that, I wouldn't be here either."

"What do you think of the house?"

Cathy wrinkled her nose.

The bedroom needed something. Perhaps some artwork. A large print there, and Michael imagined a portrait above the bed. Perhaps another print over there, and he thought a larger painting on the opposite wall. Impressionistera paintings would go well in that house, but Impressionist prints in Harare? He shaded his eyes from the glaring room light; they needed light fittings as well. They would be there for a year or more and had to get rid of the nineteen-fifties look.

"We'll go shopping on the weekend and buy a few things to make this place our own," Michael said.

"I better finish unpacking and see what the maid left us for dinner."

Michael went to Cathy and embraced her from behind. He held her loosely and nuzzled against her neck, and she rolled her head to one side. He hugged her a little tighter and she relaxed in his arms.

Cathy smiled brightly. "Not tired?"

"We slept well last night."

"Yes we did." She smiled even brighter. "Let's shower. There's a shower over the bath, which is good for us."

Cathy let him go and headed along the corridor. Michael switched on a bedside light and turned off the main light, and that looked much better. He undressed with the sound of water running in the background, and in a moment he was standing in the bath with warm water washing his remnant tiredness away. He grabbed the soap and lathered his darling all over, the beautiful curves of her slim body, her long, shapely legs, everywhere. He stood and formed a funnel with his hands, rinsing the suds away; her shining ebony skin breathtaking in muted light.

Cathy took the soap and lathered him, but it was a cursory wash and soon she was holding him tight and kissing him.

"I love you," she whispered. "And I'm glad we came."

"I did this for you."

"I know." She let him go and climbed out of the bath. "Come," she said, holding one of the two towels.

Michael turned the taps and took the towel to dry himself. In a moment he was dry, or dry enough, and he held her hand and led her to their room. They fell on the bed and Cathy stretched out. Michael lay above: kissing her and kissing her. He kissed her all over, her breasts, she gasped. He kissed her tummy, kissed her lower and she gasped again. Lower again, and she relaxed with his touch.

"That's nice, isn't it?"

"Yes."

"And this?"

"Mmmm."

"And I'll kiss you here," and he kissed inside her leg, "and I'll kiss you here," and he kissed her thigh, "and here," and he went close, "and just a kiss here," and she sighed deeply. He kissed her again and she moaned lightly, and he kept kissing and she was breathing heavily, and then he went beyond kissing and she arched her back, and then he felt her.

He knelt and their eyes met.

"I love you," he said.

She looked deeply into his eyes and he smiled. Suddenly, she smiled.

He moved and she smiled even brighter.

"This is the most beautiful thing in the world. This is beautiful, you're beautiful, you're…"

Cathy gasped and held Michael's shoulders, and he nuzzled the side of her neck.

"I adore you darling," he murmured, "I truly do."

He kissed her and she clawed him; scratching him with her long fingernails. And the pain was pleasure and their lovemaking was paradise, and it was a paradise that he once never believed possible. But he was in paradise and it was now. His lover made his life complete, and everything was wonderful.

* * *

"Ndinokuda," Cathy said quietly, "I love you."

"I love you too," Michael said. "What does kuboora ndi zwinozwino mean?"

Cathy giggled. "It's nd-i."

"N-di," Michael tried to repeat, but couldn't get it right. "What does it mean?" he asked.

"Ravish me at once. Why?"

"Just curious."

Cathy rustled his hair. "You ravished me," she said.

"We ravished each other."

"We did."

Michael felt at peace with the world. More relaxed and comfortable than he had a right to be. He rolled onto his side and traced his finger lightly over Cathy's breast.

"Don't you ever wonder about us?" he asked quietly.

"In what way?"

"How we came to be."

"Don't try to analyse it; just enjoy it for what it is."

"What is it?"

"Love."

"But you and me...?

"We met and we fell in love. I saw it that day; you ravished me with your eyes. I knew it was going to be special."

Michael nodded, remembering.

"Hungry?" Cathy asked.

"Yes," Michael replied, and she eased from his embrace. Michael watched her dress in jeans and a black t-shirt. He climbed out of bed and pulled on a t-shirt and track suit trousers. Cathy went to the kitchen and Michael went to the living room. His own sound equipment was in boxes on the floor, but there was a CD player and speakers that came with the house. He used a key to slice the packing tape on his carton of CDs, and soon 'Mr Crown Prosecutor' filled the room.

Cathy appeared at the doorway, frowning. "Oh no," she said, "I was hoping for some real music."

"Like in the taxi?"

"Yes. What's this one?"

"Cold Chisel."

"Very – I don't know what."

"Raw."

"Yeah, raw, like fingernails on a blackboard!"

"You don't like it?"

"It's not bad, I suppose."

"On the weekend you should buy your own CDs."

She nodded. "Dinner's ready, if you can drag yourself away from Cold Chisel."

Michael followed Cathy into the family room where the table was set, and he decided that a chocolate-brown tablecloth would make all the difference. He yawned.

"I thought you weren't tired," Cathy said.

He shrugged his shoulders.

"We will eat now and then have an early night," Cathy said. "A good night's sleep with pleasant dreams."

"A good night's sleep with pleasant dreams," Michael echoed. He yawned again, and there was no doubt they really needed a good night's sleep with pleasant dreams.

* * *

"What are you thinking about?" Rudo asked.

"It's late and I should go," Mudiwa replied.

"It's almost dawn. You can sleep with me until the sun comes up."

"Thank you."

Mudiwa lay on his back and Rudo curled up beside him with her right arm across his chest. Although it was late he didn't want to sleep. Even though it was dangerous for him to return to his village in the daylight, he didn't want to leave this girl.

"This is special," he said.

"Yes it is. I've seen you before, a few times, with some of the other girls."

"I've never seen you until tonight."

"Maybe that's what makes it special."

"No, it's something else."

"If you return to my village…"

"Yes?"

"If you return, remember my name is Rudo."

"Can I ask where you live?"

"You can ask for me."

Mudiwa nodded, and lying on his back with the stars so close he wished that night would never end. But the sky was getting lighter with nearby trees clear and distinct. Rudo stirred and Mudiwa let her go. She sat with her legs out straight and her hands on her knees. Their eyes met and she smiled. She was attractive with flawless dark-brown skin, fine cheekbones and a delicate face. No, she was more than attractive, from her short-cropped hair to her not-quite-fully-developed breasts. Watching her in the early dawn light, Mudiwa realised Rudo was younger than she seemed when dancing. Just of age, which was why he hadn't seen her before. Rudo reached out and touched the side of Mudiwa's face and he held her hand, intertwining her long slender fingers. She gently eased out of his grasp and slowly caressed his body.

Mudiwa sat cross-legged, and without taking her eyes from Mudiwa she sat on his lap, her legs wrapped around his waist, her hands gripping his shoulders. Mudiwa sighed: she was graceful, attractive, sensual. Suddenly, he felt a sharp pang of desire for her, an overwhelming ache that filled his entire being. He wondered how that was possible. How could he be with her and still be wanting her? But as she held him and he held her, there was no denying his strange feeling. He looked into Rudo's eyes and wondered if she felt the same way. He wanted to ask her, but then he realised that she was a girl who picked him for the night. She invited him like she invited her other men. He absorbed the softness of her skin, her breasts were pressed against his chest, and there was no doubt that it was an unforgettable moment.

* * *

It was light when Mudiwa reached the outskirts of his village of Ghanzi. In the cleared area to the right of the track, four or five women worked the soil with hoes; their singing sweet in the still morning air. Ahead was his mother's hut and Mudiwa's hunger slipped away. Indeed he felt sick. But his mother would be worried so he had to do it. He leaned his spear against the wall and went inside, while straining to see in the darkness.

His mother's voice broke the silence. "Mudiwa, where have you been?" she snapped. She was on her sleeping mat and braiding his sister Nyarai's hair.

"I went to Mufakose Mama," he said quietly while he sat on the floor.

"All night?"

"I met someone."

"But all night? You know how dangerous it is to return in daylight on your own."

"Yes, I know. But something nice happened and…."

"Elephants, hippos…," his mother's mind was somewhere else.

"I won't do it again."

"You must be hungry."

"Yes Mother."

She went outside to the cooking hearth, and returned with a plate of hot rape stew and a cup of mikaka wakakora. Mudiwa's hunger returned and he consumed his tasty breakfast in minutes. He suddenly felt strangely satisfied and at peace with himself, and he wondered why that was so.

"I must go to the men's compound," Mudiwa said.

His mother nodded and Mudiwa took his plate and cup outside and placed them in the bucket. He stretched and looked at huts gathered around the central open space, each hut spaced two paces apart. Round buildings with mud walls, each with a single doorway, and each with thatched rooves which formed broad eves as protection for cooking and washing. Outside were fire hearths and buckets, with many women cooking, or washing clothes and plates. Just beyond was the meeting area. The men from Mufakose came each night to watch dancing and more. Cousins passing in the night, tramping between the two villages. Cousins who will come for his sister, when she's of age to be initiated. The perpetuity of life: companionship and pleasure, childbirth, ageing, death. For a moment Mudiwa felt like he was high in the sky and looking down on the peaceful settlement; floating like the ancestors. Was that a premonition of his death, or something else? He shivered, and then he went to the men's huts.

Just ahead was his friend Buru: making spears by binding iron tips to sticks. But not just any sticks, the straightest and strongest saplings gathered from the bush. Around Buru were several iron tips traded from tribes downstream. Mudiwa wondered why tribes would sell useful iron in exchange for soft and worthless copper.

"Where have you been my friend?" Buru asked.

"Don't you start! My mother really gave it to me."

"And so she should. You have one spear like these, but that isn't going to help you against an elephant."

"It was worth the risk."

"Was she pretty?"

Mudiwa nodded.

"I'm glad for you," Buru said. "Now, put your spear down and help me with these. Your uncle is taking some of the older men hunting this evening."

Mudiwa rested his favourite spear against the wall of Buru's uncle's hut and sat cross-legged in the long grass. He grabbed a length of twine and tested it for flaws before taking a sapling and tip. In no time the tip was fastened and Mudiwa tested the strength of his work.

"You didn't say a word about your uncle going hunting," Buru said.

"Why should I?"

"Surely you want to hunt with him?"

"Not tonight; I'm going to Mufakose."

"She must have been pretty."

Mudiwa's thoughts were somewhere else. "Have you ever wondered about...?" he asked, but was unable to say what he really felt.

"What?"

"Nothing. No, whether there's meaning in what we do."

"What sort of meaning?"

"Well, we make spears and hoes and we hunt, and we go down the river to trade while our mothers and aunties and sisters look after their children and work in the fields. And then we go down the track, and if we're lucky one of our cousins chooses us. And then we come back here and we make more spears and hoes, and the women look after their children and work in the fields."

"Yes, that's what we do, but that's the way of the world. The ancestors gave women the power to have children, which is why men must do the dangerous jobs like hunt and sail down the river."

"But have you ever wanted to get closer to the women?"

"In what way?"

"I don't know. No, have you ever wanted to be with a woman for more than a night? To be her friend, and for she to be your friend, to..."

Buru laughed out loud. "She must have been very beautiful to make you like this." Buru put his hand on Mudiwa's knee. "You go to Mufakose tonight and maybe you will see your pretty girl. But you be careful my friend, because what you are talking of is taboo. She has brothers and she has an uncle, and they will enforce taboo against you if they have to."

"But…?"

"But nothing. Now stop talking and keep binding, or else we'll be here all day!"

Chapter Three

Michael stretched in his chair and surveyed his office. Monday, the beginning of his third week. He glanced at his computer with an inventory of systems on a spreadsheet. Through the glass wall, rendered partially indistinct by netted curtains, Cathy was staring at her computer screen.

It was quiet, eerily so, the ticking of the clock on the wall clear and distinct. A quarter-past-ten, time for coffee. Michael couldn't face instant again, and although Alice wasn't part of the project, perhaps they could invite her to the cafe.

Cathy came into his office and closed the door behind her. She was frowning and it looked like she needed real coffee too.

"Do you want to go out?" Michael asked.

She shook her head and leaned over his desk. "I found something," she said in a whisper.

"That's what we're here for."

"No, not that, something else. Something big." She looked over her shoulder before facing him again. "We need to talk."

"A meeting in the cafe?"

She nodded.

Michael led the way downstairs, across the foyer and outside. It was a pleasant sunny day, as every day was pleasant and sunny.

Harare didn't have a cafe culture and no alfresco dining at all. It was a robust and workmanlike town, almost like it was stuck thirty years ago. Especially the local cafe: complete with laminate tables, vinyl chairs, and faded posters for 'Coca-Cola'. But it had an espresso machine. Michael went to the waitress and ordered two cappuccinos because he knew they couldn't make a flat white. He joined Cathy at their table by the window.

"What have you found?" he asked.

She looked around and then leaned close. "I got Mr Chipateni to copy the financial systems onto our test server, and I was running tests on the data last Friday. By accident I found something odd. I checked it out this morning and it runs into millions."

The waitress arrived and placed the two cups on the table. Michael spooned some sugar and stirred his coffee. "What runs into millions?" he asked.

"Fraud."

Michael stopped stirring. "How do you know it's fraud?"

"Cash expenses for travel couldn't come to millions."

"Cash expenses?"

"Yes."

He took a sip of coffee and it wasn't bad.

"You don't seem worried?" Cathy asked.

"It's the way of these places," Michael said. "We're not here to audit their accounts; we're here to test and fix their systems."

"I know, but if I found it, others could as well. And if we knew and did nothing...."

Michael put his cup down. "Are you sure about this?" he asked.

Cathy nodded while drinking some of her coffee.

Michael tapped the table for a moment. "We need proof beyond the balances of their accounts."

"I can get Alice to...."

"No, just you and me for now. In accounting, every transaction's backed by documentation, isn't that right?"

"Yes."

"Find the documentation for last month and bring it to me. Then we can do something."

Michael finished his coffee and waited for Cathy. Together they headed into the bright sunshine for the short walk to the bank.

* * *

Cathy was away from her desk for most of the morning, and they ate lunch together in the tea room without her mentioning what she was doing. Michael knew her way. She was professional and thorough, and only when she had found everything would she come to him. Even so he felt impatient. He just wanted an overview so he could weigh up

36

what to do. They were alone together in Harare, and the last thing he needed was upset the locals. Although, perhaps, there was another way. An email with a recommendation. But even then, the Zimbabweans would guess that the project team was involved in a sudden financial audit. He hoped Cathy was discreet with her enquiries.

Cathy came into his office holding a manila folder of paperwork. She closed the door, pulled the guest chair around to his side of the desk and placed the file front of him. She opened it and the first document was cash reimbursement for travelling expenses, with receipts stapled behind. It was a significant amount, eleven-thousand, three hundred and ten dollars, and some cents.

"See this," Cathy said. "When I add up the receipts, they come to one thousand, three hundred and ten dollars and eight-eight cents."

Michael realised what she was telling him. "Someone has put a 'one' in front, and taken the ten-thousand."

"Yes."

"They're all like this?"

"Yes. The forms are filled out by the travellers, each using a different pen, and the extra digits always match."

Michael grabbed the next document and studied it. It was completed in red, which was bad, but hundreds of dollars had been inflated by five-thousand. Someone must have a supply of every colour of pen. They were clever but greedy.

37

Several thousand a month wouldn't be noticed, but that was bigger. "How much last month?" he asked.

"More than one-hundred thousand."

"Millions in a year?"

"Yes."

Michael rubbed the side of his nose while thinking through the consequences of what Cathy found. "We need to be careful. We need to keep these people on our side."

"But we can't ignore this. This would ruin our careers if anyone found out."

"I know." Michael reached beside his desk and pulled out the laptop carry bag. "Put the file in here and take it to the copy shop down the street. They copy in colour, don't they?"

"Yes."

"Good. Copy these in colour and give the copies to me. Put the originals away so they won't be missed."

"What're you going to do?"

"Report it to the auditors."

She smiled for the first time today. She leaned even closer to him. "You are too clever, my darling."

"With more experience, you'll be sitting behind a desk like this one day."

"I don't think so."

"Once I was like you, and I learned from others."

"So you say. Now that you've solved our impossible problem, don't forget we're visiting my sister tonight."

"Julie?"

"Yes. She got home from Mutare on the weekend and I can't wait to see her. It's been a long time. You will like her, but remember she's not like me."

"How so?"

"You will see."

Michael had a thought. "I must call the maid and remind her not to cook."

Cathy giggled. "You plan and double-check too much, my darling."

"Sorry but that's an occupational hazard. You'll catch it too, I promise."

"I will go now," Cathy said, slipping the file into the bag.

"Be discreet."

She headed out the door while Michael picked up the phone and dialled their house. The phone rang and there was a muffled something at the other end.

"Mary," he said, but there was a lot of static on the line.

"Who that?"

"Mary," he shouted. "It's me, Mr Page."

"Oh sorry Mr Page, I cannot hardly hear you."

"Look, remember not to cook dinner for us tonight."

"Dinner?"

"Don't cook for us tonight," he shouted.

"Oh yes, I remember."

"Thanks."

"Sorry?"

"Thanks," he shouted, and hung up.

That was a bad line. Just then, Michael noticed the handset on his phone was loose. He tried to tighten it, but it was cross-threaded. Odd. He undid it, and a little round silver watch battery fell on the desk. Very odd. He rolled it around his fingers. It looked like a bug. And then he smiled at his own stupidity. Bug indeed. More like watching too many movies. Who would be interested in telephone calls to his maid? He tossed the battery into the bin and screwed the handset together. He checked it and the phone should be much better.

* * *

Michael drove slowly along Mendel Road in the suburb of Avondale; looking for Julie Shoko's apartment. It was very different to Waterfalls and more like an Australian city: small blocks, plain houses, no security walls. He counted the street numbers and saw a block of flats ahead on the right.

The flats were similar to the houses in the street: red brick with white doors and white, timber window-frames. Each two-storey flat had a small but lovely tropical garden, with guava and mango trees planted along the low brick fence and hanging over the footpath. Michael grabbed the bottle of red wine from the boot of his car and waited for Cathy to join him. Under the light from a nearby street light she looked amazing: wearing tight designer jeans, a black satin blouse, a chunky gold pendant and large, gold earrings. Hand in hand they strode along the concrete path to the front door and Cathy used the brass knocker. They waited a moment until Julie Shoko opened the door.

The sisters grabbed each other and embraced with emotion. There was genuine closeness and affection, beyond anything siblings would display in Australia. Standing to one side Michael couldn't deny the family resemblance, although Julie was some centimetres shorter than her older sister, and her white dress was somewhat plainer than Cathy's expensive jeans. Julie wore her hair longer and tied into a coarse pony tail that looked quite different to Cathy's close-cropped style. They embraced for an age before Cathy let her sister go.

"Julie," she said. "This is my boyfriend Michael."

They shook hands. "Thanks for inviting me," Michael said.

"It's a pleasure," Julie replied in a clear, British-sounding accent very much like Cathy's. "Come; I will introduce you."

Michael handed the bottle of wine to Julie, and they were led into an apartment similar in vintage to the house in Waterfalls: mid nineteen-fifties. Into a cramped living room

41

which had a staircase leading to what would have been a bedroom on the second storey. The room had plain, cream-coloured walls with a bulky, brown vinyl lounge suite taking much of the floor space. Julie had enlivened the room with a brass-framed mirror with copper plaques on either side. Elephant, hippopotamus and rhinoceros figures arranged around a map of Africa on one, and more animal figures around a map of Zimbabwe on the other. Michael thought Zimbabwean copper would look nice at Waterfalls, and would make useful souvenirs of their time. A young African guy stood from an armchair to greet the guests.

"Peter," Julie said. "This is my sister Cathy and her boyfriend Michael."

Michael shook hands with Peter. Peter was similar in height and build to himself: say one-hundred and ninety centimetres and about eighty kilos. Peter had a big smile, and big hands that swallowed Michael's when they shook. Cathy then shook hands with Peter while Julie went to the other armchair.

"Please sit," Julie said.

Michael got comfortable on the sofa with Cathy.

"It's great to be home," Cathy said.

"How long are you going to be here?" Julie asked.

"About a year."

"Good.

"Are you seeing Mum and Dad?"

Cathy laughed. "Of course, silly. This weekend."

"Good. Michael, you will love Mutare."

"I'm looking forward to it," Michael replied.

"Are you enjoying it here?"

"Yes, very much. This is once in a lifetime for me."

"And you work with Cathy?"

"Yes I do." Silence for a moment with strangers getting to know one another. "And what do you do?" Michael asked Julie.

"I work as a bookkeeper for Meikles department store. Do you know it?"

"I've seen it."

"And you Peter?"

"I am a mechanic," Peter replied, still smiling brightly.

"I see," Michael said.

Julie squirmed. "I better get dinner ready. Is beef curry okay?" she asked.

"Yes, fine, but you didn't have to go to any trouble," Michael said.

"It's no trouble for the boyfriend of my sister. Cathy, can you help me?"

The two girls went through a doorway leaving the men in the living room. Nothing to say. Two men feeling awkward in each other's presence.

"What sort of car do you have?" Peter eventually asked.

"Work's given me a Mercedes. Three-twenty E."

Peter whistled and Michael smiled. Cars, the universal language amongst men the world over. But beyond the car they had nothing in common. Julie appeared at the doorway to rescue the strained conversation.

"Dinner's ready," she said.

Michael followed Peter who had the strangest loping, rolling-sort of walk, exaggerated by arms that seemed too long for his body. They reached the kitchen: cream-coloured walls with white-painted cupboards at one end, and a small, square laminex table surrounded by four green vinyl chairs near the doorway. The table was set with plates, cutlery, soft drink, glasses, his bottle of wine and a single wine glass. In the centre: beef, rice and vegetables steamed in three bowls. Michael sat with the wine and Cathy sat to his left.

"Julie, do you have another wine glass?" Cathy asked.

"Um, yes," Julie replied before going to one of the cupboards. While that was being sorted, Peter passed a bowl to Michael. He served himself, as did the others. He waited until everyone had finished, and then Julie said a prayer. That was different to Australia. He assumed the end of the prayer was a sign to start, so he poured a little wine for Cathy and some for himself. Silence while everyone ate, and it was awkward silence too. From the time he met Cathy, she had had fitted into his life like she was born to it, but that evening was very different. Michael surreptitiously glanced at his companions. Theirs was a different culture, and if it was strained it was because they were unsure of his customs and he was unsure of theirs. But Zimbabwe was his home for the next year or more and he had to learn.

"This is good," Michael said.

"Thank you," Julie replied.

"And thanks so much for inviting me."

She half-smiled.

The meal finished with dessert, ice cream, Peter announcing that was the 'best part'. And when he finished his dessert, Michael knew what was coming. The girls would wash up, leaving the men to talk about cars and sport. Only Michael wasn't really into cars and sport.

Peter consumed a second helping of ice cream while Julie cleared the table. "I will wash up later," she said. "We can go to the living room."

Julie and Peter returned to the armchairs, and Michael and Cathy took the vinyl sofa. It was so quiet.

"Thanks for inviting us," Michael said for something to say.

"You're my brother!" Julie replied with emphasis. "How are you enjoying life in Harare?"

"It's fantastic, and I'm going to learn a lot by living here. But one thing that's surprised me is how prosperous Harare is."

"Don't be fooled by what you see," Julie said. "Inside neat houses people are struggling, and in the townships life is much worse. Actually, I need to talk to both of you. Do you know of the food riots?"

"No," Michael said, surprised.

"Mum wrote to me," Cathy said. "Can you tell Michael what happened?"

"It was more than a year ago, in January last year," Julie continued. "People rioted, and they broke into shops and stole food. The army and the police were tough and eventually it faded away. It's been peaceful since but things haven't changed. Many can't afford three meals a day, and it's only a matter of time."

"For more riots?" Michael asked.

"Yes."

"How can there be food shortages? Zimbabwe is the food bowl of Southern Africa."

"All of the farms are in the hands of the whites, but they're being chased from the country," Cathy said, taking over from her sister. "You see, there must be someone to blame for the inflation, the unemployment, the shortages...."

"So the Government blames the whites for sabotaging the economy?"

"Yes, but in truth it's incompetence and corruption by the Government."

"But surely at the next election...."

"That's the biggest danger of all."

"How so?"

"The MDC, the Movement for Democratic Change. They're the first party with a chance of beating Zanu."

"The current Government?"

"Yes."

"Why is it that African countries always end up with dictators, rigged elections and military coups?"

Cathy shrugged her shoulders.

"Do you know?" Michael asked.

"Africa's past was one of kings, chiefs and villagers, where wealth was shared between all rather than accumulated by a few. This is more like Marxist socialism than Western capitalism, and those who'd been ruled by Western colonisers had no appetite to mimic the capitalist ways of their former oppressors. So African socialism came to the fore, and Robert Mugabe became a convert to that. Colonisation was by force and created urban areas for the first time, and concentrated power and control into those urban areas. African urban elites spearheaded moves to independence or majority rule, while the majority of Africans in rural areas were untouched by this, and had no experience of democracy either. This gave urban elites free reign to implement Marxist socialism while retaining the oppressive power structures they inherited from colonialism. Without the constraints of true democracies, they indulged in excesses which have blighted

Africa these past decades." Cathy looked up. "I'm sorry," she said. "This must be boring for Peter and Julie."

Peter was beaming, and Julie was leaning forward and holding onto every word.

"No, this is fascinating," Michael said. "Go on."

"Alright," Cathy said unconvincingly. "Europeans came with guns and African warriors with spears had no chance. But the lesson had been learned, and when time came for independence, a part of that was guns and armies."

Michael knew his history. "Many dictators have been overthrown in army coups," he said.

"That's true," Cathy said. "Mugabe looks after his army commanders very well."

"He's cunning."

"He is."

"Even with an army, how can he subjugate an entire population?"

"By the time the urban elites of Zanu seized power in that first election, it was too late for democracy." Cathy said. "Now, if anyone in Zimbabwe thinks we should have democracy, Mugabe has his secret police inherited from the Whites. Opposition parties have no chance."

That was interesting. "What about Morgan Tsvangirai?" Michael asked.

"He was too well known through his involvement with the union movement for Mugabe to lock him away like the others." Cathy looked up at Michael. "But this is more than Robert Mugabe, megalomaniac. African society has always cast women in a higher role than European society. When there were kings and chiefs, they never defied their wives who were often moderating influences. Mugabe's wife Sally was a part of the struggle for independence, and clearly she was a good person. Sadly she died seven years ago. By then Mugabe was having an affair with Grace Marufa who he married a few years later. Grace seems to have been a bad influence on him, and his previous moderate and conciliatory policies have become ever more radical."

"With a moderate wife Mugabe was moderate, and with a new wife he's become a despot?"

"We have an ancient culture: maybe five-thousand years," Cathy said. "Men ran the broader economy and women ran the domestic economy, which is quite different to Western culture where women were the property of men. This history of African culture is quite interesting, but that's a long story and perhaps for another time."

"When we next meet with Julie and Peter?" Michael asked.

"Yes. Next time we meet."

Michael glanced at Julie and Peter on their armchairs. Michael felt the couple should be holding hands or at least acknowledging each other's presence. Smiling Peter and serious Julie; something wasn't right.

So quiet. A car passed with the sound of tyres on tarmac very clear. So very quiet.

"It's late and we should go," Cathy said. "We had a — stressful day."

"Yes, we have work tomorrow too," Julie replied. "I know, next time we can go for a drive on a weekend."

"Lake McIlwaine," Cathy said. "No, Chinhoyi caves. Work has given us a lovely car and we can take Peter and you."

"Ah, Chinhoyi," Julie said. "We can eat at the motel."

Cathy smiled in agreement and clearly that was a special place. "The weekend after next?" she asked.

"Lovely."

Cathy got to her feet, as did Michael, Julie and Peter. The sisters embraced and held each other tightly. "It's been too long," Cathy said.

"We can make up for it," Julie said.

"One day I will come home, I promise. I miss my home, I miss my family, and I miss my mitupo."

Michael wondered what a mitupo was. The two girls parted: elegant Cathy and down-to-earth Julie.

"Goodbye Julie," and Michael shook her hand. "Peter," and another handshake.

"Goodbye Peter," Cathy said with a handshake.

Michael and Cathy left with a final wave to their hosts before the door was closed.

"You liked them?" Cathy asked while they walked along the path.

"They're good people."

She took his hand and held it tightly. "Yes they are."

They reached the Mercedes and Michael pressed the remote. He opened the door for his partner, and waited for her to settle into her German leather seat. He climbed in, started the engine and pulled out from the kerb, and soon they left pleasant Avondale behind.

Chapter Four

Quarter-past five and time enough to head home. Michael went to the open-plan area; switching off the light in his office on the way. He leaned on the partitions.

"Do you want to go?" he asked Cathy.

She nodded and shut her computer down.

"Good night Alice," Michael said.

"Good night Mr Page," Alice Kanengoni replied.

"Michael, please."

Alice nodded without saying a word.

"Good night Alice," Cathy offered, and she walked with Michael to the doorway and down the stairs to the carpark. Outside dusk was settling, and Michael got comfortable for the drive to Waterfalls. In no time they were in heavy traffic and heading south along Leopold Takawira Street. Right onto Charter Road and towards Simon Mazorodze. Buses all about: packed with commuters heading to the townships beyond the outskirts. Michael wondered about life beyond the wealthy suburbs. One day he should find out. He continued along Simon Mazorodze Road, the traffic less dense and allowing him to make good time. He kept to the left and indicated to branch onto Godfrey Avenue and saw bright lights ahead. Strange. Flashing blue, either an accident or a roadblock. The latter most likely, although in the oddest place.

"What do you think?" he asked.

"It's a roadblock," Cathy replied.

"But here?"

"It's a wealthy suburb, and good pickings to be made from rich expats like you."

"It doesn't seem right."

"Mr Suspicious."

A blue-uniformed policeman pointed to the left as a sign for Michael to stop. The policeman strolled to the car and Michael pressed the power window button.

"Good evening sir," the policeman without nametag said. "Can I see your licence?"

Michael pulled his wallet from his shirt pocket and handed over his Australian licence, and then he reached into the map pocket and retrieved his international licence and handed that across as well. The policeman studied them very closely; frowning with concentration.

"Anything wrong?" Michael asked.

"No sir, not at all. This is just a routine check. Is this your car?"

"It belongs to my work."

"Is there anything in the boot?"

"There's nothing in the boot."

"Can I see?"

Michael sighed, switched off the engine, and climbed out. He went to the boot and pressed the button. He held the lid.

"See."

The policeman lifted the edge of the carpet mat and switched on his torch, but it was just metal flooring and a spare wheel.

"Can I go now?"

The policeman studied the licences under torchlight for a moment before handing them back. "You can go Mr Page," he said.

Michael got into the car, started the engine and drove off. That was an annoyance but at least the policeman didn't ask for a bribe. That was even odder. Why stop someone wealthy and not ask for money? With inflation running at fifty percent, only a lucky few got three meals a day. The wages of many, police included, could never keep up with the continual price rises. It was no wonder they stopped cars and demanded bribes.

"That was strange," he said to Cathy.

"He didn't ask for a bribe?" she asked.

"No."

Michael turned left onto Crete Road and then right onto Leonard. Quiet and still, except for a car parked under the streetlight opposite the security gate to their home. It was a new Toyota with two African men in front, clearly visible.

It looked out of place. New cars were out of reach of all but the very rich, or foreigners like himself. Cathy climbed out and unlocked the gate, and slid it to one side so that Michael could put the Mercedes away in the garage. She unlocked the front door and they went inside together.

They went to the bedroom and Michael opened the wardrobe door.

"You should put on jeans," Cathy said, "Peter's coming at eight to take us somewhere."

"Somewhere?"

"Somewhere special."

Michael did as Cathy suggested and replaced his suit with jeans, a long-sleeved casual shirt and a pullover. Cathy dressed similarly before going to the kitchen.

The maid had left pasta, and Cathy turned on the stove to warm it before preparing a salad.

"Is this place we're going to anything to do with what you were talking about last night?" Michael asked.

"What was I talking about?"

"A time long ago."

"Oh that. No, not at all. But I can tell you about this time, if you want me to."

"Yes please," Michael said while he got a bottle and wine glasses from the cupboard.

Cathy served up two bowls and Michael helped her carry their meal to the table.

"This is a story of our history and culture," Cathy said. "There was a time in Africa when men and women ran society in harmony with each other, and marriage and relations were different to now. I will tell you a story of an African boy who went to a nearby village to meet a partner for the night, because that's the way it was in those days. So this boy is at the village, and he sees a girl dancing slowly and erotically. He hopes the girl will ask him to go with her, and she does."

"She was a pretty young girl," Michael said. "And she took the boy across a grassy field, and they slept together in a clearing surrounded by five trees."

Cathy put her fork down and looked at him. "How do you know that?" she asked.

"I dreamt it."

"That's strange."

Michael shrugged his shoulders. "I know. I can't explain it."

"Dreams can mean a lot of things. Maybe you were meant to dream this dream."

"Maybe."

"How much did you dream?"

"He's in love but the girl's too young to understand."

"No, not that. They didn't love in those days."

"But surely he could have fallen in love?"

"Yes, you're right. They didn't search for love like we do, but still he fell in love with her. How far did you dream?"

"The next night he plans to return to her village. Can you tell me what happened?

"Yes I will."

* * *

Mudiwa stood near the drummer and watched the crowd while they waited for the music to begin. No sign of Rudo so asked a young man for directions to her hut. He reached her mother's home and sat on the ground next to the hearth. Rudo appeared moments later dressed in a short leather skirt and adorned with copper jewellery: large circular earrings, bracelets on each wrist, and a pendant between her breasts. Mudiwa stood and she took his hand; silently leading the way through the cluster of houses towards the savannah. Mudiwa's heart raced. In the light of the setting sun Rudo looked delightful. How was it that out of all of the men who could be her partner, she chose him? He squeezed her little hand and she looked at him and grinned, Mudiwa realising that the tiny skirt and the jewellery were for his benefit. She dressed to arouse him!

They reached the cluster of trees and Rudo led the way inside and stopped. Mudiwa hugged her, drawing her to him, his fingers absorbing the amazing softness of her skin. He kissed the side of her neck, he nibbled her shoulder, and then he kissed her on the lips. She stiffened.

"Ssh, it's alright," Mudiwa whispered before he kissed the side of her neck again. She relaxed in his arms and he kissed her lips again. She put her arms around Mudiwa, holding him loosely while he kissed her. She gripped his shoulders, pulling him to her, wanting more of his kisses, and Mudiwa's heart ran even faster. He held her while they kissed; her first kiss. A kiss she would remember for all time.

Rudo squirmed and Mudiwa let her go. She frowned while she fiddled with the band of leopard skin around his waist. At the same time Mudiwa untied the knots on her brief skirt while his heart pounded fast. Last night was special but this was different. Tonight he desired her in a way he'd never experienced before, and to his surprise Rudo wanted him just as badly. The leather fell to the ground and Mudiwa held her again, and for a brief moment he wished they could stay like that forever.

Mudiwa knew exactly what he wanted to do. He sat on the ground with his legs crossed and Rudo straddled him, her weight easily supported by his thighs. Heaven. Mudiwa kissed her, and he was aware of nothing but the passion of their kiss. Holding Rudo, kissing Rudo, he knew he *could* stay like that forever. Two became one, body connected to body and soul connected to soul. They were born for this, Mudiwa and Rudo. His future was forever to be with his beautiful girl.

* * *

Mudiwa rolled onto his side. "I feel something special when I'm with you," He said in a quiet voice.

"Feel what?" Rudo asked.

"I have desires I can't explain."

"But we've just been together."

"Yes I know, and I still want you."

She ran her fingers lightly over his chest. "Thank you for saying nice things."

"No it's not that. These feelings are real."

"Ssh, you must be tired."

"Doesn't it feel different with me?"

"I'm – um –, you're my first."

Mudiwa admired her silhouette. "Do you believe me if I said you must be feeling something special?"

"No, I don't think so. This is just a part of life, is it not?"

"What we have is much more than that."

"Please relax and enjoy the moment."

"Yes, of course." Mudiwa paused. "Can I spend the night with you here?" he asked.

He saw the flash of Rudo's smile. "Of course you can," she said.

"Can I see you again?"

"Only if you don't talk about special feelings."

* * *

The buzzer rang and Cathy went outside to unlock the gate.
A few minutes later Peter entered the house, smiling brightly.
Michael shook hands.

"G'day Peter," Michael offered.

"Good day Michael," Peter replied.

"We should go," Cathy said.

"Where're we going?" Michael asked.

"Chitungwiza."

"What's at Chitungwiza?"

"You're going to see another side of African life."

And Michael guessed what was at Chitungwiza.

* * *

They headed south from Harare in Peter's car: Cathy in front,
Michael in the back. He felt vulnerable. He was used to
wearing seatbelts and the car only had belts in the front.

"So Peter," Michael said. "You're here to protect
me."

"He's here to protect both of us," Cathy said.

"Protect you?" Michael asked.

"I'm Manyika and this land belongs to the Zezuru."

"You said that once, before. I thought you were
all...."

"Shona," Cathy interrupted. "No. We all speak
chiShona, but we're not the same."

"I should not even talk to you," Peter said to Cathy.

She giggled. "You better talk to me, if you want to keep seeing my sister!"

He burst out laughing and Cathy stuck her hand out. They slapped together.

"Peter, you're...?" Michael asked.

"Zezuru," he said.

"Is there much trouble between the...?"

"Clans," Cathy said. "No, not really. It's more at the top. Government and politics."

"Mugabe?"

"He's Zezuru, and he's driving the larger Karanga out of Zanu. We Manyika are smaller, but we're in alliance with the Zezeru against the Karanga. The Ndau and Korekore are the smallest, so they don't play a part. Government here involves allocating power between the clans, such as deputy leaders or senior ministers."

"Ah, this explains things," Michael said. "The troubles started – probably before majority rule."

"No, not really," Cathy said. "Zanu was originally meant to represent all the Shona-speaking people, with Robert Mugabe seen as the most capable to be prime minister, as he originally was. But that utopian ideal has been corrupted."

"We are close," Peter said.

In the near distance Chitungwiza looked forbidding. No, it looked dangerous. The flat landscape was dominated by several lighting pylons forty metres or more tall: acetylene floodlights casting a ghastly orange glow over hundreds of tiny little houses. Houses yes, but nothing more than rectangular brick boxes with flat steel roofs. Hundreds of brick boxes arranged in rows: fifty or more boxes wide, fifty or more boxes deep. Smoke from kitchen fires hung low, bathed in ugly orange. And then it made sense, that was where the workforce of Harare lived. The taxi drivers, the builders, the factory workers. A legacy of white rule: Africans beyond the outskirts, commuting on overcrowded busses at the beginning and end of each working day. And under majority rule the poor still lived beyond the outskirts. Peter turned left and headed towards the township, but no people were visible. It seemed everyone was inside. Inside their own private box, two metres from the box of their neighbours. Two metres front, back, left and right.

Peter drove along a road between clusters of these houses, and ahead was an open space with four larger buildings. He pulled to the left and switched off the engine. Silence.

The door creaked and Cathy got out. Michael joined him as did Peter, who locked his car. They stood either side of Michael and walked towards the buildings of the far side of a plot of land. A poor excuse for a recreation area: a dirt patch fifteen metres by twenty metres. They closed on several people sitting on two benches. Two teenage boys and two teenage girls silently smoking cigarettes on the one, a lone woman on the other. They approached the benches and stopped. Cathy strode to the woman and bowed, and then she clapped once with her hands cupped.

"Tikukwazisei?" Cathy said. (May I greet you?)

The women got to her feet and nodded. "Kwaziwai," she replied. (I greet you.)

Cathy beckoned, and Michael and Peter joined her.

"Ndinonzi Cathy Shoko," she said. (My name is.) "Vashamwari wangu Michael Page na Peter Chirinda." (My friends)

The woman faced Peter. "Manheru." (Good evening.)

"Manheru maswera sei?" Peter replied. (Good evening; had a good day?)

"Ndaswera maswerawo." (I did if you did.)

"Ndaswera." (I did.)

"Good evening, I am Patience Rusere," she said to Michael in a thick accent.

"Good evening," Michael replied, unsure how to address her.

Cathy took Michael's hand and squeezed it. "Michael mutumbi wangu," she said. (Michael is my lover.)

Patience Rusere smiled briefly. "Ndi kufaraira ku." (I'm happy for you.) Then she frowned, "U no itireyi kudaro?" (Why do you do this?)

"Can we speak in English please?" Cathy asked.

"Why do you want to see me?"

"You're my aunt."

"I am your grandmother's cousin's daughter, and I hardly know you."

"But you're family, and I want my boyfriend to meet my family."

"Sit then."

"Can we visit your home?"

"Why do you want to do this?"

"We are family."

"There is more, this I know. Has he met your parents, and your mother's sister?"

Cathy shook her head. "In time Michael will."

"Tell me what you want of me."

"You're here and I want him to know the real Zimbabwe. He's only seen the suburbs, and he will see more of the same in Mutare."

"You ask a difficult thing of me."

"It's important for my boyfriend to know what needs to be changed."

The woman frowned and then she faced Michael. "Young man, do you love my niece?" she asked.

"Yes, very much."

She half-bowed. "You may come to my home."

"Thank you."

"This way," and Patience Rusere led them into the cluster of houses. Michael couldn't put an age on their host, he guessed about forty or so, although she could be younger. Not tall, less than five feet, and quite stocky, as many older Zimbabwean women were. She was dressed in a blue-green wrap that reached half-way down her left calf, and as far as her right ankle. She wore a bright blue scarf with just a trace of black hair visible. They passed several houses, each house a different colour, although the colours were distorted in the eerie orange light. He heard televisions, the 'Late News' perhaps. Some Zimbabwean pop music, distinctive, always syncopated with a twangy lead guitar. Patience Rusere stopped at a dark house with a darker door. She unlocked the door and led them inside.

The house was tiny, unbelievably tiny. Two rooms joined by a doorway with no door, a yellow curtain the only privacy. Not that there could be any concept of privacy in that tiny brick box. The room they stood in was the larger of the two, but it was very crowded with a bench, a sink and an electric stove. And two single beds with blankets piled high.

"This is your uncle Leonard," Patience Rusere said.

The man sitting on one of the beds nodded in acknowledgement. Leonard Rusere had a deeply lined face which made him look quite haggard. He was dressed informally in a white singlet and olive, canvas trousers.

"Tikukwazisei," Cathy said, bowing. "I am your niece Cathy, and these are my friends Michael and Peter."

"Good evening Mr Rusere," Michael said, but got no response.

"My children David and Sally."

Two teenage children sitting on the floor. Mid-teens, the girl older than the boy.

"And our lodger Albert Makamure, and his wife Lucia."

Cathy bowed. "Manheru," she said to the couple sitting on the second of the two beds.

"Manheru," Albert Makamure replied.

Michael wanted to know so much, but everything was so formal.

"Please sit," Patience said. "Can I get you something to drink? Maybe some cool drink?"

"I'm fine," Cathy replied. Michael shook his head as did Peter. Cathy led the way to the less crowded of the two beds. Leonard moved to the end to give his guests room, and probably to keep his distance.

"Aunty Patience, my boyfriend must know if we are to change things," Cathy said.

"How can you change things?" Patience asked.

"Through politics, through the MDC."

"The MDC cannot do anything against Zanu."

"With our help they can. Please, I want him to know so he can help me."

"What do you want to know?"

"Tell me where you cook."

"Here, in this room. This is my sink," she said, touching the timber bench. "And that is my stove."

"Is there hot water?"

"No water at all today, but we have cold water when it runs."

"And where do you keep your food?"

"I keep a bag of mealie meal in the room where Albert and Lucia stay. The stores here are empty, so I buy food in town and carry it on the bus. Every day a little bit."

"The buses are crowded."

"Yes, it is very hard to carry things on the bus."

Cathy nodded.

"We had sadza this morning," Patience said. "And rape soup this evening."

"You had sadza with the soup?" Cathy asked.

"The bag is nearly empty and the prices have risen so much."

"What will you do when the bag runs out?"

"God will look after us."

"Uncle Leonard, what work do you do?"

"I work for the Post Office."

"Aunty?"

"I am a maid for a family in Waterfalls."

"My cousins go to school?"

"Yes, but the school here is very bad. There are shortages of paper and pencils."

"Mr Makamure," Cathy said, "where do you and your wife stay?"

"In the other room."

"And your job?"

"I am a bus driver."

"And Mrs Makamure, what do you do?"

"I am looking hard, but I cannot find anything. I used to work as a cashier until someone from the party took my job."

"We are suffering," Patience said. "You can see this. The prices, they go up and up and up, every day more. And my husband, he has not had a pay rise in more than three years. And me; a maid does not earn much."

"So Mr and Mrs Makamure help pay the rent?" Cathy asked her aunt.

"Yes. It is very crowded, but we have no choice."

"We do not have enough money to rent a house," Albert Makamure said. "We pay for the room, and we pay for some of the food." He looked at Michael. "They are good people Mr Michael. I want you to know this."

"Yes, of course," Michael said; quite shocked by their story, or their tragedy.

"It's getting late and we should leave," Cathy said, getting to her feet. "Tatenda, sarai zvakanaka."

"Fambai zvakanaka," Patience replied. "You must come again one day."

"We will."

They left the little house and the door closed behind them. Michael held out his hand and Cathy took it. They walked to the car with Michael just wanting to get away. But he didn't want to leave those people either. It was a strange feeling. He thought about Mary. He would give her a pay rise. But even doubling her wage wouldn't be enough.

"It wasn't always like this," Michael said.

"It's always been basic, but only one family in each house, and always enough food. Now it's gone bad and it's getting worse."

"What can we do?"

"Hope for change; hope for the MDC."

Chapter Five

Michael led the way out of the house with Cathy following. He felt distracted which was not surprising after the previous night. Cathy opened the gate while Michael locked the front door. They went to the garage and Michael pressed the remote to unlock the Mercedes. Cathy climbed in, followed by Michael.

"Something's wrong," he said.

"What?"

"The sunvisor's down."

"You probably left it down after driving home yesterday."

"No, I never do that. Someone's been in the car."

"You sure?"

"Positive. Well, almost."

"It's nothing. You probably forgot, Mr Obsessive."

"Yeah, you're right."

He started the car and reversed onto the wide gravel driveway, turning around and stopping just short of the roadway. Cathy got out to close and lock the gate, and then they headed along Leonard Street. Michael turned left at the end.

"It's strange that you dreamt about Mudiwa and Rudo," Cathy said.

"It is," Michael agreed.

"I've known the story of Mudiwa and Rudo since high school, but I've only understood it these last months."

He reached across and held her hand momentarily.

Michael drove along Crete Road and then right onto Godfrey Avenue. He glanced at Cathy; the mirror of Rudo. "Perhaps it's a story we're meant to share," he said.

"We're Mudiwa and Rudo?" Cathy asked.

"Yes."

"They were a passionate couple, but they had something more precious than mere passion."

Michael checked the mirror and saw a black SUV.

"We could be," Cathy said.

"You must tell me more," Michael said.

"Of course."

Michael stopped at Simon Mazorodze and the SUV was still there. He looked left and five or six cars were coming. There was a small break in the traffic and Michael accelerated onto the main road. He thought about Mudiwa and Rudo being their parallel. One day Michael was working and something made him look up to see a tall, dark and amazing beautiful young lady enter the office. Ron introduced her to everyone with Michael being last for some reason. He stood and they shook hands, and suddenly he felt some sort of connection with Catherine Shoko. There was an atmosphere in his little space: something intense, something real. Something so real that it seemed like Michael could

71

reach out and touch this invisible force. He shook Cathy's
hand, suddenly feeling hot. All the while Cathy was
impassively looking him eye to eye. Ron said something
banal but Michael didn't hear him. Instead he held her slim
hand, until he realised what he was doing and let her go. But
that was only a momentary separation, because a few hours
later he went to the cafe and met Cathy in the queue. He
bought her a cappuccino and they sat at a table near the
window, and they talked about her new job and her past
career. And all the time Michael was spellbound by this
gentle and charming young lady. They had long finished their
coffees and there was only one thing for Michael to ask. He
would like to see her outside of work and she agreed. They
went to an Italian restaurant on Friday night. On Saturday he
took her for a picnic, and that evening she stayed at his place,
and there she gave Michael her most precious gift. From
then they were a couple, living together. Sharing a house and
sharing love.

But was that enough? Michael knew it wasn't. Living
together was superficial for what they had. He glanced to his
left, and if she was Australian he'd know when to ask. But
she wasn't. And then he realised they had a year. This
gorgeous Manyika woman; when the time was right he would
invite her out for dinner, and they would go to the best
restaurant in town. During the meal, perhaps over coffee, he
would hold her hand, look deep into her eyes, tell her how

much he adored her, and he would ask her to be his wife. It had to be in Zimbabwe. A big wedding with her family and friends. Her mother and father, Julie and Peter, and all her relatives. The Pages from Australia too.

"Have you emailed the auditors?" Cathy asked, interrupting Michael's fantasy.

"Yes."

Michael checked the mirror and the SUV was just behind, despite leaving it behind at the intersection.

"Darling, I think we're being followed," Michael said.

She turned in the seat. "That black car."

"Yeah."

"You sure?"

"We left it behind, but it overtook some cars and slowed to my speed again."

"Hmm."

Traffic lights ahead and time to check out what was going on. Michael suddenly swerved left; the sign told him it was Paisley Road. They passed into a light industrial area, bouncing over railway crossings.

"Can you direct me from here?" he asked.

"Yes."

Red light coming up and Michael slowed behind some cars. The light changed, the cars slowly accelerated with the SUV still behind their Mercedes. They continued past a green traffic light and the factories and warehouses changed to houses and a park. The street name changed too: Rekai Tangwena Avenue. On the right was the tallest building in Harare: the Sheraton.

"Samora Machel is next past this one," Cathy said.

"Can I turn right here?"

"Yes."

Michael indicated and stopped at the red light. Behind him, the SUV waited.

"I think I'm right about the sunvisor," Michael said. "Something's happening."

Cathy sighed. "I know."

"I should see the police about it."

"Police! Ha, they're useless! They're just interested in bribes and protecting important party members."

"What should I do?"

"I think they're keeping tabs on the new expat. But you're white and a foreigner, so you will be fine."

"And you?"

"They wouldn't be interested in me."

The light changed and he moved forward a few metres. The intersection cleared and he accelerated hard into Robert Mugabe Road. They entered the city centre: a criss-cross grid of streets. The next light was green.

"Left here," Cathy said. "It's Leopold Takawira."

The road that led to the office carpark, he'd looped west into the city rather than from the south. He slowed for

74

pedestrians. Intersection clear, he turned left and onto the familiar street. Still the black car followed at a distance; about thirty metres behind. Michael kept to the right and indicated, and the guard recognised the Mercedes and the gate slid open. He drove through the gap and looked across at the SUV continuing past, still heading north. Cathy was right; they were just checking up on him. He parked the car in the shade and switched off the engine.

* * *

After dinner Cathy went to have a bath and Michael went to the lounge. And then he realised 'The Main News' was on. This minister, comrade whatever, said this. That minister, comrade so and so, said that. He checked his CD collection, but nothing interested him. He thought of the radio, but all they played was the local sound or American rubbish. Then he noticed curtain was blowing lightly. Mary must have left a window open, which was unlike her. He went to close it but saw something on the white window sill. Tucked tight against the wooden frame, thin and almost invisible, a white wire. But the sill was creamy rather than white.

Michael got onto his knees and traced the wire. It led down the wall to the cream-coloured skirting board. He kept going; moving the sofa for access. And tucked into a corner next to the brick fireplace was a little silver device, a bug. A bug for sure. He touched it with his fingertip. The house was bugged. The house, his office, the car too.

Michael grabbed scissors from the kitchen and cut the wire. Still on his knees he held the two pieces of white wire in his hand while wondering what was going on.

He went to the bedroom and Cathy was in her bathrobe and rearranging clothes on a shelf in the wardrobe. He stood at the doorway watching her. She folded that lovely crocheted dress; she once wore it with a yellow slip underneath. He would never forget it, nor would the staff and patrons of the restaurant that night. She looked over her shoulder and grinned.

"What're you smiling at?" she asked.

"Me, nothing."

"Mr Innocent, something's grabbed your fancy." She went to the shelf and lifted out a blue patterned mini skirt. "Is this it?"

He shook his head. "It's the yellow dress."

She put the skirt down, and pulled it out. "This?"

He nodded.

"But you can have much more than this dress. Sorry, much less."

"Now?"

She smiled brightly and untied her robe. And then he remembered. He crossed the room and whispered in her ear.

"The house is bugged," he said while Cathy dropped her white towel onto the floor.

"Really; how do you know?" she asked.

"I found one in the living room. This room might be bugged too."

"They really are keeping tabs on you."

Michael thought her reaction was strange. "You seemed nonplussed by it," he said.

"It's the way of this place," she said, standing naked with her hands on her hips.

Cathy pulled on the short, tight dress, tugging it so it fell over her cute bottom. Coarsely crocheted, thick and chunky, leaving nothing to the imagination. She stood and checked herself in the mirror: amazingly short, unbelievably tight, covering but not hiding her at all.

"Is this what you wanted, lover?" she asked.

Michael nodded and felt flushed despite the cool evening. Cathy strode around the room; the dress was something. She turned and bent over, and it rode up high giving him a wonderful view. She went to Michael and unbuttoned his shirt, and then he remembered the little microphone in the living room. He lightly touched her hands.

"They can't arrest us for making love," she said calmly, and untied his track suit trousers and let them fall to the floor.

"This room could be bugged," Michael said, while his heart raced with arousal or stress, or both.

"Well then, let's give them something to listen to."

77

"Who?"

"The CIO, and anyone else who's out there!"

She was right; they were just making love. Michael admired Cathy lying on the bed. She rolled over and sat up and Michael knelt beside her, thinking of nothing but the love to come. He eased the dress from under her bottom and pulled it over her head. She fell onto her back and he lay against his darling and kissed her. He kissed her again and again, and she pulled her head away.

"You know what I want."

He went lower and she squirmed.

"Zwino!" she ordered. "Now!"

And he did.

"Ooh yes, just there, that's right, don't stop, more. Oh, oh – bhaudha ongu!"

He looked up, and their eyes met.

"Bhaudha ndi zwinozwino!" she ordered.

And he did. She clawed her nails into his shoulders, gouging him. "Chiradza!, Hard! Ongu, yes, kunuka, great." She scratched him deeper, and Michael winced with the pain. "Chiradza, chiradza! Ongu pukare. Pukare, pukare, pukare," she moaned, and suddenly he was there, and more a part of her than he ever thought possible.

* * *

Cathy sat cross-legged while running her fingers through his sweaty hair.

"You have lovely hair," she said.

"It's just mousy brown," Michael said.

"But so soft, not like mine."

Michael nodded.

"You're my Mudiwa," she said.

"You're my Rudo," he said.

She kissed his wet forehead.

"Mudiwa and Rudo; what happens next?" Michael asked. "I dreamt it and I want to know why. If you tell me the story I may understand the sense of it."

"The sense of it will come in good time. But now, Rudo is too young and inexperienced to realise the truth of what they have."

"That's right, so what happened?"

Chapter Six

A cold wind blew. Mudiwa shivered. They would stay in her mother's hut that night. A sudden gust whipped at him and he held his clothes to his body. The wind eased just as he smelled the fires of Mufakose. He stopped at the first hut and handed his spear to a man of the village.

"I'm Mudiwa," he said.

"I'm Tinashi, son of Rutendo," the man replied.

"You're the brother of Rudo?"

"Yes I am."

Mudiwa nodded and then he headed towards Rudo's hut, disappointed that they wouldn't share her special place beneath the stars. More disappointed that in her mother's hut he wouldn't be able to stay with Rudo for the night. He passed men talking, turned the corner and saw Rudo with Farai from his village! How could she do that to him? Surely she knew what they had was special? Mudiwa stopped as the couple passed by. Despite the cold they were heading into the savannah. Not just the savannah, they were heading to *their* place. He watched them pass and it seemed to take forever. Walking side-by-side, not holding hands, not talking. Mudiwa waited for them to disappear into the blackness and then he felt dizzy. The wind blew again. Cold, cloudy, no moonlight at all. In such darkness, Farai wouldn't be able to see her exquisite beauty. *Stop, what thoughts!* Rudo with Farai when it should be him!

Just then he heard women talking and two girls passed by. The talking stopped, the companions parted, and one of the young women came to him.

"I'm Tatenda," she said.

"I'm Mudiwa from Ghanzi."

"You're visiting our village?"

"Yes, but I can't stay."

She put her hand on his arm, holding him lightly. "But it's cold and I can take you somewhere warm."

"No, I must go."

"It's early and surely you're thirsty after such a long walk."

"No, I'm not feeling well."

"Oh, that's too sad, and you've come such a long way too. I can give you something to drink. That might make you feel better."

In the glow from the doorway of the hut, Mudiwa's companion was fine-looking indeed. But she wasn't Rudo.

Mudiwa held her hand and looked into her eyes. "Thank you for your invitation Tatenda," he said. "But I'm not feeling well and I must go."

"I hope you feel better soon."

"Thank you."

Mudiwa headed towards the track, and stopped where Tinashi waited patiently. Mudiwa took his spear and strode into the bush.

* * *

Mudiwa paced up and down with dirt and dust swirling around his feet. Back and forward, back and forward, until he realised his legs were sore.

He sat on an upturned jug and gazed across the grassy plain. The endless plain; two villages connected. Mudiwa got annoyed with himself. His thoughts were straying. But still a week and it seemed like forever. It *was* forever. The longest time since his initiation. And who was he punishing? Himself! Not Rudo, not Farai: they enjoyed their night together. As if she cared?

Buru strolled towards Mudiwa with that ambling gait of his. Mudiwa smiled at his friend, realising that some men just don't have what it took.

"Hello my friend," Buru cheerfully greeted.

"Hello Buru," Mudiwa replied.

"Are you alright?" Buru asked.

"I'm fine."

"You don't look it. I watched you from over there, and something's on your mind."

"Ah, yes. I need…"

"What?"

"I'm going to Mufakose."

82

Buru nodded.

"Do you want to come?" Mudiwa asked.

"Why not?" Buru said. "It's safer for two to walk in the bush, isn't it?"

"Let's go to the river and wash

Mudiwa rose, and with Buru by his side they walked towards the part of the river where the men bathe. On the way Mudiwa heard women singing while they worked in the fields, with their voices sounding so sweet. Yes, it was time for Mufakose.

* * *

It was a cool but lovely evening and Mudiwa felt cheerful as he approached the outskirts of the village. Maybe he would meet the pretty girl from last week. He struggled to think of her name and then it came to him: Tatenda. She was a sweet girl and so worried that he was feeling unwell. It would be nice to see Tatenda and even better if Rudo saw them together. He smiled to himself. Such a lovely evening. He imagined Tatenda under the full moon. The full moon would make his evening complete.

No men waiting so Mudiwa left his spear at the first hut and ventured into the village. He strolled towards the meeting area with sweet voices on his left. Mudiwa glanced at girls talking amongst themselves, but not Tatenda. He went to the bright, crackling fire and let it warm him for a moment. A young man came to the fire as well.

"Good evening, I'm Mudiwa from Ghanzi."

"Good evening, I'm Tichaona."

"Can I ask you for a favour?"

"Yes, what is it?"

"Do you know of Tatenda and where I might find her?"

Tichaona smiled briefly. "Yes I know of Tatenda. Walk between those huts there," he said, pointing directly opposite. "The fourth hut on the left belongs to her mother."

Mudiwa suddenly felt weak. The fourth hut on the right belonged to Rudo's mother. "Thank you for your help," he said.

Aware he was being watched, Mudiwa walked across the open space and between the huts. He tried to appear calm while he passed the huts: one, two, three and he stopped. Fourth on the left, a pleasant young woman. On his right, someone more than pleasant, someone who was once in a lifetime. But she felt nothing for him, or nothing special at least. Mudiwa took one step to the left and stopped again. And then he turned right and headed towards the doorway. But he couldn't enter, he had to wait. A woman emerged and Mudiwa bowed.

"May I greet you?" he asked.

"I greet you," Rudo's mother replied.

"I am Mudiwa from Ghanzi," he said.

84

"I am Rutendo."

Mudiwa bowed again.

"And you know Rudo?" Rutendo asked.

"Yes I do," Mudiwa said.

"Do you wish me to tell her that you are here?"

"I would be very grateful if you could do this."

"I will tell her."

Rutendo went inside and moments later Rudo burst through the opening and roughly grabbed Mudiwa, holding him tightly without saying a word. Mudiwa hugged her, relishing the touch of her soft skin against his body. Rudo gently squirmed out of his embrace, took his hand, and led him out of the village and towards her special space. She was walking briskly, and Mudiwa walked fast to keep up with her. Still holding his hand, she broke into a steady run. Mudiwa jogged alongside while admiring her delicate beauty. How could he have thought another woman could be a worthy substitute for Rudo? He silently wondered at his stupidity; his determination to make her suffer. After all she was a woman and she picked her men. She decided which partner to share her special pleasures with. How pretentious of him to think he had some sort of right over her? All week he punished himself for nothing! They reached the circle of trees and Rudo stopped.

She grabbed Mudiwa roughly, dragging him close, holding him tight in her arms while they kissed. Mudiwa felt her fingers on his waist, and in a moment she untied his clothes and they fell to the ground. He reached for the delightful curves of her hips, and tried to unpick her leather skirt but it was too tight! Rudo stepped backwards and quickly undid the criss-crossed leather cord on her side, and her skirt parted. She knelt in the grass and Mudiwa knelt in front of her. Again she grabbed him and held him and kissed him. Mudiwa tried to hug her, but it lasted a brief moment. Rudo pulled away and pushed his shoulder and Mudiwa knew what she wanted. He lay on the soft grass and she knelt above him. She looked down on Mudiwa; smiling brightly. Mudiwa's heart raced, this was happening so fast, too fast. One part of him wanted to slow things down but another part was desperate for what was to come.

"Chido ndi, kuboora ndi, bhaudha ndi," she said slowly and deliberately.

Rudo took him. Still smiling she bent to kiss him lightly. Mudiwa wrapped her in his arms, holding her to him; hugging her and kissing her. Rudo eased out of his embrace and sat up, her eyes closed while she moaned gently. Rudo moaned again, and then she dug her fingernails into Mudiwa's chest, but he didn't notice. Instead, he was entranced by his partner's arousal. Rudo gouged Mudiwa until drops of blood appeared, and yet he didn't feel any pain. She dug him as hard as her strength would allow, and then she shrieked!

She consumed his entire being, and only when it was over did he realise what happened. Slowly he returned, opening his eyes, looking up at his beautiful girl with a mixture of satisfaction and surprise.

Rudo still knelt astride him, and Mudiwa thought he saw her cheeks glistening in the blue light. He touched her face with his fingers and wiped her tears away. She took his hand and brought it to her mouth, and gently kissed his fingers.

"I don't know how to say this," she said in a very quiet voice. "Every night I waited for you, but you didn't come."

Mudiwa said nothing.

"But you came for me," Rudo said. "And you saw me, yes?"

"Yes, I saw you," Mudiwa said.

"Tatenda told me she spoke to you, but you weren't feeling well."

Mudiwa nodded.

"But you weren't sick," Rudo said. "It was me, wasn't it?"

"It was."

"You have special feelings for me, I know this now. You're different to other men."

"No, it's not me. It's us together."

"It's us together like this." Rudo bent forward and placed her head on his chest and he embraced her.

"It's more than this," Mudiwa said quietly. "I want more than this."

"How so?"

"I want more than just evenings here. I want to be part of you and I want you to be a part of me. I want to share meals with you, share your children with you, live with...."

Rudo sat up straight. "What, are you mad?" she snapped. "You can't do that!"

"I feel mad," Mudiwa said quietly. "But I also feel saner than any time in my life."

"No! My village, my family, my brother.... Yes, my brother, he would kill you for that. What are you going to do? Live in my mother's house; eat her food, live with us?"

"But...."

"But nothing. I like you, I won't deny it. And you like me, I know this too. But this is just sex in the bush. It's good sex, but sex just the same. And in the mornings, you go to your mother's village and I return to mine. And in the evenings we meet here again."

Mudiwa searched for the right words to say but they wouldn't come to him. He looked at her for a sign and she smiled. She bent forward and kissed him on his forehead.

"My dear sweet Mudiwa," she said. "You're such an unusual man."

"I'm sorry for upsetting you."

"Ssh, it's alright. It's just your way, that's all. Do you want to sleep here with me?"

"Yes."

Rudo got up and Mudiwa watched her lay on the soft grass. He cuddled up to her and she placed his hand on her breast.

"None of this silly talk about living together," she said. "We will see each other here, and we will sleep together too."

"I'm a lucky man." Mudiwa whispered.

And she pressed his hand tighter against her breast.

Chapter Seven

Michael stared at the dark blue Toyota while he waited for Cathy to lock the gate. Still parked across the street with two men sitting impassively in front. He wondered if they'd heard their lovemaking; listening through headphones and snickering like a couple of schoolboys with a girlie magazine. He shivered slightly; that was eerie. Cathy climbed in and Michael drove along Leonard Street and away from the gazes of men who knew too much.

The journey annoyed him: too many buses and trucks belching sooty diesel fumes: that couldn't be healthy. Too many cars trailing oil hazes: that wasn't healthy either. He was relieved to reach the bank and park the car in his reserved spot. He went to his office and switched on the laptop, and then wondered what to do next. Check his emails. Maybe there was a reply about his recommendation for a financial audit. He scrolled the inbox and there it was. A typically Swiss response, formal and stilted, thanking him for bringing the matter to their attention and promising action. He frowned, but he had to do the right thing. Now he could get on with his real job, which were the head office systems followed by the finance company, followed by the branches. A lot of travelling for the project manager and analyst in the coming months. That would be interesting.

Michael looked up to see Washington Mabada standing near Cathy's partition. Something was happening: Mabada and Cathy were facing each other with body language that said much. Cathy had her hands on her hips and Mabada was waving a finger close to her face. She stood her ground, and then pointed to Michael's office. Mabada left Cathy and entered Michael's office; closing the door hard.

"I am very angry with you!" he snapped.

Michael wondered what was going on now.

"I said I am very angry," Mabada repeated with sweat glistening on his forehead.

"Tell me about your problem," Michael said; not wanting to destroy his relationship with the most important local for his project.

"You come here, you take over, you run things, you dazzle our women with your ways."

"Is this about Cathy?" and Michael remembered the confrontation in the office. "Cathy's a grown woman who's made her own way in life."

Mabada leaned over Michael's desk while wiping his forehead with a handkerchief. "This is not a colony Mr Page, we have independence now. Foreigners have to respect their place in society."

Michael stood and gripped his desk tightly. He had to stay calm and not make a bad situation worse. "I do my job and I live with my girlfriend, nothing more."

"You are being disrespectful to me."

"I'm trying not to be."

"There are more important things than Catherine Shoko. You should know this."

This was about the project, the highest priority for the next nine or ten months. "I'm here because you couldn't find anyone locally." He bit his tongue, he had to be calm.

"Mhata!" Mabada snapped.

"What?"

"I'm angry!" Mabada snarled.

And then things made sense. "Do you know anything about a car outside my house?" Michael asked.

"You keep out of things you have no right to meddle in, Michael Page." Mabada opened the door and marched into the general office area, leaving Michael standing at his desk. Michael shook his head and suddenly realised he was holding his desk so tightly that his hands hurt. He checked through the net curtain but Cathy had left her desk. Coffee, even instant, good idea. He went to the tea room and Cathy was boiling the kettle.

"Mabada confronted you about our relationship?" Michael asked.

"Yes," Cathy replied.

"He's jealous of us."

She nodded in agreement.

"He said it's something else too, probably my job," Michael said. "He's not fit to be a manager. You know he got his job through the party."

"Through the party?" Cathy asked, sounding surprised.

"Political appointment, tokenism."

"Really?"

"I'm wondering if he's involved with the bugging."

The kettle clicked off and Cathy poured two mugs. "He could be," she said. "He had to be high up in Zanu to get a job like his. We should be careful with him."

"How careful?"

"Very careful. How did the email go?"

"They thanked me, and they'll get in touch when they set the schedule."

Cathy sipped her steaming drink. "That's not good. They're going to be here soon."

"We'll finish here as quickly as we can, and then we'll get onto the finance company."

"I will ask Alice to help me."

"We'll both ask her."

Michael took his mug to the partitioned area and sat in Cathy's seat. Alice looked across and froze. "I want to talk with you," Michael said.

She looked around and put her head down. "Not here," she said quietly.

"Okay. Cathy and I often have lunch in the Harare Gardens. Perhaps we can talk over lunch."

"Only if we go separately."

"Meet you at twelve?"

She nodded and Michael left her.

* * *

Michael and Cathy walked in silence to the park, carrying tubs of yoghurt and fresh bananas and mangoes. Busy Harare had a lunchtime crush of city workers, but the gardens were peace and calm. Perhaps the local's didn't realise the gem they had, but after the bleakness of Melbourne, the gardens was like an oasis in a city centre. They found a bench in the shade of a palm tree and Michael shared out their food. Michael finished his yoghurt and started on a mango while wondering if Alice was coming. And then he was aware of a presence, and looked into the sun to see Alice Kanengoni standing over him.

"Sit please," Michael said, and she sat beside him.

"Why do you want to see me, Mr Page?" Alice asked.

"Michael please, and I was wondering if you could help us on the project."

"No, I could not do that. Mr Mabada would get very angry with me."

"I understand." Michael guessed she knew a lot about the branch. Indeed she probably knew everything worthwhile. She was a good communicator; she listened a

94

lot. "Alice, this is safe here so you can talk to me. You understand this, don't you?"

She nodded.

"And whatever you say is just between you and me," Michael continued. "You can trust me."

She nodded again.

"Do you know what's going on with Mr Mabada?" Michael asked.

"He is angry with you and with Cathy," Alice said.

"Do you know why?"

"I do not know for certain. But I saw him talking to Liz and Jenny just before he came to speak with Cathy."

"Who are Liz and Jenny?"

"They do data entry."

"Data entry of what?"

"Invoices, credit notes and receipts."

"Financial data entry?"

"Yes."

"Cash advances and claims for expenses?"

"Yes, those as well."

"Do Liz and Jenny work for Mr Mabada?"

"Yes. Information technology provides a data processing service for accounts."

"Okay. I understand why you can't work with us, but thank you for talking with me."

"I can go now?" Alice asked.

"Of course, and thank you."

Alice got up and Michael watched her head towards Julius Nyere Way.

"Mabada's behind the fraud," Cathy said.

Michael ate some mango and thought about what was going on.

"He can't be, it's too big," Cathy corrected herself. "It's Mabada, but it has to be Mukoko and probably Katsvete as well."

Accountant and branch manager. She was probably right.

"They take a share each," Cathy said. "And everyone's doing well until we come along."

Michael nodded in agreement and finished his mango. Cathy started on her mango and Michael waited for her to finish. He was impatient to get back to the office and get things going. And it was time for the project manager to help with testing, because the sooner they were finished the better. Cathy had finished her fruit and was staring at the green grass at her feet.

"Let's go," Michael said.

* * *

Michael spent the rest of the afternoon recording keystrokes on their computer test programme; mindless repetitive work. And he loved it. It was relaxing to follow Cathy's script while she wrote the next one. And satisfying to be making solid progress, and satisfying that they worked well as a team too. Perhaps more satisfying to think that Michael Page and Catherine Shoko, despite their differences in background, had many things in common. It was a shame that the year 2000 project in Zimbabwe was unique, and it was unlikely they would work like that again.

Michael kept at his task until weariness overtook him. Making too many simple mistakes. Cathy's scripts looked a bit ragged too, and by five-thirty it was more than late enough to be heading home. Another thing they had in common, they both didn't cope with long hours terribly well.

It was a slow drive home in heavy traffic and Michael was glad to see Leonard Street, despite the dark blue car parked across their house. It really was absurd and he wondered what they hoped to achieve, beyond listening to trivial conversations or a couple making love. Or perhaps there was something more than surveillance and bugging. Perhaps they were there to affect him. Michael stopped his car and Cathy got out to open the gate. Moments later, Michael climbed out and strode across the road to the Toyota under the streetlight. Two heads turned in synchronisation. Two men looked at him approaching.

"No!" Cathy screamed, and she ran towards Michael, grabbing his arm and pulling hard. "Don't do it," she said.

Michael turned to face her.

"No," she said again. "It will make it worse."

97

"But it's time for this to be over."

"Not this way. Please come with me." Still holding Michael's arm she led him towards the Mercedes. "Those men have no more power than you or I," she said.

"But it's invading our privacy."

"I know, but it's pointless. And they would report you, which could make it worse."

"How do we stop it?"

"Keep out of Mabada's way."

Michael glared at Cathy even though he knew she was right. He parked the Mercedes in the garage and went inside to change his clothes. They ate yet another meal of pasta, but in silence.

After dinner Michael wanted something to brighten his mood, and not The Main News either. He went to the bookcase in the lounge room and contemplated the rows of novels. Suddenly a door slammed and he jumped a metre!

"Sorry," Cathy called from the far end of the house.

Michael sighed and decided he didn't want to start a book after all. Perhaps some music, but something suited to how he felt. He flicked through the rack and pulled out the black and amber-coloured double-CD and put the first disk in the player. The music started slowly, haunting and mournful. It was achingly simple and beautiful, and within moments he felt better.

"That's nice," Cathy said, settling into one of the armchairs.

Michael looked across the room. "Music by Ry Cooder, it's a collection of his soundtrack music. This is the theme from Paris, Texas."

"Paris, Texas?"

"It's a marvellous film. You know the Scottish band Texas named themselves after it."

"I don't know what you're talking about."

"It's okay," Michael said while he got comfortable in the other leather chair. Despite the lovely music there was no denying how he felt inside. "I'm worried about – you know," he said.

"That's natural, but there's nothing we can do about it. In any case we're going to...," but left their destination unsaid. "We should take our minds off things."

"Yes, but how?"

"I think something inn.... Some more of the story?"

"Why not?"

Why not indeed.

* * *

Mudiwa lay on his back in the grass. All was perfect in the world. He glanced to Rudo lying beside him. "Rudo...," he said, and then he remembered last night's conversation.

She looked at him and their eyes met.

"Rudo, kunaka chikomba wangu," Mudiwa said.

She smiled brightly. "Kunaka hanzwadzi wangu," she replied.

They lay on the grass in silence: Mudiwa's pretty lover, Rudo's handsome cousin.

"I like you," Rudo said quietly.

"I like you too," Mudiwa replied, and then he rolled onto his side to admire his beautiful companion.

"No!" Rudo said, moving to sit cross-legged. "I like you but I can't put it into words. I have such strange feelings. I crave you even though we're together like this. It's confusing and I don't like to be confused. But it's a beautiful feeling too, and I don't want to lose it." She punched his shoulder. "I hate you for what you've done to me. You've put me under a spell; you've done strange things to me."

"I have the same feelings, which is why I come to see you every night. Every day, all I can think of is being with you for the night."

"Are these nights enough?"

"Without these nights I don't know what I'd do."

"You didn't answer my question."

"No," he said quietly. "They're not enough."

"Why do we feel like this?" Rudo asked.

"I don't know."

"What can we do about these feelings?"

"Yesterday I suggested...."

"No, we can't do that."

"Perhaps there's a way."

An elephant trumpeted in the distance and Mudiwa shivered with the mournful noise.

"You should go," Rudo said.

"Can I see you tomorrow night?" Mudiwa asked.

"Yes – no – I don't know."

"Please?"

"Just go."

Chapter Eight

Mudiwa struggled to concentrate, and then he stumbled over a baobab tree root and swore. He rubbed his eyes and continued towards Mufakose. Again his thoughts drifted. Would Rudo see him again? If she did, would they share anything more than nights in the scrub? And even if she agreed to more, what could they do? She was right. Mudiwa could never share her mother's home, and relocating to the men's compound at Mufakose would be just as ridiculous. And yet he needed to be part of her life. And her reaction yesterday, telling him to go. Would she blame him for the way she felt? Would she even see him?

Mudiwa stopped and handed his spear to the man waiting for visitors. In the darkness, something about this man seemed familiar.

"You come to see my sister again," the man said, and Mudiwa realised he was Tinashi, brother of Rudo.

"Only if she wants to see me," Mudiwa replied.

Tinashi held Mudiwa's spear horizontally, blocking the path. "That is understood," he said. "But it's wrong for you to see her all the time."

"Why is it wrong?"

"No-one has ever done such a thing before."

"It's her right to choose a man to spend the night with."

"If you hurt her, I will kill you."

"I'm not going to hurt her."

Tinashi slowly brought the spear around, pointing it at Mudiwa's throat. "It's wrong for her to get involved with a visitor like you."

"That's right; I'm just a visitor for the night."

"No, you're more than that. You know it's my job to protect her just as it's your job to protect your sister, and I say this thing between you and her is wrong."

"It's...," and Mudiwa didn't know what to say.

"It's my right to say what's right or wrong!" Tinashi said firmly. "If you hurt my sister in any way, I will come after you. Cousin or not, I will find you and kill you."

"This is Rudo's decision".

"No it's not."

"Yes it is! Now, I must go."

Mudiwa stepped away from the spear, took a breath, and continued towards Rudo's hut. He felt light-headed; almost dizzy. Was it the confrontation with Tinashi or the confrontation to come? Both, most likely. He rounded the corner and in the near darkness he spotted her fine form, standing next to the cooking hearth like she was waiting for him. Mudiwa strode faster, almost racing to his beautiful woman. Rudo rushed to Mudiwa and grabbed his arms, burying her head against his chest. He held her, and she looked him in the eyes.

"My brother came to see me," she said.

"He spoke to me too."

"I don't know what to do."

"What do the voices in your head tell you?"

"That I'm sharing something very special with you."

"Then you know what to do."

"But what, how?"

"Tonight, after everyone's asleep we can slip away. We will leave this place, we will leave your brother and start somewhere new."

"But...."

"It's easy. All we need are you and me. I can hunt and you can grow vegetables and we will have enough food for the two of us, and your children if the ancestors wish it."

"I don't understand."

"With the feelings we have for each other, we can do anything."

"Just you and me?"

"Yes."

"After the clearing?"

"Yes, when everyone's asleep."

Rudo eased herself out of Mudiwa's embrace and took his hand, leading him out of the village. For a moment, Mudiwa wanted to look over his shoulder to check for Tinashi, but then he realised everyone knew. They were Rudo and Mudiwa going into the bush to have sex, and tomorrow he would be gone, or so they thought. Rudo was running now, and Mudiwa jogged beside his darling towards the circle of trees.

Although Rudo was wearing just a tiny leather skirt, Mudiwa couldn't wait to remove it and have her naked in his arms. He patiently unlaced it, and she watched him undress her. Naked, she undressed him and then she looked him over. Mudiwa hugged her, and she buried her head on his shoulder.

"Do you think we were made for each other in some way?" she asked.

"Perhaps the ancestors have something special planned for us," he said.

"Every time I see you, I want you."

"Me too."

"And now we're naked in each others arms."

"As the ancestors intended."

He ran his fingers over the curves of her body. She was so small, so young, so lovely; it seemed impossible to believe that soon she would be his and his alone. She touched him and he was ready for her. He sat on the grass, she sat on his lap, and they became one. For a moment that seemed to last forever, or seemed to pass in a flash, nothing else in the world mattered.

And then came the ultimate realisation of their love, even though they didn't know the existence of such a word.

But they knew what they felt for each other was very special, which is why they couldn't let it go. They held each other that quiet night, alone on the African savannah.

"I'm scared," Rudo said quietly.

"I know," Mudiwa replied.

Noise in the distance and Mudiwa froze. Animals closing. He looked for a refuge and it was time to climb a tree. Rudo climbed off Mudiwa's lap and got up, and he joined her. He took a step and stopped. He heard voices. Too close and not enough time to climb a tree. He held Rudo's hand and waited.

Four men entered the clearing.

"Brother, Uncle Munashe," Rudo said.

Two men strode to Mudiwa and got very close to him. Tinashi and an older man, Rudo's uncle; both with angry faces. Mudiwa let Rudo's hand go and she backed away. The men stood their ground, with the two other men in the background holding spears. Mudiwa's heart pounded and he struggled for breath.

"I warned you," Tinashi said.

"Is this him?" the older man asked.

"Yes Uncle."

"I'm here for my niece," Munashe said.

"I'm a grown woman and I make up my own mind," Rudo snapped. "Mudiwa's good with women, which is why I see him." She looked her brother in the eyes. "By this you have brought shame on me!" she shouted. "You dare to question which man I choose! And you Uncle Munashe, you're the brother of my mother and my guardian, but you know it's my right to be here with a lover!"

"You're too young to realise what shame you bring to your mother and yourself by getting involved with one of your cousins."

"I'm old enough to know there's nothing wrong with seeing a man who is kind, and who knows his way with women."

"I'm here to take you from this place," Munashe said, grabbing Rudo by the forearm and holding her tight. Rudo squealed with her face contorted in pain.

Mudiwa grabbed Munashe's hand to prise his fingers apart. "You're hurting her," he said.

Tinashi suddenly pushed Mudiwa who stumbled backwards in surprise. Tinashi lashed out at Mudiwa who grabbed at his assailant and dragged him down to the grass. The two men rolled on the ground. Mudiwa struggled to land a blow in Tinashi's side but they were too evenly matched. With Mudiwa on his back and Tinashi above, Mudiwa stopped resisting. Tinashi relaxed and Mudiwa struck him as hard as he could. Tinashi gasped and Mudiwa easily rolled him to one side and got to his feet, only to have the two other men grab him and hold him tight. Mudiwa squirmed to break free, but two against one was impossible. Breathing hard with the exertion of his brief fight, he looked the old man in the eyes.

"You've got what you wanted," he said. "You can take Rudo, but you disgrace her this night."

"You're not to see my niece again," Munashe said. "Or the consequences will be serious."

Tinashi slowly stood; obviously in pain. The two men released Mudiwa and he watched the foursome lead Rudo out of the clearing and towards the village.

* * *

Mudiwa advanced on Mufakose from the north. Ahead all was peaceful and still. Everyone asleep – he hoped. Mudiwa kept his head low and crept between the huts. Carefully he advanced to where Rudo should be sleeping. Slowly moving from building to building. He reached the doorway, peeled the leather strip away and went inside.

Even though Mudiwa's eyes were used to the night, it was much darker inside the hut. Mudiwa noticed a shape in front and another to his left. He reached out for the hanging leather where it met the wall and lifted it back, peering inside the sleeping quarters. A woman on her sleeping mat, but too well-built for Rudo. It must be her mother. At the other sleeping quarters Mudiwa parted the screen and....

"The young man returns."

Munashe and Tinashi! On the far side of the sleeping area, he just made out Rudo sitting against the wall.

"Mudiwa, you must go," Rudo said in a flat voice.

"You heard her," Tinashi said.

"Please go," Rudo said.

Mudiwa turned and headed out the doorway.

Chapter Nine

It was the morning of the last Saturday in March, and the air was crisp and still with the sun shining from a deep blue sky. Michael was more than pleased to be getting away from Harare for a few days. An early start, eight, for the almost three-hundred kilometre drive to Mutare. A bug-free drive too. Michael eventually found the little silver disc wedged into the roof lining behind the rear-vision mirror. He guessed they should get to Cathy's parents just before lunch for what was going to be an enjoyable weekend.

Many intimate conversations, especially over the past few weeks. Pasts laid bare, futures discussed. Dreams, hopes, disappointments, ambitions, desires. Her father was a school headmaster and Cathy was inspired by him in many ways. For her excellent English, not just to communicate but to be a citizen of the world. For her degree, the opportunity of her lifetime. For her move to Australia, to turn her qualifications into a career. And many things unspoken: her quick mind and her organised approach to everything she did. She certainly was the oldest daughter of the school headmaster.

Julie was quite different to her older sister, getting a simple qualification from the polytechnic, and satisfied with a job which paid her way with enough money to spend on small luxuries like new clothes and journeys home on the bus.

But she was a personable young lady. Apparently Julie was close to the Baptist Church while Cathy had different views. As always, Cathy's enquiring mind analysing – before she decided that the bigger picture was more complex than middle-eastern writings of two-thousand years ago. Cathy was proud of her African-ness, and followed her own path through Africa's spiritual heritage. Michael wanted to learn more of what she believed.

They cleared Harare by driving along the Mutare Road beyond the suburb of Green Grove and the light-industrial area of Msasa. The landscape was surprisingly familiar: flat plains fenced into fields. Big farms of crops and pastures. Brown grass, wire fences, scrubby road verges, trees here and there. They could have been driving through the farming areas of Australia. And not. Pedestrians walked along the highway; something never seen in Australia. On the left a family group: a man followed by his family. Several steps behind was his wife, dressed in a red and orange wrap topped by a dark-red head scarf, balancing a bag of maize meal and a large sack of something else on her head. Tied on her back was a baby, held in place with a brown scarf. Holding her hands were two children, aged about two and four. On the right was another family group heading east. Husband ahead, brightly-dressed wife following, two youngsters at her ankles. In the trees monkeys jumped from branch to branch. A packed bus roared past with all manner of items strapped to the roof. And then the army: three personnel carriers in brown and green camouflage, with soldiers in green uniforms surrounded by machine guns. A sign beside the road, 'Marondera'. Another sign, sixty, Michael slowed.

Marondera had a dozen or more shops on either side of a broad main street. Each shop was white-painted brick, flat roofed and with a veranda supported on brick pillars. Many parked cars were shaded by jacaranda trees. Old cars like the rest of Zimbabwe. Men sat under shady verandas while women bustled about. It was a sexist society. Michael glanced at his companion and he understood her better because of their journey. Indeed, he understood the headmaster's daughter extremely well. They continued along the main street until the town petered out. Marondera gave way to farmland with thick, green crops.

"Tobacco," Cathy said.

Michael cruised along at about one-ten or so, while noticing the road was steadily climbing.

"We're close to home," Cathy said, "Manicaland."

"Homesick?"

"Yes."

The road continued to climb and there were many curves. The landscape changed to dense forest for twenty or so kilometres. No people walking either. And then another tobacco farm and Michael noticed a dirt track leading to a

112

group of small white buildings, with several men and women heading towards the main road. He glanced at Cathy.

"A village," she said.

"A traditional village?" Michael asked.

"Sort-of. They have electricity, although just cables strung in the air. But they live in huts and work on the big farms, and listen to the radio in the evenings."

"They work on farms owned by white farmers?"

"Yes, the farms are owned by whites."

"Does this cause resentment?"

"Yes, of course. Mugabe has talked of land reform for so long, but he knows things can't change. If we broke these farms up; what would the villagers do? Subsistence farming: a patch of mealie, a patch of yams? Subsistence farming won't feed the cities. And our export crops? Without beef and tobacco, how can we pay for imports like fuel and other essentials?"

"Do you think he'll do land reform?"

"In my heart I hope not, because that would be a disaster. The economy would be ruined and the country would starve. It would be terrible."

"What does your head tell you?"

"Ha, my head's too logical! My head tells me that Zimbabweans want change, and the MDC is our first hope in twenty years. But Mugabe will do anything to keep power.

Land reform will buy him votes in rural areas, even if he destroys my country in the process."

"But he'll do this only if he feels politically threatened?"

"Yes. These are dangerous times, and we must always be careful of what we say and what we do."

They were climbing through a series of curves, slowed by a truck. The fumes were sickening, so Michael turned on the airconditioning. The road straightened so he checked the mirror and accelerated. And just behind was a black SUV. He turned off the airconditioning and wondered. He gripped the leather wheel tighter. Maybe it was about time to deal with this, or maybe not. Would Mutare, amongst Cathy's clan, be safer? He continued onwards, they had done one-hundred and eighty kilometres, well over half-way. A crest in the road, the highway blind. A white car was ahead with brake lights on and slowing. *What now?* Michael lifted his right foot and checked the mirror; the SUV still about fifty or sixty metres behind. Over the crest and just before the next curve, a roadblock. Damn! The white car, brake lights off and through the gap in the white barrier. And then a soldier strode forward and put his hand up. Emerging from behind trees on the road verge were four more soldiers holding black machineguns. Michael stopped the Mercedes and the nearest soldier walked towards the car with a machinegun casually hanging over his shoulder. Michael lowered the window.

"Mr Michael Page, Miss Catherine Shoko, step out of the car please," the soldier asked.

"What's this about?" Michael snapped.

The soldier raised his gun.

"Do it Michael," Cathy said flatly.

Michael opened the door and climbed out. The other four soldiers closed with guns ready as if Cathy and he were dangerous criminals.

"Look," Michael said, "this is getting..."

"Silence!" and Michael staggered backwards in excruciating pain, his jaw on fire. *Fuck, where'd that come from?* The bastard must have hit him, but he was fucking quick.

Cathy screamed! Michael looked up and she was being held with her arms pulled painfully hard behind her.

"Let her go!" Michael bellowed.

"Silence!" and Michael ducked, avoiding a second blow. A machinegun barrel was poked against his ribs, just hard enough to hurt. "Do not make a noise."

Michael nodded while he looked at Cathy squirming to get her arms free.

"Stand up Mr Page."

Michael straightened and one of the soldiers grabbed his arms like Cathy, but he didn't pull them tight.

"This way please."

They were taken past two soldiers dismantling the barrier. The commanding soldier led, Michael walking side-by-side with Cathy, and two soldiers followed, holding wrists tight. Cathy looked straight ahead while Michael scanned all around for something, anything, to get them out of this. But there wasn't anything.

They rounded the curve to a brown and green-patterned jeep parked on the gravel verge; almost hiding behind a large baobab tree. Cathy was pushed and half-tripped, but she regained her footing. Michael wanted to yell at the men to respect her, but that would be futile. Cathy stumbled on ruts in the dirt, and her stiletto ankle boots were not made for rough ground. The soldier forced her towards the rear of the jeep. The rear panel was open, exposing two rows of green metal seats. Cathy was pushed and she fell, hitting the ground hard.

"Fuck!" Michael shouted, and such pain! His head – excruciating! Michael felt himself on the ground with no idea how he got there. Everything was blurry and the ground started to move. He reached out to stop falling, but that didn't help. Something dark was nearby, and he grabbed at it and missed. He grabbed a second time, and again he missed. In the background, strange noises, distorted and indistinct. And his head, it hurt so much, the only thing in the world was the ache in his head.

* * *

Michael woke and he was sore all over: his hips, his shoulders, his knees. He stretched, and groaned when a sharp stab ripped through him. He rolled onto his back and that felt better, except for an intense headache. And his head, it felt really strange. He touched his head and there was cotton on it. He touched again, a bandage. Aaah, someone hit him.

It was dark and it smelled bad. No, it smelled awful. And he was tired, so very tired.

Michael rolled onto his other side and closed his eyes, and that felt better. He decided to sleep for a few moments, just a few moments. With his eyes closed he saw four men; who were they? And then he recognised two of them. Ah yes, that made sense.

* *

They were close to Mufakose. Passing the small lake near the track, with the waterhole ringed by a herd of giraffes. Mudiwa turned to his companions.

"Let's stop and go over the plan," he said.

"What, again?" Buru replied.

"This is dangerous and we can't afford to take chances.'

"You're more worried that if this goes wrong, you won't see your pretty girl again."

Mudiwa glared at his friend.

"Alright, let's go over it again," Buru said wearily.

Mudiwa led the way off the track and sat behind a baobab tree. The sun was close to setting, with scrub

117

silhouetted black against an orange sky. In the foreground a flock of flamingos suddenly took to the sky, noiselessly skimming just above nearby trees. Mudiwa was entranced by the scene. By that time tomorrow, Rudo and he would have a home somewhere safe by a river. He imagined the two of them sitting on the ground, hand-in-hand and watching a sunset like tonight. But first, business.

"Buru and Dakarai," he said, "Tinashi is tall, as tall as me, and well built. He's easy to recognise, he's got a scar on his arm here," Mudiwa continued, touching his own arm half-way between his shoulder and elbow. "He often waits for travellers, so with luck you won't have to search for him. If not there, he may be at Rudo's hut protecting her from me. To get to Rudo's hut you cross the meeting area, and her hut is fourth on the right with a leather hide hanging across the doorway."

"And if we find him?" Dakarai asked.

"Tell him you're from Ghanzi, and that you've seen me at the meeting area. Encourage him to come with you. If that doesn't work, overpower him so that I can grab Rudo and get away."

"But you said he's big and tall," Dakarai said.

"Yes, and there's two of you. I beat him on my own in a fight, so you two can do it."

They said nothing. Buru and Dakarai were old friends of Mudiwa; they were initiated together. Tafadzwa was different, an acquaintance of Buru's brother, two years younger and recently initiated. Mudiwa wondered if he was up to the task of dealing with Rudo's uncle. Mudiwa frowned.

"Tafadzwa," Mudiwa said. "Your job is to find Rudo's uncle Munashe and distract him. Most likely he will be in the men's compound, which is over there," he said, pointing to the left of the village. "Your story is that you were coming from our village and you came across Tinashi lying in the grass next to this track You think he's been bitten by a snake. As his uncle, Munashe will come straight away. Lead him here."

"But what happens when there's no Tinashi lying in the grass?"

Mudiwa shrugged his shoulders. "It wasn't a snakebite; it was something else."

Silence.

"We can do this," Mudiwa said. "I don't need much time to get to Rudo, and for the two of us to get away."

"Where're you going?"

"Far away," Mudiwa said, wanting to tell his friends Buru and Dakarai, but deciding not. Even though they wouldn't deliberately tell anyone, accidents could happen. "One day, when things settle down, I can return to Ghanzi."

Buru nodded.

"I will head into the bush and get close to Rudo's hut. Then I will give you enough time."

"Good luck friend," Buru said.

Mudiwa used the faint light of a setting sun to guide him through trees and scrub, heading towards Mufakose but keeping to the right of the village. Something moved ahead and Mudiwa stopped. The story about Tinashi's snakebite made him nervous. But still, walking in long grass in early evening was dangerous indeed. Mudiwa waited a moment, snakes rarely attacked unless provoked, and then moved onwards, with a faint glow from the village helping him find his way. He continued south with Rudo's clearing on his right and the village on his left. Mudiwa emerged from scrub into grassland and the going was much easier. He kept low and closed on the worn pathway that led towards the nearby hills. He used that pathway to advance on the outermost hut of the village. There he waited, guessing it took him twice as long to get there as if he used the main track. In the quiet of the cool night, biding time seemed to take forever. If only he knew what was happening! Impatient, he got up and entered the village, walking tall so to not appear suspicious. He passed the outermost huts, getting closer. He reached the rear of Rudo's hut and stopped, but all still and quiet. He kept close to the hut and circled it towards the doorway. Still not a sound. He wondered if that was a good sign or not. He reached the leather hide and paused, sweaty despite the cold. Mudiwa peeled the hide away and slipped inside to where it was warm and bright from a small fire. On the left was Rudo's mother, and Mudiwa had to do the right thing. He knelt before her.

"May I greet you?" he asked.

"I greet you."

"We have met before. I am Mudiwa from Ghanzi and I have come for your daughter."

"I remember you," she replied. "And I know why you are here."

"I want your blessing."

"Will it stop you if I don't give it?"

"This is Rudo's choice."

"Rudo," Rutendo called. "Come here."

Rudo emerged from behind a leather screen and sat beside her mother.

"Your cousin Mudiwa is here for you," Rutendo said. "Do you wish to see him?"

"If it pleases you Mother," Rudo said.

"And if it doesn't?"

"I would rather it did."

"What is it that makes you behave like this?"

"It's something very special that the two of us share," Rudo replied. "An exhilaration that's beyond description. Have you ever felt this way about a man?"

Rutendo turned her head and looked her daughter in the eyes. "Yes my daughter, a long time ago, just before I had you. But the ancestors decided I would have a child and I was no longer able to see him."

"And after?"

"You know the tradition." She looked to the ground. "No, I never saw him again."

"Do you bless us Mother?"

"Mudiwa, I want you to protect my daughter, and I want you to treat her like the treasure that she is. And if the ancestors decide for her have a child, I want you to stay with her until she is ready for you again. I want you two to share your wonderful gift for the rest of your lives. Will you do this for me?"

"Yes," Mudiwa replied.

"Rudo, you have my blessing. Now, you must go. Your uncle and your brother don't know of the feelings that special people have for each other. I wish I could make them understand, but they know of nothing but traditions."

"Thank you Mother," Rudo said.

"Rudo, are you ready?" Mudiwa asked.

"I've packed my things."

Rudo went behind the leather and returned moments later with a package wrapped in a skin. Mudiwa stood and bowed.

"Goodbye Rutendo," he said. He took Rudo's hand and led her out of her mother's hut.

Outside all was still. His companions must have been successful.

"Where are we going?" Rudo asked.

"We will head towards the Odzi River and walk upstream until we find somewhere to build a home."

They walked through the grass and past her special clearing for the last time. Mudiwa felt a pang of remorse. Wouldn't it be lovely to be able to remain in her village and continue to visit that special place for all time? But such things would never be. Still holding hands, they trudged westward through the long grass with Mudiwa alert for dangers. But everything was quiet that lovely evening, while they headed away from Mufakose and towards a new life.

Mudiwa stopped because he sensed a presence. No sound, but something was out there. Only one animal was smart enough to track in the dark without making a noise.

"It's your brother and uncle," Mudiwa whispered.

"Where?" Rudo whispered back.

"Close. Can you run?"

"Yes."

"Give me your things."

Rudo handed her bundle to Mudiwa and he began to jog with Rudo keeping up with him. He ran faster and still she matched his stride. She was a young girl and fit, and

Mudiwa was relieved. Silently they ran across the plain with Mudiwa trying to think for a solution to their problem. Their tracks were clearly visible before, and now they were running their tracks would be even easier to follow. They could run all night and still be in danger. *Bechenura!* They were so close to getting away and now it was hopeless.

They were climbing and Mudiwa realised he'd never been that far west before. He half-stumbled over some uneven ground, but Rudo was surprisingly swift and sure-footed. This girl was full of surprises! He was a lucky man, if they got away. Still they climbed and still the men followed. How many? Their scent was easy to pick, so at least three or four or maybe more.

The ground became rougher and they were running downhill. Suddenly, Rudo fell, hitting the ground almost silently. Mudiwa stopped and held out his hand for her, and she got up but was gasping for breath. *Dhodhi!* She was almost done for and the men were even closer.

"Can you do it?" Mudiwa asked.

Heavy breathing. "I'll try," she said, panting hard.

"Please."

He took her hand and they stumbled onwards.

"Look!" Tinashi's shouted.

"My brother," Rudo said.

"He's close," Mudiwa said.

"Mudiwa...," she panted.

"Please run."

They ran with Rudo almost spent. Mudiwa pictured being surrounded by four men, probably the same men from the other night, with Rudo flat on the ground and unable to take another step. Trapped and cornered like animals. All they could do was run until exhaustion, and then what? And suddenly, above Rudo's laboured breathing, Mudiwa heard noise. Water. Water running. A river nearby. They had to get to the river.

"The river," Mudiwa gasped. "We'll make for the river."

No response but Rudo kept on running, struggling to keep her footing on the increasingly rough ground. Careering downhill with the noise of the water much louder. Ahead Mudiwa saw scrub and trees. At last, they must be close to the river. He headed towards the dark mass and stopped. He looked all around. *Now what?* There seemed to be a break just over there, so he took Rudo's hand and they headed to the left. Mudiwa felt the world closing in on him, the bush surrounding him and crushing him down. Nothing but a useless break in trees and shrubs. They went into the break, and in the darkness Mudiwa noticed the river was moderately wide running steadily, and animals had trampled the scrub and were using a fallen tree to cross the water. It was a big tree, and almost as wide as a man was tall. Not a moment to lose.

"Under the tree," he whispered.

"What?" Rudo asked.

"Down the bank and under the tree."

Mudiwa slid down the steep bank while holding onto branches poking from the fallen tree. Rudo slid past and he reached out and grabbed her left arm to stop her from slipping into the water. Using all his remaining strength, he pulled Rudo onto a ledge. She was breathing harder than ever, but Mudiwa hoped the noise of the water....

"Mhata!" Tinashi swore. "Where are they? We should've caught them."

"They were too fast," Munashe replied.

"For you, but not for me."

"Quiet!"

"But she's just a girl."

"Quiet."

Silence.

"A tree across the river," Munashe said. "They've crossed that way."

Mudiwa's heart beat heavy as he heard them get closer and closer. He smelt their scent, clear and sharp. Sweaty male bodies. Her brother Tinashi with brute strength, and her uncle Munashe with brains. Closer and closer, the tree rocked. The men crossed the river. He heard them, smelled them, and they were gone. And being an animal trail, they wouldn't be able to track. They'd lost their prey and had

126

no way of knowing. The scent of the men was fainter and fainter until it was gone.

"Can you go on?" Mudiwa asked.

"My legs are too sore."

"It's alright."

"But they will catch us."

"No, not for a while. Four men crossed the bridge, but on the other side are many animal tracks. They know that I know how to use those tracks, so they won't be surprised that they've lost us."

"So we're safe?"

"For now. They will return, and by then we must be gone."

"When?"

Mudiwa rubbed his chin while he thought. "We have enough time to recover," he said.

Rudo kissed his cheek, and Mudiwa got as comfortable on the rocky ledge as he could.

Chapter Ten

The deep voice boomed out of nowhere. "You are in trouble white man."

Michael sat up and winced in pain. Where was he? He was sitting on a thin mattress on a concrete floor with coarse blankets at his feet. Unpainted brick walls all around and a green steel door hanging open. His clothes, orange cotton overalls. At the door two men: a middle-aged African about as tall as himself, and a slightly shorter African policeman in a blue uniform. The middle-aged guy was dressed casually, and looking relaxed while he smoked a cigarette.

"Stand up Mr Page."

Michael got up and he ached so badly. And thirsty. He was so thirsty.

"Some water please," Michael asked.

"Over there."

In the corner was a bucket, and above the bucket was a shelf with a shallow basin and a stainless steel flask. Michael grabbed the flask and half-emptied it. That felt better. He put it down and slowly turned around.

"What's this about?" Michael asked while wondering why he was in that place; dressed in those clothes. It didn't make sense.

"You are in trouble," the African with the cigarette said.

"Yeah, you said that. Why?"

"You have been deliberately undermining the good government of Comrade Mugabe."

"How?"

"You have been spying for MDC."

"Pardon?"

"You heard me. You have been giving secrets to the traitorous opposition. You have been helping those who wish to trample Zanu into the dust!"

"Bullshit."

Crack, the policeman slapped Michael's face hard! Michael rubbed his stinging cheek.

"You will show respect!" the policeman snapped.

Michael nodded while feeling more confused than ever.

The talkative man got up close; smelling of cheap scent. "The party is everything and you have been trying to destroy it." He moved away. "Come with us," he said. "To discover what secrets you have given to the treacherous scum who wish to destroy our country."

The policeman grabbed Michael's arm and guided him out of the cell and into a corridor. About twenty metres long, with bare brick walls illuminated by naked globes hanging on wires. On the right were three, green steel doors, each with a head-high barred opening about one metre by one metre. And then he realised where he was. Michael was led around a corner and into a brick room painted white, garishly illuminated by a large fluorescent light fitting. The room was quite large, about ten metres by ten metres. Near the door was a woodgrain laminate table with three steel-framed, vinyl-covered chairs. Opposite was a two metre long wooden bench about waist high. Against the wall was a small timber cabinet with a reel-to-reel tape recorder.

"Sit."

Michael sat at the nearest chair, and the middle-aged man sat in a chair across the table. The policeman stood next to the door.

"I am David Mandipaka," the casually dressed man said before butting his cigarette in a tin ashtray on the table. "I have some questions to ask you, Michael Page."

Michael nodded while he took in all that was around him; trying to make sense of it.

"You work as a project manager for the CBAC bank?" Mandipaka asked.

"That's right," Michael replied.

"And you have access to account information on clients of the bank?"

"No, not really."

"Yes or no?"

"Well, I have password access to all systems, but I only use them for testing."

"So you have access?"

"I have, but only for testing."

"The accounts of our president and his wife?"

"I don't know anything about the president, or his wife."

Mandipaka got to his feet and walked slowly to the green wooden bench, Michael watched him pick up a thin cane about a metre long. He returned to the table and slapped it hard with an almighty 'thwack'. Michael jumped involuntarily. Mandipaka leaned forward.

"You know the financial details of the president and his wife," Mandipaka said. "And you have told the Australian Government, and they have told Morgan Tsvangirai."

"Leader of the MDC?"

"That is right."

"That's ridiculous!"

Mandipaka cracked the cane against the desk again. "Tell me the truth!"

"I have."

Mandipaka stood up straight and flexed the cane. "I could hit you with this," he said.

Michael jumped to his feet. "The fuck you will!"

A sharp blow to his side, and Michael doubled over with the pain. The policeman.

"I'm an Australian citizen and I demand to see the Australian ambassador."

"Sit down," Mandipaka ordered.

Michael sat and cradled his aching stomach. This had something to do with the bank, or perhaps the surveillance. And then he remembered the black SUV. This was definitely about the fraud at the bank.

"Criminals under investigation have no special rights," Mandipaka said.

"You've no proof," Michael said.

"I think a confession from you, or a statement from a credible witness."

"Washington Mabada?" Michael asked, remembering Mabada's position in Zanu.

Mandipaka shook his head slowly. "Miss Catherine Shoko is better."

"She'll never...."

Mandipaka caned Michael's hand and the pain seared hot. Mandipaka held the weapon in both hands. "Maybe this will encourage a witness to speak the truth."

Michael jumped up and grabbed for Mandipaka across the small table. "You bastard!" and then he was hit over the head with the cane; stinging his skull. Mandipaka half-smiled.

"We have done enough for now. Now we should talk to your girlfriend and find out how much she knows."

Michael glared, but to prevent another beating he didn't say a word. The policeman grabbed his arm and Michael didn't resist. He was led into the corridor, around the corner and towards his cell. The last two doors were open, and inside the first open cell was Cathy in orange overalls. Cathy was in the cell next to his! Michael was pushed into the second cell and his door was left open. They were close, separated by a brick wall. Michael went to the doorway and peered along the corridor. At the end, sitting on the chair, was the policeman. There was purpose in that.

"Cathy, are you okay?" Michael asked quietly.

"Yes I'm fine," Cathy replied equally quietly. "What's going on?"

"They've accused me of – um – spying."

"What?"

"Of sending Mugabe's and his wife's financial details to Australia, and the Australians giving the details to the MDC."

"That's absurd!"

"They're going to interrogate you about it."

"They can interrogate me as much...."

"They're going to beat you. He's got this cane."

Silence for a moment. "They can beat me 'till my skin comes off, but I won't lie for them."

"Darling...."

"No I won't. Anything I say will be used in a trial. I cannot, and I will not!"

Michael sat on the floor, his back to the doorframe. "I don't know what to say."

"I won't give in."

"I wish I could help."

Footsteps on the concrete floor, closer and closer.

"Catherine Shoko, come with me," Mandipaka ordered.

Michael's cell door closed with the lock rattling noisily. He heard footsteps on the concrete, fainter and fainter. Michael leaned against the wall with his hands shaking. He was confused about how a chance discovery of fraud had turned into arrest and torture. He was even more confused about being followed along the highway and stopped in Manicaland. He wondered what was going on.

* * *

Michael didn't know how long Cathy was gone: one hour, two hours, maybe longer. He paced his cell, sat on the mattress, lay down, stood, paced again. And then he heard the door of the interrogation room. Footsteps and scraping, closer and closer, a thump and Cathy squealed. That was agonising; worse than being hit himself. His door opened, and it was Mandipaka.

"Your girlfriend is very brave," he said. "I will leave this door open so you can talk sense into her. She should not suffer for your crime."

Michael waited for a moment and looked into the corridor. The policeman was sitting on a chair.

"Darling, what'd they do to you?" Michael asked in a quiet voice so the policeman wouldn't hear.

"He hit me with that cane like you said," Cathy said. "But don't worry, I told him you didn't do anything."

"Darling...."

"It's okay. He hurt me, this is true, but nothing I can't recover from."

"I wish...."

"We can't do anything except be brave," Cathy said. "This is my fault."

"No, it's not."

"It is. If you hadn't come here with me, none of this would have happened."

"Don't ever think like that. I love you and I wanted to see your country."

"I adore you my darling."

"We're Mudiwa and Rudo."

Silence for a few seconds. "Yes we are, but not here. This is the wrong place to tell a love story."

"Of course."

The policeman appeared carrying two plates. Michael got up and took one. The policeman left.

"Sadza," Cathy said.

It was a coarse, dry porridge-like something. Probably made out of corn, given that maize-meal or 'mealie meal' was so common. No cutlery, he sat on the bed and used his fingers. It was near tasteless but at least filling. Probably nutritious too.

The door closed and the lock clanked.

Michael finished his meal and rinsed his hands in the basin of water before drying them on his overalls. A drink of water, all the comforts. He sat on the mattress and the light went out. He lay on his back in semi-darkness, with light shining through bars in the door. He stretched and got as comfortable as he could on the lumpy mattress, but he couldn't sleep. And in the still and quiet, it came to him. Perhaps they were followed out of Harare because he was Australian. Perhaps that was a ploy to get the foreigner far from his ambassador in Harare. The normal course of events would be for the ambassador to interview Michael and to offer assistance, but not in Manicaland. Cathy and he had disappeared and there was nobody to save them. They were isolated for as long as it took.

Chapter Eleven

The door clanged and rattled; Michael woke with a start. It was Mandipaka and the policeman. Michael rubbed his eyes; how did he manage to sleep?

"Up Page," Mandipaka said.

Michael got to his feet and stood next to the mattress. Mandipaka was strange. An ordinary man; he could have been any Zimbabwean. Dressed in cheap grey trousers, a white shirt, a wedding ring on his finger; casually smoking a cigarette. Michael pictured David Mandipaka going home to his wife and two children at the end of his day of torture, with a meal waiting for him in the oven. Did his family know? His neighbours? His friends? And the policeman: stern and unsmiling. A job in brutality was a serious responsibility for that man, or so it seemed.

"I need water," Michael said.

"Later."

The policeman grabbed Michael's arm and dragged him out of the cell. Shoved along the corridor past closed doors; maybe Cathy was asleep. He imagined her lying in the dark breathing lightly. Pushed around the corner and into the big room; the light hurt his eyes. The policeman forced Michael towards one of the vinyl covered chairs.

"Take off your shoes," Mandipaka said while butting his cigarette in the ashtray on the table.

Michael looked up, and crack on his knuckles with the cane. Michael reached down and slipped off the cheap, Velcro-fastened sandshoes. The policeman wrapped a leather belt around him. No, not a belt, it was too long. He was strapped to the chair and held tight around his chest.

"Put your feet up there."

Michael tried, but the belt took away his body leverage.

Crack on his arm and it stung. He made a bigger effort, and put one foot after the other onto the table.

"Today we get serious," Mandipaka said. "First you and then your girlfriend. That way you will know what she will be in for."

"I'm not going to confess to something I didn't do," Michael said with trepidation. He knew this would be bad.

Crack on his arm again. Mandipaka leaned forward and Michael caught his foul breath. "You are a traitorous spy Michael Page, and traitorous spies deserve no mercy." Mandipaka flexed the cane. "I am going to enjoy today. And I warn you, the longer this interrogation lasts, the better it gets." He smiled. "Better for me."

Mandipaka stood back and swung the cane a few times. And then he swung it hard and low, smack onto Michael's feet. Michael jumped as the pain seared hard. Mandipaka did it again and the pain burnt. And again, and again, and again. Mandipaka stopped.

"Do you have something to tell me?" he asked.

Michael shook his head; unable to talk.

"You are a brave man, Mr Page.

Mandipaka swung and Michael gasped. With Each blow the pain was worse. It was cumulative – and then another blow. Another, another, another. No, no, no, please, please, please.

"Stop!" Michael shouted.

"You want to tell me?" Mandipaka asked.

"I can't take it anymore."

"That is the point."

Mandipaka hit him again and again: excruciating. Michael moaned and Mandipaka smiled. And again, and again, and again.

"No!" Michael shouted in agony.

And another blow.

"Will you talk?" Mandipaka asked.

Michael shook his head.

Mandipaka hit him twice more. Michael felt woozy; he was on fire from his knees down. He didn't register the blows anymore; it was continuous agony. He closed his eyes and suddenly he was drenched. He looked up, and the policeman was holding a bucket and the pain was less. Mandipaka watched while holding the cane.

"Talk," he said.

"No," Michael replied in a husky voice.

139

Mandipaka grimaced. He left the room, but returned a couple of minutes later with a plastic device like a car battery charger. Mandipaka moved the ashtray to one side and placed the device on the table, while the policeman plugged the power cord into a wall socket. Michael's heart beat fast, that was for him. There were two wires with probes, one with a red handle and one blue. The probes were centimetres from Michael's bare feet.

"Tell me what you know?" Mandipaka said in a steady voice.

Michael didn't move, didn't respond. Frozen, unable to register.

Mandipaka touched the probes together and a spark jumped. Michael watched Mandipaka hold a probe against his toe with the other probe close to his skin.

"Talk."

Michael closed his eyes and pain scorched his foot. He cried out. It was so much worse than the beating.

Mandipaka sneered. "That was only the start," he said.

Again Mandipaka did it, and again Michael shouted, as much as he tried not to. It was too intense, like someone was cutting him with a knife. A sharp knife slicing his foot. Mandipaka did it a third time and Michael tried to pull away, but the policeman held his leg with both arms. He couldn't escape and he couldn't talk. But if he lied? No! Another shock and Michael saw black and white. It was strange, it swayed and curled, moving and shaking.

Consciousness, soaked in water.

"We lost you Mr Page, and so mild too." Michael watched Mandipaka put the probes down and turn a switch on the machine. "We will take you to your cell so you can think about things. In the meantime, your girlfriend might say more."

"No," Michael tried to shout, but his voice came out husky and indistinct. "She knows nothing."

The policeman loosened the leather strap and Michael felt himself falling. His weight lessened, and then he realised they were carrying him, dragging him, along the corridor. Three doors open, and he was guided to the third. Suddenly he fell, hitting the thin mattress hard, a deep throb from his wrist against the concrete floor. He lay there unable to move. And then – a voice. Sweet and light, Cathy. Michael tried to talk but the words wouldn't form. His feet: beyond excruciating and to another place. His throat, he needed water. An orange blur and he was wet. Someone touched his face, wiping him gently. His head was lifted, and he felt cold against his lips. He drank and spluttered. He drank again, and continued drinking the cold liquid until it hurt. It was Cathy; she was in his cell caring for him.

"Darling," she said.

"I'm alright."

"You're not."

"I'm fine." His head was fuzzy, aches overwhelming him so much that he couldn't think clearly. He tried to focus and one thought came out. "They're going to beat you," he said.

"I know."

"And electrocute you."

"They did this to you?"

Michael nodded.

Cathy cradled him and he felt at home.

"If you or I talk," she said. "We will never see each other again."

Laying like this, being held, being loved. Yes, he could survive the pain. "But can you...?" he asked.

"I'm Rudo."

"I know."

"We have a saying: where there's love, there is no darkness."

Michael hoped that was true. Movement at the door and that ugly voice. "It is not too late," Mandipaka said.

Michael looked up before looking away.

The policeman grabbed Cathy and she beat against him, but the policeman didn't seem to notice. She was a woman; not strong enough. The policeman dragged her and she squirmed and wriggled. She fought while they pulled her through the door and out of sight.

Silence.

The scream startled him! A woman's scream, Cathy. And again she screamed. The bastards, they left the door open! And Cathy, what were they doing to her? Again she screamed, and again and again. Michael sat on his mattress, back to the wall, the screams filling his cell, his head, his heart. He ached, not in pain but something more. He ached with love; he loved her more than he ever dreamed possible. He loved her; please let her go. The screams continued and his ache got stronger. The screams went on and on, forever and ever. He was full of love for her. In her suffering maybe she could feel his love; maybe it would help her. They beat her and electrocuted her for longer than he, or so it seemed. And then it stopped. Silence. Silence was bad. He heard a voice, footsteps. He jumped.

"Your girlfriend is strong," Mandipaka said, and then he drew on his cigarette.

"Bastard!" Michael spat.

"We have someone else; you should hope he talks."

"Who?"

"Thokozani Chipateni."

"From the bank?"

"Yes."

"You really believe this lie, don't you? You really believe I did it?" Michael put his head down, that was worse, much worse. That was beyond revenge, that was real. They were going to torture Cathy and he and others until – what?

Mandipaka was gone and it was quiet.

"No!" a deep voice bellowed. "No, don't do it."

The torturers dragged another victim along the corridor. The cries started and Michael knew he was safe. In the distance, a heavy voice begged and pleaded and shouted and swore. Michael crept into the corridor; he went to Cathy who was lying on her mattress, curled up tight in her orange. He sat beside her and touched her wet cheek. *Cry my sweetheart.*

"I didn't talk," she said quietly.

"I know, you're a brave girl. I love you."

"I love you too."

She put her head on his lap and he held her. Her little heart was beating so fast. In the background there were screams and shouts, and in his mind he made love with his darling.

* * *

"No, not again!"

The shriek stung Michael awake. Cathy, they were starting on Cathy! He got up and Mandipaka appeared at the open door.

"You," he ordered.

Things were so bad they couldn't get worse, so Michael went to the bench and drank from the steel flask.

Mandipaka hit him with the cane and the Michael dropped the container; it clanged onto the floor. Thirst relieved, Michael felt better. The policeman grabbed him but Michael twisted free. Michael stood, glaring at Mandipaka. Mandipaka left the cell and walked along the corridor, with Michael following to the ugly room of pain. Inside, Cathy was strapped to the seat. No shoes, her legs on the table, the transformer in place. The policeman grabbed Michael and shoved him towards a chair, close to his lover. He turned his head away.

Crack on his skull, agony! The policeman grabbed Michael's head and held it, forcing him to look. The probes, waiting. Mandipaka picked up one, and then the other. He held them millimetres from her bruised flesh.

"Talk," he said.

Mandipaka touched Cathy and she jumped; pulling her legs away. He touched her again, and she squealed. He touched her again and she screamed louder.

"Talk!" Mandipaka shouted.

Silence. Michael heard his heart beating fast, the sound echoing in his ears.

"Bechenura," Mandipaka swore. He put the probes down. "Get the other one."

The policeman let Michael go and left the room. Michael caught Cathy's eyes and he saw her pain.

Scuffle, a crash – silence. Thokozani Chipateni came through the doorway, in prisoner orange overalls and with his head down. Poor bastard. A thirty-eight year old family man, a wife and two children, he probably couldn't believe his good fortune when he got the job at the bank. The policeman followed. Chipateni lifted his head and Michael caught his eyes. "Sorry," Michael mouthed.

The policeman went to Cathy and released the belt. She lifted her feet from the table.

"Kusimuka!" Mandipaka shouted.

She stood.

"Bisa numbi dzaka," he ordered.

"Kwete!" Cathy snapped, and she was belted three times with the cane. She glared at Mandipaka.

"Bisa numbi dzaka," he said.

Michael watched Cathy undo the buttons on her overalls, one after the other, slowly, steadily. Mandipaka watched with his arms crossed. And suddenly Michael had a terrible thought. No, it couldn't be. Cathy peeled her outfit down to her hips and Mandipaka caned her naked arm.

"Kwazwo."

With her hands shaking Cathy struggled to unbutton the fly. Mandipaka hit her and she tore a button free. She pulled the suit off, awkwardly freeing it from her ankles. She waited with black panties hiding her modesty.

"Dzose."

She looked at Mandipaka and Michael saw the whites of her eyes. He lifted the cane and she tore those panties off. She stood with her hands between her legs.

Mandipaka went to Chipateni, right up close. "Bisa numbi dzaka," he said in an even voice, and Chipateni didn't hesitate. Shoes off, overalls onto the ground and he stopped. Whack with the cane. Chipateni put his head down and removed his last garment. He stood like Cathy with hands protecting himself.

Mandipaka poked Cathy's hip with his weapon and whispered in her ear. Michael couldn't hear, but she went to the bench and sat on it with her hands still wedged in place. Mandipaka whispered something else and she lay on her back, still covering herself.

"You," he said to Chipateni. "Rape her."

"No!" Chipateni bellowed.

Crack against his palms and Chipateni's hands pulled away with shock. Crack on his genitals; Chipateni bellowed and doubled over in pain. Crack on the back of his neck and Chipateni fell on the floor. Mandipaka kicked him hard and Michael winced.

"Stand up." Mandipaka shouted.

Chipateni put his hands out to brace himself and slowly got to his feet with sweat glistening on his body.

"Make yourself ready for her."

Chipateni looked up with his eyes wide, and then he touched himself. Michael turned his head. The policeman grabbed Michael's ears and forced him to watch.

"Sick bastard," Michael snapped. "You'll destroy them."

"Talk," Mandipaka snapped.

Sweat stung Michael's eyes and his hands shook. Over there, on the table, Cathy. And in front of him, that poor man. Cathy, raped by her friend. Cathy, darling Cathy. No, that would ruin her.

"I'll tell you," Michael said.

"No!" Cathy screamed.

"I did it. I accessed all the account transactions and sent them to Australia, and they sent them to Morgan Tsvangirai."

"Which accounts?" Mandipaka asked.

"The personal accounts of Robert Mugabe and his wife."

"His wife is…?"

"Um."

"Grace."

"That's right, Grace Mugabe."

"How?"

"Um, I copied the screens using a utility program, pasted them into Word, and attached the document to an email."

148

"Who did you send them to?"

"A mailbox at the Department."

"An email could be traced."

"Um, ah – the Word document was encrypted."

Mandipaka half-smiled. "Good, good. Do you have this on tape?"

"Yes," the policeman said.

"Turn the machine off."

The policeman went to the small timber cabinet. A clearly audible 'click' and it was over.

"Stop this now," Michael said

"Chipateni; put your clothes on." Mandipaka ordered.

Michael wiped the palms of his hands against his overalls. He looked across at Cathy who was sitting and protecting herself.

"Can I….?" she asked.

"Lie down," Mandipaka shouted, but Cathy didn't move. "Lie down you whore of the MDC!" and she lay on her back. Mandipaka was unbuttoning his shirt; fumbling with the buttons.

"You bastard!" Michael shouted.

The policeman punched Michael hard; everything swirled for a moment and he felt dizzy. Hands on Michael's head. He was turned towards the bench and Mandipaka was there. Trousers at his ankles, Michael tried to look away but the grip was too strong. Mandipaka was there, on her, and she just lay still. Michael wanted to shout at her, make her resist, do something, anything. But no, Mandipaka violated her, just like that. So close, and Michael couldn't do anything. So close and useless. Michael focussed on her face, her head moving back and forward. Moving with inertia, her body a mere receptacle. It was too much.

"Stop!" Michael shouted.

The policeman hit him and nothing changed. No, something changed, it was faster. The movement forcing her movement was faster. Faster and faster, and a noise. An animal noise, appropriate for an animal. Mandipaka slid off the bench and pulled his trousers up. Michael heard the noise of a zip.

"Get dressed," Mandipaka snarled.

Cathy climbed off the bench, and with her hands in place she went to the table. Michael put his head down and looked away from her last humiliation.

Mandipaka reached into his shirt pocket and pulled out a packet of cigarettes. He lit one and then bent over, and Michael almost gagged on his stink and the smoke.

"Tsvangirai can't help you or your whore now." He straightened. "Take these traitors to their cells."

The policeman grabbed Chipateni and led him out of the room. He returned a moment later and grabbed Cathy with one hand and Michael with the other. They were guided out of the room, along the corridor and into respective cells. Doors shut, locks slid home. Alone, silent, it was over.

Chapter Twelve

"You, up, now!"

No, not more torture. Michael sat on his mattress with Mandipaka and his silent companion at the door. Michael rubbed his eyes and sighed. If they killed him, that would be good.

"We take you to Harare," the policeman said.

Michael got to his feet. "Can I drink?"

Mandipaka gestured at the flask on the shelf. Michael drank, and then he splashed some water from the basin. He felt much better.

"What time is it?" he asked.

"Eight."

"In the morning?"

Mandipaka nodded. "We must go."

Michael went to the door and waited while the policeman unclipped handcuffs hanging from his belt. Michael's arms were pulled in front and the 'cuffs fastened.

"Okay, good." Mandipaka said, already striding along the corridor, and heading right and away from the torture room. Past the policeman's chair and left into a concrete staircase. They climbed, turned, and climbed and then Mandipaka stopped. There was a grey timber box fastened to the wall; Mandipaka opened a door to the box and hung a key amongst others. They continued onwards, passing a brown wooden door into an office. It was a very nineteen-sixties office in a very nineteen-sixties building. A large room painted white with several yellowing notices stuck on the wall, along with a stock-and station agent's calendar from nineteen-eighty-nine and some faded girlie photos: a well-endowed young blonde in the most unlikely of surroundings. There were several varnished timber desks and black vinyl chairs; one desk was covered in paper and the rest were clear. A few files in a bookcase, some telephone books on a bench, and a counter on the right facing a waiting room with brown timber benches. Next to the counter was a brown door marked 'Gents'.

"I need to go," Michael said.

"Now?"

"I haven't, you know, since...."

Mandipaka glared at Michael.

"It's a long way," Michael said.

"Okay, go," Mandipaka said while reaching into his shirt pocket and extracting a packet of cigarettes.

The policeman unlocked the handcuffs and Michael went into the toilet and locked the door. On his left, a cracked, white, porcelain washbasin. Ahead, a lavatory with black plastic seat. Above that a fixed louvered window with thin glass panes set into a brown timber frame. He got up close and on both sides the timber had warped. He grabbed the timber and wriggled it back and forwards. He wriggled

153

them harder and was able to bend them out of the way. Working carefully, he slid the bottom piece of glass out of the frame and placed it on the floor resting against the wall. And the next one, and the next, and the next. *How long, five minutes maybe?* He stood on the lavatory, grabbed the frame and lifted himself; the pain! The beatings, his feet ached. He took a deep breath and lifted himself again, sitting on window-ledge with his legs hanging out of the building. He slid forward and dropped onto the ground in agony! Michael looked around with his heart beating fast. He was outside a cream-brick building with the toilet window the only opening along that wall. Opposite was a cyclone wire fence about a metre or so high, and then a red-brick house, possibly the policeman's home. Part-way along the fence was a locked gate, and it was the policeman's or Mandipaka's home. Michael climbed over the woven wire, and in dull pain he jogged to the back of the house and waited for a moment. Nothing, not a sound. The house looked like the houses in Avondale where Julie lived: late nineteen-fifties brick with a timber garage in the rear corner of the block. The back yard had several large fruit trees surrounded by lush lawn. Michael jogged towards a fence on the far side, protected from view by the house. He jumped the low timber fence, and continued across a vacant, weedy block, feeling exposed. Ahead was a rickety brush fence about two metres tall, with a gate! Michael ran to the gate and pulled it, but it struck fast against the soft earth. He pushed and it creaked open just wide enough for him to slip through.

Michael was standing behind a clothesline built out of two rough-hewn posts and a single wire strand. Hanging were two quilts which almost reached the ground. Just then, a siren in the distance, louder and louder, more intense and more intense, closer and closer. Michael pressed himself against the fence with the quilts protecting all but his feet from view. The siren was very loud as it raced past, clearly heading towards the police station. Moments later the noise stopped; reinforcements had arrived.

Think, think. But his mind was blank. Clothes, money. Priorities – clothes and money. He tapped his chin and willed a solution.

A squeak and then a clatter. Michael peered around the edge of the quilt, and a woman approached the line. *Fuck!* He backed away towards the gate, and then he heard voices in the empty block. He was trapped. He moved along the fence, away from the householder, but the police in the vacant block were getting closer.

"Who are you?" she asked.

Michael started, and put his fingers on his lips. He moved towards the woman holding a cane basket, with his hands down and his palms facing out.

"Can you help me?" he whispered

"Who are you?" she snapped.

155

Michael put his fingers to his lips again. "The police, they beat a confession out of me, and now they want to try me for a crime I didn't commit."

"They beat you?"

"Yes, and much worse."

"Aiwa, this Mugabe and his Zanu cronies! What was it they said you did?"

"Spying for the MDC."

She smiled. "Ah white man, the MDC. It is no wonder they beat you, the MDC is very dangerous to Zanu, isn't it? One day we will win."

"You support the MDC?"

She paused. "Maybe."

"Can you help me?"

Just then voices from the street. Through a gap between the quilts, Michael saw two men: Mandipaka and his blue-uniformed offsider.

"A ri payi?" Mandipaka asked.

"U kumbirire mukadzi uyo," the policeman replied.

Michael smelled Mandipaka's sickening cologne. Closer, very close, hemming him in. Would the woman protect him?

"Nda banditi shaya?" Mandipaka asked, standing next to the quilts, just centimetres away.

"Apana banditi," the woman replied. *What did that mean?*

"Ndi no pfidza," Mandipaka said, and silence. Michael looked between the quilts and they were gone.

The woman came to him. "They are looking for you," she said.

"I know. He's the man who tortured me, and who raped my girlfriend."

"I am very sorry to hear about your girlfriend; such things are tragic." The woman put her basket on a wooden stand. "I am Therese Nyathi," she said.

"I'm Michael Page."

They shook hands.

"Come, I will help you," she said.

Therese was what age? Older than Cathy, almost thirty perhaps. Dressed in a blue cotton-print dress, and with leather or vinyl sandals. She had the loveliest smile. She led the way across her yard. Across thick green grass and past shrubs growing against a beige-coloured, cement-rendered house. They followed a concrete path around the back and she opened an old-fashioned, timber flyscreen door.

Michael was in a cool house. Peaceful and it felt homely. They were standing in the kitchen. No frills: stove, gloss-green timber cabinets, a wooden table and four sturdy wooden chairs.

"So Mr Page, are you a spy or not?" she asked.

"Michael and I'm not a spy, it's really about a fraud my girlfriend discovered."

"She is a spy?"

"No, not at all. There's a lot of money involved and I reported it, so they framed me to get me out of the way. And there might be something else. I think the manager, who's a member of Zanu, is attracted to my girlfriend."

Therese frowned. "Someone from Zanu wants a white woman?"

Michael smiled. "She's Manyika."

Therese laughed the biggest laugh. "You are full of surprises Michael Page! You are not from here, are you?"

"No, I'm Australian, and I'm working in Zimbabwe for a year with my girlfriend."

"Oh, you poor man. You must think terrible things of our country for what happened to you."

"I know the people here are kind and good. But there are problems with, um, democracy."

"There are big problems, as you say. How long did the CIO hold you?"

"Why do you say the CIO?"

"That man with the policeman, he looks CIO."

"I see." Michael thought hard, but the details were blurry. "I don't know how long; all I know is we were taken on Saturday."

"Today is Wednesday, so they had you for four days."

"Yes, four days."

"I will run you a bath and then we will find some clothes; my husband's clothes should fit. Do you want some tea?"

"You're too kind."

"Nonsense! It is my duty to help you so you can rescue your girlfriend."

Therese turned on the stove and filled an aluminium kettle. "I will run the bath," she said, and left the room. Michael heard water running. By the time she returned, the kettle was close to boiling. She switched the stove off and poured two mugs.

"This will help you."

Michael rubbed his chin. "Not as much as the bath."

She laughed.

* * *

The bath was glorious. So much grime to wash away. And his aches, the hot water was a miracle treatment. Michael touched his feet; they were tender but it didn't seem like permanent damage had been done. Or so he hoped. He lay in the hot water thinking through options. He had one chance, and it had to work. And he needed help from Julie and Peter. He would go to the post office, look up the directory and ring Julie. But he didn't know anything more than she was a bookkeeper for a department store. If he could get to Harare by that afternoon, by bus or train perhaps, that would be better. Face to face would be much better.

After so long the water was getting cool, and Michael didn't want to abuse his welcome by topping the bath up. He climbed out and dried himself, and then held the clothes left by Therese. He sighed; her husband must be close to his height but bigger-built. Michael used the belt to tighten the waist, which made the trousers hang funny. The shirt too was baggy, but it would have to do. To finish, he slipped on his Velcro-fastened shoes. A shave would be good, but Therese had done enough already. He left the bathroom and smelled cooking.

As soon as Michael appeared at the kitchen, his kind host served some maize porridge and stew, as well as a mug of coffee. She must have been reading his mind, for the coffee at least, although the maize was okay with vegetables and a little boiled meat.

"Therese, you've been too kind," Michael said. "I don't know how to thank you for all you've done."

"Do you love your girlfriend?" Therese asked.

"Very much."

"Then you must help her, because she has suffered."

"I know. Her sister and a friend will help me, but they're in Harare."

"And you have no money. I know this because I threw away your overalls."

"Yes, my wallet was taken from me."

"I can give...."

"No," Michael interrupted. "I'd appreciate it if you could lend me some cash, and I'll return it as soon as I can."

"A loan to get you to Harare; I can do this."

"Thanks."

Michael ate the rest of his breakfast in silence.

"Thank you again Therese," Michael said after he finished. "I need to know one thing from you; how can I get to Harare?"

"The Express Motorways bus from Mutare comes through about twelve. You should catch that to the Holiday Inn. I can take...."

"Can I walk to the bus stop?" Michael said.

"You're a wanted man, so I will take you in my husband's car."

"But you're putting yourself in danger."

"I insist. I will lend some money, two hundred should do, and you use that to buy a ticket from the driver. When you get to Harare, catch a taxi. There are many criminals waiting for the bus and it is dangerous. Will your girlfriend's sister pay for a taxi?"

"Yes."

"Good. I will get the money now, and we will leave for the bus at half-eleven."

"Thank you again."

"Enough with the thanks! You get to Harare, you rescue your girlfriend and you help her. Understand?"

Michael nodded. And despite the tragedy of their country, the people of Zimbabwe were the most likeable and generous he'd ever met.

* * *

The taxi stopped outside flat three of twelve Mendel Rd where lights glowed through curtains.

"Wait here," Michael said to the driver.

He limped to the front door and knocked. He heard noise inside and the door opened.

"Michael, what happened?" Julie asked.

"I've got a taxi waiting; do you have a hundred dollars for the driver?"

"Um, yes."

Julie went inside and returned carrying a black handbag. She went to the street and a few moments later the taxi drove off.

"Dad called and he said you and Cathy never showed up. So I rang the police and there weren't any accidents reported. You two just disappeared. Ah, where's Cathy? Sorry, please come in."

Michael followed her into the living room and sat on the brown sofa.

"Tell me what happened?" Julie asked.

"The CIO arrested us," Michael said.

162

"The CIO; why?"

"We found a fraud and I reported it, and then a manager at the bank made up a story about me being a spy. But I think he had problems with me well before the fraud."

"And the CIO found the truth and let you go?"

"No, I escaped."

Julie put her hand to her mouth. "And Cathy?" she asked.

"Probably in custody at Rusape."

"My God, poor Cathy! And you too, you were limping."

"It's getting better."

"So what do we do?"

"We rescue her."

"How?"

"As far as I can tell there's only two involved, a CIO agent named Mandipaka and a local policeman. I thought about this in the bus. We'll create a diversion, get the key to her cell, and get her out of there."

Julie frowned.

"This isn't a movie so we can't go in with guns blazing," Michael said. "A fire could work though. The policeman or the CIO agent lives next door, so we'll burn their house down."

"Next door, that could work. Ah, our parents. If we get Cathy free, they will go after them."

Michael rubbed his forehead. "Do you think Peter can help?"

"Yes, he's family. Peter can borrow a car for us to drive to Rusape, and he can drive to Mutare to warn my parents."

"You should drive to Mutare, and Peter and I'll go to Rusape to rescue Cathy."

"I can't drive."

Michael frowned. "This is dangerous," he said.

Julie frowned in response. "I know," she said. "How's Cathy?"

Michael didn't want to burden Julie with the full story. "She was tortured," he said.

Julie gasped.

"Let's get her free," Michael said.

"Yes, of course," Julie said. "And you, some food?"

"Not, um what do you call it?"

"Sadza."

"Please."

"Wait here; I will warm something for you."

"Thanks."

Julie returned about ten minutes later and sat beside him.

"I called Peter and he's on his way."

"Good. I need to get to my house. I need clothes that fit, and I need my passport and some money. But the house might be watched."

"Your maid...."

"What?"

"Your maid can bring your things to us." She got up. "Your food should be ready."

Michael followed Julie to the kitchen where she dished up rice and stew while he waited at the table. She sat with him.

"This seems like a dream," she said.

"This is real enough," Michael said.

"This country...."

Michael put his hand on hers. "It'll be fine."

A knock at the door. Julie left the room, and returned a few moments later with Peter. Michael stood and they shook hands.

"Please sit," Julie said.

Peter sat.

"Something terrible has happened," Julie said. "The CIO has Cathy."

"Why, what is it?" Peter asked.

"Nothing she did," Michael said. "But we've got to get her out. Julie and I are going to Rusape to rescue her, and we'd like you to go to Julie's parents."

"What for?"

"They must leave the country."

"And I should tell them this?"

"Yes."

"Cathy and I were arrested and tortured by the CIO, and because of the torture I confessed to something. Julie and I will rescue Cathy, and you must tell Mr and Mrs Shoko to leave the country in case of retribution for our escapes. Do you understand?"

"Yes."

"Good."

"There's another thing Peter," Julie said. "We need a car."

"I can borrow my cousin's car."

"And we need some petrol in a tin," Michael said. "Twenty litres should be enough."

"I can get some."

Julie kissed Peter on his cheek.

"You are my family," Peter said.

"How do we get in touch with your maid?" Julie asked.

"I can't call her; the phone at my house is bugged. We'll have to visit her tonight."

"Where does she live?"

"Chitungwiza."

"Can you take us Peter?"

"Yes, but there is not much time for all these things."

166

"We have to do it right," Michael said while wishing he wasn't a project manager. Too much planning, too much detail, and what if it went wrong?

* * *

From a distance, Chitungwiza looked as forbidding as ever. Closer it was orange lighting and a haze from cooking fires. Michael was in the back of Peter's old, yellow Volvo.

"Where does your maid live?" Peter asked.

"Four Gokoro Street."

Peter turned onto the access road and headed towards the clusters of houses while Michael thumbed through a map book.

"I do not know this place," Peter said.

"First on the left is Chaminuka Road, and maybe half a kilometre on the right is Ingwe Drive. Gokoro Street is about half a kilometre on the left."

Peter followed Michael's directions and the main roads were clearly marked with large signs. The smaller streets were not marked, so Michael counted to four on the left.

"Next on the left, Peter," he said.

Peter turned the corner and parked. They climbed out of the car and Peter locked it, which was necessary in a place like Chitungwiza. Gokoro was a short street and number four was easy to find. In the background, the television was on. Michael knocked firmly. A scrape and the television went silent. A paunchy man in his fifties slowly opened the door.

"Mr Mufaro, I'm Michael Page. Your wife cleans for me."

A big smile. "Mr Page, thank you very much for her pay rise. What can I do for you?"

"I'd like to speak to Mary please."

"I will get her for you. Please, just a moment."

Moments later, Mary appeared at the door.

"Mr Page, you not at home."

"Something's come up. Mary, I want you to do something important for me. In the bottom drawer of the cabinet beside my bed are two passports, a plastic bag of traveller's cheques, and about five-hundred in cash."

Mary frowned. "What is traveller's cheques?"

"Um, pieces of paper about this big, with American Express in large, blue writing," Michael said, holding his hands just so. "They're in a plastic bag with some Zimbabwean dollars and two passports; one blue Australian and one red Zimbabwean."

Mary nodded.

"I want you to put the money, the passports and the traveller's cheques in my brown backpack along with some clothes," Michael said. "I need my dark blue trousers, a couple of blue shirts, my black suede boots, and a few sets of underwear and socks. We also need clothes for Cathy: say jeans, a couple of blouses, leather shoes or boots, and underwear for her."

"What is this about Mr Page?"

"It's best you don't know. Tomorrow morning, pack my things and take them to the supermarket. My friend Peter Chirinda will be inside waiting for you."

"This is Mr Chirinda?"

"Yes."

Michael was worried; Mary was a nice person and a good worker, but perhaps that was too much for her. "Mary, can you do this for me?" he asked.

"Yes."

"First thing in the morning, when you start?"

"Yes Mr Page."

Michael shook her hand. "I won't keep you then, and thank you very much."

"Goodbye Mr Page."

Mary closed the door.

"Can she do this?" Peter asked.

"I hope so; we need the money. Look, we'd better get back to town, there's lots to do.

"Is all this going to work?"

"For Cathy's sake, it has to."

Chapter Thirteen

Michael crossed the room to the window and looked though the curtain netting, but no yellow Volvo. He returned to the armchair and sat. And then he went to the kitchen, but forgot why. He came back to the living room and sat in the armchair again.

"It will help if you relax," Julie said.

"There's too much on my mind."

"We should occupy ourselves." Julie looked at the floor, and then she looked at Michael. "I know," she said. "There's something I would like to know. This might be the last chance before...."

Michael leaned forward and their eyes met.

"You see," Julie said, "Cathy's my sister, which means if you get married I will be your sister too. This is different to where you come from, isn't it?"

"Yes it is," Michael replied, uncertain about where this was heading.

"What I'd like to know is how you met Cathy."

"We met at my work the day she started."

"Is that all?"

Michael kept his gaze on Julie. "No. I'd just broken up with my partner of five years, and then I met Cathy. I fell in love with her the day we met."

"I thought it was something like that."

"I never believed love at first sight was possible, until it happened to me."

Julie nodded and Michael looked at his watch. He was curious about her relationship with Peter, and how close they were to each other. "We might have some time before Peter gets back," he said. "So if you're going to be my sister, do you mind if I ask you something?"

"Of course not."

The front door opened; Peter entered the room.

"Hmm, we'd better get ready," Michael said.

"What do you want to ask me?"

"Some other time."

Michael got up and Peter handed the brown backpack to Michael.

"I'll get dressed," Michael said.

Michael went up the stairs to the bathroom and got changed. He returned, carrying the bag.

"Peter; you have the address in Mutare," Michael said. "Julie, we need to meet somewhere. Do you have any ideas?"

"Ah, I know. The Yeoville Cemetery, at my grandparent's graves."

"Yes, good, very good. Peter, can you take Julie's parents there?"

"Yes."

"Is there anything else?" Michael asked.

"There is one thing," Peter said. "I will get it when we leave."

"We'll leave now."

Peter led the way, with Michael and Julie following. A young man leaned on a Toyota.

"This is my cousin, Richard," Peter said.

Michael shook hands. "I'm Michael and thank you very much for the loan of your car."

Richard nodded. "I must catch the bus home," he said.

"I can drive you."

"Peter said you have problems and you need this car, so I will catch the bus."

"Goodbye and thank you again."

Richard left while Peter went to his Volvo and opened the boot to extract a metal rod more than a metre long.

"You might need this," he said.

"What is it?" Michael asked. It was big and solid, with a socket fitting at one end, and a broad crowbar-type point at the other.

"We use them to change wheels on cars. If you hit someone with this…."

Michael held it in both hands and it would make a useful weapon.

"Fuel's in the car?" Michael asked.

"Three tins," Peter replied.

"Thanks."

Michael went to shake hands, and his hand was swallowed by Peter's giant paw. "Good luck."

"You too."

Julie was in the passenger seat of the white Toyota, and Michael put his bag in the boot. He climbed in and started the engine, and waited until the Volvo pulled out and headed away. He followed the yellow car at a safe distance, forming a small convoy heading east to Manicaland. He rubbed his hands together; they were slippery on the wheel. The clock glowed eleven twenty-two in the morning and it was a two-hour drive. He tried to get comfortable, but the mid-eighties Corolla wasn't built for comfort. Especially the vinyl seats, aged and split after many years of African sun. Michael squirmed again, and found a sort-of compromise. He glanced out of the corner of his eyes and Julie looked so much like her sister it was uncanny, especially in blue jeans and a blue t-shirt. Suddenly, he felt a glow of warmth. Michael looked away and studied the road ahead, feeling confused. Feeling very confused.

* * *

Michael traced his route from the bus stop towards Madsen Street. He parked just across the road from the cream brick police station and switched off the engine. Silence, except for the engine ticking while it cooled. He looked at Julie and she looked at him.

"I think the garage," Michael said. "We'll carry the tins to the garage and I'll drive the car around the corner. Then we'll burn it down, and do the house if we have to."

Silence again. Michael got out of the car and went to the boot.

"Who's that?" Julie asked.

Michael looked up, and – fuck – it was Mandipaka!

"Get down," he said forcefully but quietly, ducking behind the car. He looked around the boot, and Mandipaka had already reached the front door of the house, pausing for a moment before entering. The door closed, and with a man in the house it was too risky.

"That's the man," he said.

Julie nodded.

"It's good; we know it's the right house," Michael said. "We'll wait."

"This is dangerous," she said.

She was right. "We don't have much choice; we have to know when he's out of the house." Michael looked around, but it was too open, too exposed, and too suspicious-looking. "You get in front and I'll hide in the back."

Julie got up and went to the driver's door, while Michael opened the back door and climbed in to lie on the floor. They waited with Michael cramped on the hard and uneven surface. How long: twenty minutes, half-an-hour, longer? What was Mandipaka doing? Having lunch, something else? A brief flash, celebrating torture with his wife. Probably not, which was why he was so twisted.

"Any sign?' Michael asked.

"Sssh."

"What are you doing?" a deep voice boomed.

Mandipaka! A creak as Julie opened the door and got out.

"I'm waiting," she said.

"Waiting for what?"

"A friend."

"Wait somewhere else."

"She will be here soon, and we're going to Harare together."

"Go away from here." Pause. "Go away now."

A scrunching on the seat, Julie behind the wheel. Clonk, she closed the door.

"You can't drive," Michael said.

"I can, a little."

Michael fished in his pockets with his trousers too tight. He pictured Mandipaka just metres away, watching, waiting for the slightest wrong move. He found the keys, and put them on the floor between the seats.

"The keys are there," he said.

A tinkle as Julie took the ring, and moments later the engine started. Grind – *more clutch Julie*. Suddenly they took off, Michael thrown against the back seat with the jerk. God he hoped Mandipaka didn't get suspicious. They roared down the street in first gear, engine screaming, and then a rough change to second.

"Left at the next street," Michael shouted above the bellow, they must have been doing sixty. A rough jerk left – correcting right –and then veering left again. A gentle bump into the kerb, engine off.

"I'm sorry," Julie said.

"Where is he?" Michael asked.

"I can't see him."

"Good. You did well."

"Thanks. If we return...."

Michael sat up, opened the door, and half-fell onto the nature strip with cramp. He stood and held the car for support. After a few moments he felt better. Julie was right; if Mandipaka saw their car again. What to do? They had three tins of petrol and it would be too suspicious to carry those up the street. If Therese Nyathi was home, perhaps they could use her car. No, wrong, too dangerous for her to get involved. And then the answer.

"We'll go to the main street and hire a taxi," he said. "We'll go now."

Michael looked up and noted they were in Bank Street, and then he limped to the driver's door and got behind the wheel. No wonder Julie had problems driving the car; she hadn't adjusted the seat. He drove to the next intersection, turned left and headed towards the highway. At the highway, he turned right and sped to the shopping centre. Time was getting away, how long did they have, how long would Mandipaka hold Cathy in Rusape? Ahead the shops and no taxis, or at least taxis in the obvious sense.

"I will find one," Julie offered.

"If you can, get them to follow me."

Julie walked towards the shops, and Michael noticed just how delightful she looked in jeans. Wrong thoughts, very wrong. Julie went inside a grocery store, and then she emerged with a tall young man. Julie pointed at Michael, and then she pointed at a car across the road and Michael got ready. He did a 'u' turn, and pulled over to wait. The taxi emerged, and Michael checked his mirrors before easing onto the highway and returning to Bank Street. He parked, and the taxi parked behind. Moments later, jerrycans and socket bar transferred, Michael in the back seat, and they were cruising along Madsen Street.

"Here," Julie said, and the driver stopped.

"How much?" she asked.

"Fifty."

Michael got out and went to the boot which the driver had already released, and moments later Julie joined him. Michael handed one, ten-litre jerry can and the steel bar to Julie, and grabbed two cans himself. Michael shut the boot, and the taxi drove away while Julie and he crossed the grass and marched up the concrete driveway. That was dangerous in broad daylight! Ahead was the garage and in it was a late-model blue Peugeot; clean and well cared for. Michael carefully placed the tins on the floor, and helped Julie with hers. Michael took one of the cans and unclipped the cap, and then he poured the fuel around the garage. He emptied the tin and another one. He took the remaining jerrycan and the socket bar to the rear of the house. Julie followed at a distance, like she was scared. Of course she was scared! Michael pulled the small box and a roll of cardboard from his pocket, struck a match, lit the card; and tossed it to the left side of the garage. The fire caught with a 'whoosh', just like a movie. He took a second roll of cardboard, struck another match and lit it, and after a few seconds he tossed it to the right. Another 'whoosh' and the timber was already crackling. Michael spread fuel around the back of the house, and suddenly the door opened and he was facing a woman. *Fuck!*

"Inside, quick, now!" Michael snarled, reaching for the bar and holding it in both hands.

"What's happened?" the woman asked.

Michael smashed the bar against the door frame near her head with splinters falling to the ground. "Inside now!" he bellowed, and the woman backed away from him with the whites of her eyes showing.

"Who are you?" he snapped.

"Mrs Carole Mandipaka," she said.

"Where's your husband?"

"At work."

"Next door?"

"Yes."

"Call him; tell him the garage's on fire, and don't say anything about us."

"What?"

"Call him and I'll be listening."

She went to an old black telephone on a stand in the entrance corridor and dialled the number. Pause. "Is David Mandipaka there?" Pause. "David, it's Carole. Please come, the garage is on fire." Pause. "Yes, on fire. No, I will do it now. Come quick." She hung up and looked at Michael.

"He is on his way," she said. "You lit the fire, why?"

Michael swung the bar and belted the telephone table to smash it to pieces. "You're coming with us!" he shouted, and then he looked at Julie. "Keep an eye on her."

Michael went to the open door and grabbed the last jerrycan of petrol. He doused the base of the kitchen cupboards until it was empty, carefully putting the tin on the

179

floor to avoid making a noise. He stood in the entrance hall; took a match and his last piece of cardboard, lit it, and threw it across the room. Moments later, the kitchen was blazing.

The two women watched from a few metres away.

"We go out the front," he said.

The timber and frosted-glass front door had an old-fashioned snib lock, not a deadlock. Michael released the lock, eased the door open, and checked around. No-one there. He opened the door wider and put his head out, and heard loud voices and then a crash. Shouting from the rear of the house and possibly the garage collapsing.

"Now, quick, hurry."

Michael grabbed Carole Mandipaka's arm and dragged her towards the street, along the footpath and across the grass to the front door of the police station. The door of the station was wide-open, like Mandipaka left in a hurry. Michael pulled Carole through the doorway beside the counter, and across the office to the door that led to the stairs and the cells. Michael tried the handle but it was locked.

"Hold her," Michael said to Julie, and then he jammed the pointed end of the socket bar into the gap between the door and frame. It fitted, but Michael couldn't lever it open. *Damn!* He looked around and spotted the two telephone books. He grabbed the thickest, the yellow pages, and put it between the iron and the door as a type of wedge. He shoved the iron into the gap to the frame and pressed against the thick book. Some movement and the iron dug into the plywood door, but it remained fast. He tried again and the door frame splintered, but the door still held. He moved the book closer to the edge of the door for more leverage, dug the iron into the gap and pressed hard. The door moved, stopped, and suddenly burst open. Michael dropped the bar and went into the concrete stairwell.

On his left was the grey timber box; Michael opened it and grabbed all six keys. With Julie still holding Mandipaka's wife he went down the stairs as fast as his sore feet would allow, around the corner, down again, and into the corridor of pain.

The first two cell doors, his and Cathy's, were open and the next two were closed. Michael checked his old cell, nobody there. He checked the next, also vacant. He checked the third and the door was unlocked. He opened it and Thokozani Chipateni was lying on the mattress, on his back with his eyes closed. Michael gingerly got onto his knees and touched Chipateni, but he was very cold. Michael looked up at Julie.

"He's dead," Michael said.

"Who is he?" Julie asked.

"He's from our work."

Julie put her hands on her mouth. Michael stood and grabbed Carole Mandipaka by her shoulders and shook her hard. "This is what your husband does, look at him! He's dead; why? Because someone made up a bullshit story about me! Your husband tortures and rapes and kills."

"It's for the party."

"There's no excuse for this." He pulled her arm, and she nearly fell. "Get down on that mattress!"

She gingerly got onto the floor with her heels making it awkward for her.

"On the mattress," Michael ordered.

Carole Mandipaka sat beside the body.

"We'll lock her in," Michael said.

Julie waited in the corridor while Michael clanged the door closed. He tried two keys before he found one that worked. He sighed and went to the last cell. He looked through the barred opening and it was empty. He felt unsteady and held the wall for a moment. One place, but unlikely. He led Julie around the corner and into the room of terror, and the light was off. He groped for the switch, and the fluorescent flickered. Garish bright, painful memories, but no Cathy. He looked at Julie, and she looked at him. Michael rubbed his forehead; surely there must be a solution. And then it came to him.

"Upstairs, we'll check the office for paperwork."

A siren in the distance, probably the fire brigade but maybe the police. Either way, they didn't have much time. Up the stairs, past the damaged door and to the desk.

"Look for anything that might give us a clue.'

Julie rummaged through the papers on the desk, while Michael sat in the black chair and checked the drawers from top to bottom. Nothing. He searched again, but all the documents were dated weeks and months before. He looked up and knew he didn't need to ask Julie. He sighed, but there was nothing they could do.

"Let's go," Michael said. "There's no point in us being caught."

"But...."

Julie put her head down and went through the waiting area towards the front door. Michael cut her off and checked outside through a smeared window. An old, red fire truck was in the street, and men in black protective clothing bent over a hose that ran out of sight; no doubt to the garage and the rear of the house. Fireman in black and no police in blue, but it was too dangerous to walk past the fire to get to their car. Michael decided to walk around the block instead.

"It's safe," he said.

They went down the steps, and Michael put his hands in his pocket while he strolled along the concrete path towards the driveway that ran along the side of the police station.

"Michael, look," Julie said.

Julie led the way to a white utility van parked next to the station. It was relatively new, quite clean, and the rear part was box-like with blue 'police' signwriting. No windows in the rear. Michael opened the passenger door and inside was muddy, scuffed and littered with rubbish and soft drink bottles. He climbed in and checked the glovebox, but only found the vehicle handbook.

Thump! Julie hammered on the back of the van.

A muffled response. "Who's there?"

That was Cathy's voice!

"It's me, Julie," she said.

"Julie, get me out."

Michael tried the handles to the rear doors, but they were locked. He tried each of his six keys, but none fitted. He raced to the front and climbed into the driver's seat to search. He checked the ignition, above the sunvisor, the glovebox again; no keys. He ran to the back doors and tried them again, but they were secure. *Fuck! Maybe?*

"I'll get the bar," he said.

Despite his pain, Michael ran to the police station, across the waiting room and though the office to the staircase. He grabbed the socket bar and raced to the van, and in agony by the time he reached Julie. He jammed the pointed end through the gap between the doors and twisted it. The edge of the doors bent, but they didn't move. He jammed it deeper and levered again, and the doors bent more. Michael held the tyre iron tight and wrenched it as hard as he could, the doors sprung open, and Michael fell on the ground in agony! His wrist, his right wrist! He sat up and Cathy slowly climbed out of the van; still dressed in orange overalls. Michael stood, held his right arm and wondered if it was broken. Cathy rubbed her eyes.

"Cathy, we have to go," Julie said. "Ah Michael, what happened?"

"I hurt my wrist," Michael said.

"Is it broken?"

"I don't know."

"What do we do?"

"We go. Are you okay Cathy?"

She nodded and burst into tears. Michael hugged her with his good arm and she buried her head into his shoulder. "They didn't touch me, but poor Thokozani. It must have been the shock, but he...."

He squeezed her tighter and she sobbed desperately.

"I knew you'd escaped, and I knew you'd come for me," she said. "I hoped you wouldn't, in case.... But you did." She pulled away. "Darling sister, you saved me." They held hands.

"We have to go," Michael said.

A siren screamed and that was probably the police. The siren was close; very close. They could never get away with Cathy's orange overalls, outstanding as they were meant to be. And then a car turned into the driveway, the engine rattling and clanking as it closed on them, and Michael's heart fell. He spun around to see a faded, formerly red, Datsun. The driver in blue overalls climbed out, holding a handgun.

"You must come with me," he said.

Chapter Fourteen

Michael was shocked. "Mr Nyathi?" he asked.

The African man nodded. "I'm Albert Nyathi. Therese told me you're in trouble," he said, while he jabbed a key into the boot lock. The lid sprang open and he rummaged for a moment. Bang with the lid and a tartan blanket handed to Cathy. "Climb in the back and hide under this," he said. "You two get in as well."

Michael climbed into the front. "Thank you so much," he said.

"Where are we going?"

Michael drew a deep breath, but that was asking too much. "Just to Bank Street," he said.

"Are you sure?"

"We have a car there."

Albert started the engine. Soon they were on their way, to the main road and not past the scene of the fire. Then to Bank Street.

"That Toyota," Michael said, and Albert did a u-turn and parked behind. He switched off the engine.

"Are you sure?" Albert asked again.

"I'm sure."

"Take this then," Albert said, while holding the gun for Michael.

Michael was startled. "I can't."

"You need this against Zanu. They will kill anyone in their way."

Michael wondered for a second, but no, never. "I couldn't shoot someone," he said.

"I can come with you."

Out of the question. "Thank you Albert but no. You rescued us and with luck we'll be okay. We must go."

Albert turned in the seat. "Take that blanket and hide in the back of your car."

"Yes," Cathy said quietly.

They all got out while Michael wriggled his wrist and grimaced with the pain. Tyre noise getting closer; a car was approaching.

"Get down!" Michael shouted to Cathy, bright in her overalls.

"What?" she asked.

"Down beside the car."

She got onto her knees while a car rolled by, and Albert leaned against the car aiming his gun. Michael was startled. It was as if Albert really would shoot the CIO or the police. Silence. No, something. Michael squatted beside Cathy and she buried her face against his shoulder, crying so quietly. She was a mess.

"I – thought – it was – them," she said between soft sobs.

"I know. But we're safe now."

Cathy nodded and Michael held her. Time passed: seconds, a minute.

"We have to go," he said.

Cathy got up and wiped her cheeks.

Michael unlocked the car with his left hand. Cathy got in the back, down low with the blanket over her. "Julie, you get in the front. That'll look less suspicious."

The door creaked and she climbed in.

"Thank you so much," Michael said to Albert, but avoided shaking hands.

"You have hurt your hand," he said.

Michael sighed. "I'm okay to drive."

"Are you sure?"

"Yes."

"Good luck and God speed."

"Thank you so much," Michael repeated, but those words sounded trite. "You go home and look after Therese, and if you don't hear anything on the news you'll know we got away."

He smiled brightly. "Zanu only broadcast their victories.'

"I know."

Michael climbed in, turned the key and the pain from his wrist! Worse, the engine didn't start. He tried again for several seconds, and no response. They were stuck. He waited a moment and tried a third time, and the engine struggled into life, but spluttered and ran rough. He pressed the accelerator and it cleared to a degree. Into first, left hand on the wheel and away, parallel to Madsen Street towards Mutare Road. He drove carefully, third gear, neither fast nor slow. There was more smoke now that the fire was out. He waited at the intersection for a tractor to pass, and pulled out onto the main road. They headed south-east and Michael rolled along behind the bouncing tractor until they reached the last of the houses. He checked his mirrors, road clear ahead, and pulled out to pass.

"I should see a doctor," Michael said. "Got any ideas?"

Julie frowned. "We will head towards Mutare and see if we can find someone at Nyazura."

Michael nodded, placed the car into fifth, and drove left-handed with his arm on the door rest. It was three-eighteen by the clock, and then a sign: Nyazura Fifteen. Not so far.

"Nyazura is only small, so we may not find a doctor," Julie said.

"What's the next town after that?" Michael asked.

"Mutare, but we will get there too late. Doctors close at four."

"If I can't treat it, I can't treat it."

"Is it okay?"

"I'll survive. How are you Cathy?"

"Good."

They continued along the highway with shadows getting longer in the mid-afternoon. Michael had so much he wanted to say and so much he wanted to ask. They crested a hill and Michael saw a house on the left in unpainted timber, with a sagging balcony protecting it from the sun. And a house on the right, leaning backwards. He looked at Julie.

"On the right, just down there," she said.

Michael slowed, and past the second ramshackle house there was a sign pointing at the sky. Nyazura. And a narrow back road that seemed to lead to nowhere; it wasn't promising. Michael indicated and turned onto a very rough road. A sign for a railway crossing, and the narrow-gauge track ahead. He slowed to a crawl with the crossing in bad repair. Further along were a few houses and a store. He pulled left and parked under the shade of a palm tree.

The general store may have been white in years gone by, but much of the paint had peeled giving it a dappled orange and cream appearance. A balcony had a couple of sheets of tin missing. In the shade sat a pile of maize-meal sacks and two steel barrels of 'Chibuku'.

Inside was dark and cool, and Michael couldn't make out much. It took his eyes a while to adjust. Nobody around, or so it seemed. It was a real general store, a little bit of everything. Wooden racks of vegetables on the left, shelves of clothing ahead, and a counter on the right with

191

several soft drink bottles standing at one end. And there, in the shade, a man sat on a timber crate.

"Good afternoon, I'm Michael," he said. "Do you know where I can find a doctor?"

The floor creaked and the two girls entered the shop. Silence.

"Excuse me sir, is there a doctor who can help my boyfriend?" Cathy asked. Michael looked over his shoulder and she was dressed in the jeans and the black blouse that Mary packed for her.

The man got to his feet and walked slowly to the counter. He picked up a soft drink bottle and rolled it in his palms.

"Maybe," he said.

"Please," Cathy asked. "His arm is hurt and he needs help."

"Three bottles of orange," Michael ordered.

The man slid three bottles of 'Fanta' along the counter, along with an old-fashioned bottle opener. Michael flipped the top from a bottle and handed the opener to Cathy.

"Thirty dollars," the man said.

Julie fumbled in the pocket of her jeans and handed over a handful of notes. The man slowly counted them, opened a drawer and put the money away.

"Can you tell me if there's a doctor nearby?" Michael asked.

"Yes, he is near the farm. His name is Doctor Nash and he can help you."

"Near the farm?"

"Yes, it is along this road for two kilometres," he said, pointing to the left. "The doctor's house is on the corner of the dirt road to the farm."

"Thank you."

Michael sipped some of the lukewarm drink and headed out of the door. The girls followed, also drinking. He got into the car and Cathy joined him in the front. Suddenly, things seemed better. He headed along the rough road, past a rusting steel shed and a few more timber houses. And then a large red-brick wall with two burgundy-coloured steel gates. There were buildings behind and overlooking the countryside beyond the town. The wall was massive, surrounding grounds of a hundred hectares or more. A boarding school perhaps. Next was a paddock of weeds rather than grass, and then a dirt road on the left. On the far side of the dirt road was a small fibro building, in the natural grey of unpainted cement sheeting. Very small, maybe six or seven metres wide and about the same deep. Very plain: two natural aluminium window frames and a dull-white plywood door, split and warped at the bottom. Opposite the house, a large green letterbox with the name 'Lincoln Stud'. That

193

might be what they were after. Michael pulled onto the gravel verge.

"I'll see if this is it," he said to Cathy.

Michael strolled across a yard of dust and dry weeds to the front door. Quiet, not a sound. He knocked and got no response. He knocked again and heard the clank of a bottle. Footsteps approaching, fumbling at the lock and the door opened.

He was white, maybe late fifties. Untidy grey hair, thin on top. Bloodshot eyes, face lined and wrinkled; skin blotchy. Stained and creased white shirt, crumpled khaki shorts, bare feet. He smelled of alcohol as if he'd been drinking, while he held the door frame, swaying slightly.

"Doctor Nash?" Michael asked.

"Who wants to know?" he grumbled.

"My name is Michael Page, and I've hurt my arm."

"You better come in."

Michael followed Nash into a corridor walled with unpainted Masonite and floored with bare boards. Nash went through a doorway, and Michael followed him into a small room also lined with Masonite, but painted dull white: a desk with two vinyl kitchen chairs on one side, and an old, vinyl-covered office chair opposite. To the right was an examination table with a white timber cabinet beside, while books and papers were spread around a bookcase attached to the wall. On the desk was a half-full bottle of Johnny Walker Red.

"Sit," Nash said.

Michael sat on one of the kitchen chairs and Nash sat beside him. Nash squeezed and flexed Michael's wrist.

"Sprained," Nash said. "I'll bind it."

Nash went to stand but didn't make it, flopping onto the chair again. He grabbed the desk for support and levered himself to his feet. He swayed for a moment, and then he went to the cabinet and slid a drawer open, rummaging for a while. He returned with a wide roll of bandage.

"Unbutton your sleeve and roll it to your elbow."

Michael did as he was told, and Nash started at the top of Michael's forearm, stretching the broad bandage all the way to the palm of his hand. He doubled the bandage back again, and used an elastic clip to fasten it. Just then, Michael heard steps echoing in the bare corridor.

"How's your arm darling?" Cathy asked from the doorway.

"Darling's arm is fine," Nash said without looking up. Michael watched Nash look over his shoulder, and then hold the table to stand. "Ah, a young African. You've got a pretty little African."

"Careful Nash," Michael warned.

"I know why you've got...."

"I haven't got anyone; she's my girlfriend."

195

"You've got an African whore!"

Michael jumped to his feet and didn't know what to do. He wanted to grab Nash and shake him, but couldn't. He stood, glaring eye to eye. "Fuck you Nash!"

"Pretty African whore....."

Cathy lashed out and kicked him in the shin.

"Fuck!" Nash staggered and fell into the chair. "Bloody Africans."

"You're in the wrong country," Michael said.

"Yeah, and you think I want to be here? This place, it's gone to shit."

"And why do you think that is?" Cathy asked. "Why's it gone this way?"

"Your people," Nash said.

"Your people Doctor Nash. I know how it was: university for whites, trade school for coloureds, year twelve for Africans, those who could make the sacrifice that is. Is that not so? And then what, majority rule and the whites clear out, or the ones who could. And we're left to pick up the pieces. Not educated, not trained, not experienced. We had to run the country, run the businesses, make things work."

"Yeah, and you fucked up."

"Yes, we fucked up as you put it. We had a European democracy dumped on us that didn't fit our culture. If whites had never come here and we were left to our own ways, things would be very different."

"What, living in the bush like savages?"

"They may have lived in the bush, but they weren't savages. They knew their rights and obligations, and there was honesty and integrity. I know stories of my ancestors, and I'm proud to be African."

"This is pointless," Michael said flatly.

"But he insulted us!" Cathy exclaimed

"I know, but you will never change him and his type."

Cathy stood stiffly with her arms crossed, glaring at the two men.

"He's a bitter old man and he'll never understand," Michael said. "Nash, you have no idea. I've been to hell and back, and so many kind African people helped me. They put their lives at risk for a stranger as if it were the most normal thing in this world. I wish the people in my country were half as kind and half as good as the people here. If they have a weakness, it's that they're too kind and too accepting of things."

"That's our culture," Cathy said.

"I know," Michael replied. "How far does this go back?"

"For us Bantu about five thousand years."

"Tell Doctor Nash of your culture."

"Our culture is about collective moral obligations, collective justice if you wish. Justice for our tribe, our mitupo and our village. European culture is all about the rights of the individual. The two don't fit, and we can't make them fit."

"Savages….," Nash muttered.

"This is pointless. Look Nash, is my arm okay?"

"Avoid using it for a couple of days, and keep it elevated as much as you can," he said. "Take the compression bandage off after four or five days and you'll be fine."

"How much do I owe you?"

"Two-hundred."

Michael put two notes under the bottle on the desk, and he took Cathy's hand and led her out the door.

"That man…," she fumed.

"You're better already."

"I'm not. I'm angry, but I'm crying inside too."

"Come, it's getting late."

Julie sat on the bonnet of the Toyota. She slid off, brushed the seat of her trousers and got into the back seat. Cathy joined Michael in front, and soon they were heading towards the highway. Michael turned right, and accelerated up to one-hundred. The shadows were long with sunset approaching. Michael continued to rest his right arm even though it felt better with the bandage in place. They closed on a bus belching diesel fumes. Suddenly brake lights flickered on and the bus slowed.

"Is there anything near here?" Michael asked.

"No, nothing," Julie replied from the back.

Michael braked hard, and the increasing gap allowed Michael to see past the bus to white barriers across the road. He braked harder and pulled onto the gravel.

"Roadblock," he said.

Cathy tapped her fingers on the dash. A voice from the rear, "Nyazura," Julie said. "Go there and wait for the train."

Michael turned the car around and retraced the route to the dishevelled little town. As they approached the railway line, he slowed and spotted a track leading to buildings on the right. A platform, a stone station building with a veranda, and a couple of sheds on the other side of the tracks. He took the narrow road and turned left onto a rocky trail leading to the steel goods shed. Michael drove slowly on the stones, and he pulled up behind the rusting building. Car hidden.

The sound of cicadas, a light breeze blew, and no-one around.

"I will check the station," Julie said.

"I'll do it," Michael offered.

"No, you're limping. I won't be long."

Michael sat on the bonnet of the car and Cathy sat beside him. "She's a good sister," he said.

"She is," Cathy agreed. "Do you like her?"

"Of course, as family."

"Remember she's a good person."

"What do you mean?"

"Just remember."

Julie returned with her head down. "The train's due at two fifty-four," she said.

"In the morning?" Michael asked.

"What do we do?"

"I need to wash," Cathy said, "I can still feel that....," and she turned her head away.

"There's a washroom," Julie said, "I need to wash myself."

"We'll all go," Michael suggested.

They stumbled over stone ballast to the lonely station building.

* * *

The blast from the locomotive horn woke Michael. He stretched and the horn blew again, and it was a miserable sound. He sat up on the wooden bench and looked across at Cathy who was rubbing her eyes. On the other side of the waiting room, Julie watched her sister. Michael swung off the bench and stretched again, and Cathy came to him.

The train was closer now; the diesel engine whining as it slowed for the station. Michael looked along the platform and nothing stirred: just three in the open waiting room. The locomotive headlight lit the track, brakes squealed, and the train eased to a stop. A single locomotive, red with a silver stripe, trailed by a dozen or more steel carriages, also red with silver stripes. Michael checked his watch under the balcony light, and it was just after three.

At the head of the train were three first class carriages. Michael, Cathy and Julie were standing opposite a carriage marked '2'.

"We will take second class," Cathy said. "Third is uncomfortable."

Third class must be something like wooden seats.

Michael waited for the girls to climb on board and then he followed them. The girls opened the door from the vestibule, and Michael entered an empty saloon. Cathy took a seat by the window. Michael tossed his bag on the luggage rack and sat beside her on the aisle. Julie put her bag on the opposite rack and sat next to Michael, but on the other side of the aisle. The carriage was in good repair: walls lined in pine laminate, cream ceiling, dark green vinyl or leather seats. The locomotive horn blew, muffled by double-glazing. A moment later the carriage jerked and they rolled out of Nyazura station. Michael stretched and got comfortable on the soft seat.

"Peter must be wondering what happened to us," Cathy said. "I hope he waits."

"Me too," Michael said. "How do you feel?"

"Dirty." She looked away. "I don't know if I will ever get over it."

Michael put her arm around his darling, and she rested her head on his shoulder. He could have said soothing words to comfort her, but everything seemed trite. "I can't imagine what it was like and how you feel now," he said quietly.

Cathy snuggled into him tighter and Michael felt his eyes going moist.

The conductor staggered along the gently swaying carriage. "Tickets please," he asked.

"How much to Mutare?" Michael asked.

"Forty-two dollars."

"Three please."

The conductor pulled rectangular cardboard tickets from his pouch and punched them one after the other. He handed them to Michael, who handed a two one-hundred dollar notes across. He received his change and carefully slipped it into his pocket; he was running low on cash. If only he could cash a travellers cheque.

It was unbelievable that they were on their way to Mutare at long last. No obstacles at all. Julie was clever for thinking of this. Why was it so easy to get away? Maybe they weren't important enough to chase around the Eastern Highlands. More likely it was the African way of doing things. Erect a couple of roadblocks, sit back and wait.

The train rocked easily, they weren't travelling very fast. And then vibration and noise, brakes on. They were slowing, more vibration, and stop. Lights outside, it was a station, but nobody around. The horn sounded and they pulled away. Within a few minutes they reached cruising speed, whatever that was. Forty, fifty perhaps. Onwards through the dark and Michael wished he could sleep like Cathy, but he slept too well at Nyazura. Onwards for about quarter of an hour or so, and they slowed for the next station. A sign on a light post, 'Pounsley'. They waited only moments. Michael listened to Cathy's gentle breathing, and she was such a darling. He closed his eyes with the easy rise and fall of her chest comforting against his shoulder. He didn't sleep, he just allowed love to wash over his body. No wonder Mudiwa found love with Rudo, African women were precious.

Stop after stop and the sky lightened as dawn approached. Quarter-to-five, very close to Mutare now. Cathy stirred and moved her head. She drifted into sleep for a moment and then woke. He watched her in the lights of the carriage.

"Did I sleep long?" she asked.

"About an hour," Michael said.

"I wish this ride would last forever."

"Me too."

The train stopped and a sign showed 'Feruka'.

"It's not far now." Cathy said.

The horn bellowed and they were on their way; the ride wasn't going to last forever. Outside was brighter with morning approaching. Michael eased away from Cathy and went to the washroom to freshen up. He returned and Cathy went along the corridor, so Michael took the window seat. She returned about ten minutes later.

A few houses near the railway with lights on. A car passed with headlights illuminating the way. Zimbabwe was waking and life seemed so normal. And yet the country was collapsing. The collision of European values and African culture didn't fit. On one hand the community assumed collective justice, and on the other hand a small group of elites struggled with the complexities of modern governance while taking advantage of European-styled individual rights, helping themselves to whatever they felt was their 'right'. As Cathy once explained, African socialism didn't work economically. And with a long history of free and fair justice, the community never questioned incompetence, until it was too late. And for Zimbabwe, regardless of the MDC, it seemed too late. The elite weren't going without a fight.

The train slowed and Julie stirred, as if she sensed they were reaching their destination. Slower and slower, and the brakes squealed sharply. Journey over.

Passengers bustled around the train, especially at the rear in third class. Luggage, boxes, sacks, livestock; there were more goods than people on the platform. The threesome kept clear of the pandemonium and headed through an exit gate onto the street. Ahead a taxi, Julie opened two doors. She got in the front, and Michael and Cathy behind.

"Yeoville Cemetery please," she said.

The driver pulled away from the chaos and drove along a quiet street.

"It isn't far," Julie said.

Minutes later, they were in a hilly suburban street, outside a lush grass-covered field with trees scattered about. Julie paid the driver and got out of the car.

"This way," Julie said, and Michael and Cathy followed her along a bitumen driveway. They climbed a hill, it was cooler there, and rounded a bend and climbed again. Julie stepped onto the grass and headed towards a tree. Peter stood and Julie ran to him.

"We're so sorry," she said.

"What happened to you?" Peter asked.

"It wasn't easy. First we had to get Cathy, and then Michael sprained his wrist. And then the road was blocked so we came by train. Ah, where are our parents?"

"They will not come; your father did not want to leave."

"Why?"

Peter shrugged his shoulders.

"Tell me Peter?" Cathy shouted.

"I do not know," Peter said.

Cathy grimaced. "Drive us home."

"My car is this way."

They followed Peter down the hill to a carpark. The yellow Volvo was parked to one side and Peter unlocked the doors. Without prompting, the girls got into the back, which left the men to share the front.

"I do not know the way," Peter said, "I just followed your parent's car to get here."

Julie gave directions and Peter drove across town. It was early morning and traffic was sparse. It took about quarter of an hour to reach a tree-lined street that could have been in Harare or even in Rusape.

"Turn right here," Julie said, and they turned into the driveway of a red-brick house.

Cathy was out of the car and at the front door before anyone else. She pressed a button, waited a few seconds, and pressed again. Michael arrived just as the door opened.

"What are you thinking, Mum?" she shouted. "They're after us; don't you understand?"

"Cathy, what…."

"Do you know what I've been through? Peter must've told you I was arrested and tortured and Julie had to rescue me."

"But darling…."

"Don't 'but darling' me, this is serious!"

"Come inside darling."

Cathy ripped the flywire door open and stomped into the house.

"And you're Cathy's friend?" Mrs Shoko asked. Michael wasn't surprised by Cathy's mother: tall, slim and dressed smartly in black slacks and a white blouse, and she had an accent like her daughters'.

"I'm Michael Page, Cathy's boyfriend," he said, offering his hand. "I'm really sorry; I've never seen her like this before."

"I think she's been through a lot."

"Do you know what happened?"

"Mr Chirinda told us she'd been arrested over something and we should leave the country, but I didn't know anything about torture."

Michael glared at Peter.

"Come in please," Mrs Shoko said, standing to one side.

Michael went inside, and headed towards raised voices.

"But Dad this is dangerous; it's the CIO. If they can't get me, they will start on you!"

"But why?" the man, Cathy's father, asked.

"They don't need a why; they're evil sadistic bastards and any excuse will do!"

"Let's start at the beginning – oh sorry."

"I'm Michael Page, Cathy's boyfriend."

"Joe Shoko," he said, and Michael shook hands. They were in the kitchen and Joe held a mug of what smelled like coffee. "Please sit," Joe offered.

"Excuse me Mr Shoko," Michael said. "But we've been travelling all night and, um...."

"You would like a cup of coffee," he said, and chuckled.

"Yes please."

"Please sit Cathy, and I will get you a cup too."

They sat at the table while Joe switched on the electric kettle and got busy in the kitchen. He was what Michael expected or maybe not. He was quite chubby in fact.

Mrs Shoko came into the room and Michael half-stood for a moment, before sitting again.

"You've met my wife Sally."

"Yes."

The kettle switched itself off; Joe poured two mugs and brought them to the table.

"What's this about?" Joe asked. "The story we got from that man was very confusing."

"We found fraud at the bank and reported it," Cathy said. "But one of the managers is a member of Zanu and he made up a story about Michael spying on Mugabe's bank accounts and giving the information to the MDC, and we both were arrested and tortured. Michael escaped, and Julie helped him to rescue me."

"This is awful," Sally said. "We had no idea it was this serious. And this was about fraud?"

"We think so, or perhaps he's attracted to me. I thought they were just keeping tabs on Michael, and I never guessed things would get as serious as they did."

"Maybe he started something that got out of control," Joe said.

"Possibly."

"Are you alright darling?"

"I'm fine, but I'm worried about you."

He took her hand. "We will be safe here," he said. "Just because this happened to Michael and you doesn't mean...."

Julie burst into the room. "They're here!" she shouted.

"Who's here?" Joe asked.

"Police, CIO, I don't know. We heard a car and we saw them."

"Fuck!" Cathy exclaimed. "Sorry Dad. Look, they've been watching the house. You have to come now."

"Where?" Joe asked.

"Mozambique."

"What, now? Just leave everything and go?"

"We have to."

"But who will look after the school?"

"Fuck the school!"

"Darling...."

"Michael and I have to go, and once we go we can't come back."

"But...."

"We can't come back, and I don't want to never see you again."

"I just can't leave everything."

"Please Dad. Mum, tell me you will come."

"Only with your father."

"I'm new here," Michael said. "But I know what these people are like. Cathy's right, until there's change at the top, I don't see any...."

"Michael, they're here!" Julie shouted.

"Please Dad," Cathy was crying.

"We have to go," Julie said, grabbing Cathy's arm and pulling her from the table. "Please Dad, come with us."

"You too Julie?"

"They're after me for helping Michael."

"Is there someway out of here?" Michael asked Julie.

"When we were young, we used to climb a tree to get over the back fence."

"Okay, let's go. Mr and Mrs Shoko, please reconsider."

"No, we will stay here and tell them you weren't here."

"Dad...," Cathy pleaded still crying; tears on her cheeks glistening.

"It's alright. This can't last forever, and once things change we can meet again."

"That will be years."

"No, it won't be that long. You should go."

Cathy kissed her father and mother while Julie grabbed Peter. Heavy knocking at the front, and Joe unlocked the back door.

"Hurry," Joe said. "We will stop them for as long as we can."

Michael took Cathy's arm and ran across the back lawn towards trees against the fence. Julie went first, scrambling from branch to branch to get herself about two metres off the ground, and then she edged along a thick limb and slid down to be hanging above the ground. She swung and dropped with a gentle thud. Peter went next, and

211

Michael pushed Cathy forward. She climbed and he watched, and when she reached the limb he followed her up. Painful, his feet! Poor Cathy must be in agony on top of everything else. Michael reached the limb just as Cathy dropped onto the one-metre high compost heap. Just then, loud voices in the Shoko's back yard. Michael dropped, and such agony when he landed! Julie was already across the yard and running between the house and fence. Peter and Cathy followed, and Michael brought up the rear.

"Va ri ko," and shots crackled over the fence. It was eerie, it sounded like a television news broadcast, only much louder and sharper. Another burst, but Michael was protected by the house. Peter ran, no galloped, across the street to a silver Nissan parked on a front lawn. He picked up a rock from the garden and threw it hard at the driver's window with the glass smashing into pieces. By the time Michael arrived, Peter opened the driver's door and released the boot. Michael watched him loosen the tool roll and grab the tyre iron and a screwdriver. He jammed the screwdriver into the ignition lock and hit it hard with the tyre iron.

"You drive," Peter said.

Michael shook his head.

"I cannot drive manual gears well," Peter clarified.

Michael swept glass off the seat and climbed in. He turned the screwdriver and a miracle happened, the engine started. Army green at the end of the street: soldiers and guns. Michael shoved the car into first, bounced off the kerb, u-turned and away. A rattle of gunfire, but Michael kept his foot into it. A second rattle while Michael took the right-hand bend as fast as he could. As long as the army didn't chase them with a vehicle, things should be okay. Yeah, right; it was only a matter of time before the roadblocks went up. He continued heading east, away from soldiers and towards Mozambique.

Chapter Fifteen

"Which way?" Michael asked.

"Turn right at the end," Cathy replied.

"What should we do about the border?"

"Pardon?"

Michael wished Cathy was sitting up front. "The border might be blocked," he shouted.

"We will go over the mountains."

"Is it far?"

"No, not at all. Turn left here and then next right."

Michael checked his mirrors and nobody behind.

"Go along here for about three or four kilometres," Cathy said.

They were running through a neat, middle-class suburb, and on the right were jagged mountains. Tall tree-covered peaks stretched as far as Michael could see. They were going over *that* in a Nissan Sunny?

"This is Morningside, we're close," Cathy said. "Turn right up there."

Michael slowed and turned at the intersection, and they were on a wider suburban street with the mountains ahead. He continued, the road climbed, houses overlooked the town centre on the flat plain below. The road veered left and right and still they climbed. It was hard work on the curves, driving one-handed as much as he could. The houses were interspersed with grassy paddocks, tall trees here and there, and the climb was steeper. Michael changed down to second, the little car struggling with the hill and with the weight of four adults. The grade eased and they left the outskirts of Mutare behind. He drove through thick forest, and downhill in third for engine braking. He checked the mirror, and another vehicle was behind, but he lost his view as they rounded a bend and headed uphill again. Climbing hard, ears painful. Michael checked the mirror and it didn't look like a car, and then he rounded another bend. Down a short straight section of road; he checked and it was a jeep!

"The army's behind," he shouted.

"What?" Cathy shouted in reply.

"A jeep."

"Go faster."

"It's flat."

The road climbed and snaked left and right, Michael taking the poor car around the bends as fast as he dared. Although he wanted to get away, it wasn't worth wrapping it around a tree.

"The border's close," Cathy yelled.

Michael kept his foot flat in third, the speedo hit 90 which was as much as the Nissan was going to give uphill. The jeep was pacing them, neither catching nor falling back. He noticed Cathy looking over her shoulder.

"It's not far," she said. "Where the road changes to dirt."

The road straightened, the grade easier, 100 in fourth. Downhill 140, the car wandering, suspension not able to cope with the uneven surface. A curve coming up, brake, down to 90, third and away. Yellow surface ahead, the border. They'd done it. Michael kept it flat, and bounced onto the dirt road. He eased down to 70, and the jeep continued onto the dirt too.

"They're still behind us," he said.

"But they can't!" Cathy exclaimed.

"No-ones gonna stop them."

Fuck! He accelerated up to 80 and the dust they raised blocked his view. A sharp bend, he braked, turned, and flat in second up a hill. The dust cloud eased and the green jeep was still there. A steep hill, temperature gauge against the red, the car struggling. And the suspension was bottoming all over the place.

The trees diminished and they raced beside a grassy plain. One-fifty on the straight with the car moving around on the dirt, but how fast could a jeep go? He didn't know; the dust cloud blocked his view. Ahead was an intersection with a road diagonal left to right.

"Which way?"

"Right."

Good, he wouldn't lose momentum. Michael slowed and nudged the car onto another straight. In the door mirror he caught sight of the green jeep and it was further back. It looked like 150 would do it. He was in fourth again and the lack of power and worn suspension were evenly matched. The car bottomed and snaked badly, and didn't have enough power to go faster. The road swung left and Michael eased, knowing the jeep would be better on curves on a dirt road. He had to make ground on the straights, so he put his boot into it and the steering kicked in his hands. Dangerous. Trees surrounding the road with a curve to the left; Michael braked and washed off a lot of speed. Too slow; left and right, and then climbed with the engine labouring. That was it, they had no chance. Any moment, Michael expected the sharp crackle of guns. The road veered left, and ahead was a black line.

"The main road," Cathy shouted above the noise.

Michael slowed and checked, road clear and away. Look in the mirror, dust cloud gone, jeep about a hundred metres behind. A good long straight, the car flat in fourth and the gap growing. Over a concrete bridge, speeding across farmland, climbing, temperature gauge red, still flat. Climbing hard, down through the gears, sharp left ahead. Change up, and a sharp right. Brake and turn, and the road was blocked. Michael lifted off and pressed the soggy brake pedal, it suffering with his driving. He slowed and checked, and the

217

road behind was clear. Michael's heart skipped a beat and he checked again, and no jeep. He slowed, and the soldiers looked different. Michael stopped, and watched a solider in a sandy-coloured uniform butt his cigarette on the road before strolling towards the driver's door. A door hinge squeaked and Cathy got out of the car. She walked towards the soldier while Michael got out and leaned on his door.

"Mangwanani," she said. (Good morning.)

"Mangwanani, marara sei?" the solider replied. (Good morning; did you sleep well?)

"Ndarara mararawo." (I slept well if you did.)

"Ndarara." (I slept well.)

"Ndinonzi Cathy Shoko, u no gona kunzgwa English?" (My name is Cathy Shoko; do you speak English?)

"Ongu, kunyatsodo reva. Yes, but please speak slowly."

"This is my boyfriend Michael Page, my sister Julie Shoko and her friend Peter Chirinda."

"I am Sergeant Khumalo of the FADM." He slung the rifle over his shoulder. "Can I see your – um – passports please?"

Michael pulled them out of his trouser pocket and gave them to the sergeant, who flicked through the pages.

"You do not have visas," Sergeant Khumalo said, handing the document back.

Michael shook his head.

"And you?" Sergeant Khumalo asked the others.

"We don't have passports," Julie said.

"Talk slowly please."

"We – do – not – have – passports."

"You must come with me then."

"But we were escaping the CIO," Peter said.

"What is the CIO?"

"The Zimbabwean army."

"You are in trouble with the Zimbabwean army?"

Michael glared at Peter.

"You must come with us," the sergeant said. "Please get into the car and follow my jeep. We have these," Khumalo said, lifting his weapon from his shoulder. "Just in case."

"Where're you taking us?" Cathy asked.

"Chimoio."

* * *

They approached Chimoio along a highway lined with hundreds of pedestrians. Some walking, some passing time, some selling home-made clothes hanging on makeshift lines. There was a market next to the road, a steel roof supported on wooden posts with dozens of small timber stalls around and about. They closed on the city centre, and it was very different to Zimbabwean towns. It bustled noisily, with dirty, dusty streets thronging with colourfully dressed Africans. It had a Portuguese feel with run-down colonial buildings lining the main road. The jeep led the way slowly, forcing its way through crowds and avoiding errant drivers. Michael followed: despite the chaos he had no chance of getting away through such crowds. They left the central business district and drove through a suburb of dilapidated houses: paint peeling, windows and doors missing, rooves incomplete. The jeep turned left onto a side-street, and ahead was a white wall with a charcoal-grey gate. The gate swung open and the jeep passed through with Michael following.

It was a modest, walled compound with two white buildings ahead, and two more to the right. A tin shed took up most of the left of the compound, and through the open door Michael saw jeeps and personnel carriers under repair. Behind, more jeeps and personnel carriers were parked against the wall. Sergeant Khumalo came to the car and Michael climbed out. Cathy joined him, while Peter and Julie were on the other side of the Nissan.

"Come with me please."

Khumalo led the way into the largest building and to a darkened room. After the bright sunshine Michael struggled to see, but it seemed they were standing in a wide hallway with three closed doors on the left and a single open doorway on the right. Michael glanced inside, and saw rows of straight-backed wooden chairs facing an altar with a cross on top. Curtains to the rear, rich burgundy with golden crosses for trim. In the corridor behind, two of the soldiers from the jeep guarded the entrance with their machineguns ready. Khumalo knocked on the first closed door, waited a moment; opened it and went inside. Michael overhead a conversation in chiShona.

"Do you understand what they're saying?" he whispered to Cathy.

"Yes. The sergeant is talking to Lieutenant Shumba, who thinks we should be returned to Mutare."

"That's terrible."

"But it's not settled. They're going to wait for Major Nhema to return, and he will make the decision."

"Do you know when?"

"Saturday."

Tomorrow. Sergeant Khumalo emerged from the office.

"Ndi Manyika u fana," Cathy said. (I'm Manyika like you.)

"Ndi no pfidza, ndi gone," Sergeant Khumalo replied. (I'm sorry, I can't.)

"Ndi kubatidzo." (Please help me.)

"Ndi no pfidza." (I'm sorry.) "Now, all of you must come with me."

The Sergeant left the building and strode briskly across the dusty yard. The foursome followed, with the two soldiers trailing. Khumalo was heading towards a smaller, shabby white building. Badly stained with black mould, a rusty steel door, and with rusty bars over two windows. He reached into his right pocket, pulled out keys and unlocked the door. He held it open, and Michael and Cathy went inside with Julie and Peter following.

It was a dark corridor with white brick walls and four open doors.

"You two go there," Khumalo said, pointing at Matthew and Peter. "You go there," he said to Cathy. "And you go there," he said to Julie. The fourth door, whatever it was, remained closed.

It was a cell, full circle. A double bunk bed and a bucket the only furniture.

"You must wait here for my commander to return," Khumalo said.

Michael nodded.

Khumalo closed the steel door and clanked the lock. At least they had natural light through the grimy window, although the bars meant they weren't going anywhere.

"I said the wrong thing," Peter said.

"Yes you did."

"I am very sorry."

"Can't be helped. Look, I'll take the bottom bunk, you take the top."

Michael climbed onto his bed and stretched out. Imagine being taken to Mutare and handed over to the CIO, to be locked away for the rest of his days. Wouldn't that be tragic?

Chapter Sixteen

Being held in custody by the FADM was more civilised than the Zimbabwean CIO. Two meals a day including coffee with breakfast, followed by a shower and a walk around the yard. But it was frustrating, especially as Saturday dragged by without any indication of their fate. Michael had a restless sleep that night, not made any easier by Peter's snoring. He woke when the door to their cell creaked open, and breakfast was served by a young soldier. Sadza, a roll, black coffee. Their cell door was left open, and he heard the soldier at the door opposite. There was a muffled conversation, Cathy's voice, and the soldier replied with 'ongu' which meant yes.

Michael started with the coffee and roll. He was about to have some sadza when the soldier returned.

"Kubuda na ndi."

"Sorry, I don't speak chiShona," Michael replied,

"Venha comigo."

Michael shrugged his shoulders. Portuguese was equally confusing.

"He said to go with him," Peter said.

The soldier marched across the corridor and opened the door to Cathy's cell. "Kubuda na ndi," he said. A few moments later Cathy appeared at the door.

"We're to go with him," she said.

"Do you know where?"

"Don't worry, it's safe."

Outside was bright and Michael shaded his eyes from glare reflected from the concrete paving. The soldier led the way to the largest building, the one they were taken to on Friday. They entered into cool darkness and the soldier led them to the first doorway on the right. He stamped his boots on the floor and stood at attention. A few moments later a white man emerged: thinning grey hair, deeply lined face, and wearing a long black robe. A priest. The priest beckoned and Cathy went inside.

"Come with me," she said.

Michael went into the small chapel. Three rows of varnished wooden chairs faced an altar covered in a red cloth, decorated with gold crosses as a border. On the altar were two brass candleholders, candles unlit, and a polished brass cross. The priest turned his back and put a bowl on the altar before turning to face Michael and Cathy. Cathy went to the space between the chairs and the altar and looked over her shoulder at Michael.

"Come here and kneel," she said.

Michael was perplexed, but when Cathy knelt he did as she asked.

"Do you speak English?" she asked the priest.

"I do," he replied.

"I want you to hear my confession."

"If you come with me to...."

"I want to confess with my boyfriend."

"This is unusual."

"Please, I want to."

"This breaks the sanctity of confession."

"This does no harm if I want it to be this way."

The priest sighed. "If you wish."

Cathy closed her eyes and the priest knelt and made the sign of the cross above Cathy's head. "In the name of the Father, and of the Son, and of the Holy Spirit. Amen."

Cathy put her head down. "Bless me Father for I have sinned, I have never confessed."

"Never?" the priest asked.

"I'm not Catholic."

"Then I cannot hear your confession."

"Please."

"No, this is not possible. I cannot offer absolution to you."

"There's more to life than religious dogma."

"Confession is sacred to Catholics."

"Dreadful things have happened and I want to confess."

"I am sorry, but I cannot."

"Maybe I can just tell you, and then you can say a prayer for me."

The priest rubbed his chin. "A prayer for you, this I can do."

"Thank you father."

The priest bowed his head. "In the name of the Father, and of the son, and of the Holy Sprit. Amen," he said.

"Michael is my boyfriend and my lover. We were arrested and tortured by the Zimbabwean Intelligence Agency, and then I was raped and Michael was forced to watch. Because of this, Michael confessed to a crime he didn't commit."

"But this is not your sin."

"The sin is the army in this place are going to send us back. Don't let them do this; Michael will go to jail for something he never did. And me, I can't return to a country where the Government rapes its daughters."

The priest frowned and then he stood. "Please take a seat," he offered.

Michael and Cathy sat on two of the chairs, and the priest sat next to Cathy. He turned to face her.

"Your name is Catherine," he said.

"Yes it is," Cathy replied.

"Tell me what happened."

Cathy put her head down. "To be violated is every woman's nightmare. It can happen to any of us, we know this, but we always hope. And then...." Cathy looked up, looked at the priest, looked deep in his eyes. "It was awful, the most horrible thing, I just can't describe it. I felt – I don't know – helpless. To my grave I will never forget and I will never forgive."

"You said the Intelligence Agency?"

"It was. But it was really about a twisted man's greed, and his attraction for me."

"I am very sorry for what has happened to you."

"Do you believe me Father?"

"I know you have suffered because I feel your pain. Is there something I can do to help your soul?"

"My soul is in good hands."

"What hands are those, Catherine?"

"I believe in greater spiritual powers known to you as God and known to me as Mwari, and known to others in this world in many different ways and by many different names. Mwari is man and woman, creator and destroyer, the God of above and the Goddess of below. Mwari gave us the ability to think and to reason, to love and to hate, and to act for good or to act for evil."

"How about your soul, Michael?"

"I've always been confused, and I was looking forward to learning more about Cathy's beliefs."

"Do you wish to pray?"

"Please Father," Cathy said.

The priest bowed his head.

"Dear Father. Bless these two lovers, for they have suffered. Bless Catherine, for she understands that which remains a mystery to many, including me. Bless Michael, and help him to learn from Catherine. And bless me, for I must rescue them. Amen."

"Amen," Cathy repeated. "You will help us?" she asked.

"I cannot let you return to such a place, so I will help you."

"Thank you so much."

"I am Father Santos Almeida." He went to the door. "Você pode tomá-los às suas células," he said. "The soldier will take you to your cells and I will contact the commander. Give me luck, for I will need it."

"Thank you again Father."

The soldier stomped into the chapel, and Michael and Cathy waited to be escorted to the cell block.

* * *

Clang, crash, the door opened. It was Sergeant Khumalo, frowning while he smoked a cigarette. Michael followed him out of the cell and waited while Khumalo retrieved Cathy. They were escorted to the white building, and Khumalo went into the second of the two offices opposite the chapel. Moments later he beckoned them inside.

A bulky uniformed officer sat behind a large, varnished timber desk. He looked important with dozens of bright ribbons on his breast pocket. Father Almeida sat in a timber chair opposite. Michael and Cathy stood and waited.

"I am Major Nhema; the Father told me of your request."

"Major, this is more than a request," Cathy said. "This is a matter of life and death."

"But why should I believe you?"

"Which woman would make up such a story about herself?"

"As you say. And you, you are very quiet."

"I'm a visitor to Africa," Michael said. "Whereas my girlfriend is better able to deal with this – situation."

The Major rubbed his chin. "You have admitted escaping custody, and you make serious accusations about the government of our neighbours. You have the potential to create much trouble for me."

"It isn't our intention to make trouble, but what happened, happened. Both my boyfriend and I wish that the whole thing could be undone, but it's too late."

"Even if I help you, what of your sister and the other man?"

"They helped us escape, and for that they will be punished. If we are spared, they must be spared too."

"Father?" the major asked.

"I believe Catherine suffered and she deserves our mercy."

"Perhaps she is trying to manipulate you, to get your sympathy."

"I believe she is genuine."

"It is Sunday, and the Father called me at home because of this. For now, I will not repatriate you. Instead, I will contact my superiors in Maputo and let them decide. Sergeant Khumalo, take them to their cells."

"Please tell them what happened," Cathy said. "So that they can make an informed decision."

"And what really happened?"

"Someone made a false accusation against me," Michael said. "We were interrogated and tortured by the CIO. The CIO officer threatened to rape Cathy, and I confessed to stop it happening. But he raped her anyway.

"Please Major," Cathy asked.

"Sergeant," the major said.

Khumalo grabbed them by their arms and led them outside. Cathy took Michael's hand and held it tight for the walk across the yard. And then they were separated and locked away.

* * *

Michael enjoyed his exercise period in the yard, and especially being away from Peter. Then he spotted the priest heading towards him fast, with his black cloak swinging about.

"Good morning Father," Michael said.

"Good morning Michael. Do you know where Catherine is?"

"Over there," Michael replied, nodding towards the cell block. Cathy and Julie were on the step in the shade.

"Please come with me, I must talk to you both," Almeida said.

Father Almeida strode towards the dilapidated building, Michael following.

"Good morning, you are Julie, are you not?" Almeida asked.

"I am," Julie replied.

"I want to borrow your sister please."

Julie nodded and Cathy got to her feet.

"This way," Father Almeida said while marching towards the big building with the chapel. They went inside and to the right, and Father Almeida shut the door and sat on one of the chairs. Michael and Cathy sat beside him. The Father reached inside his cloak and handed a sheet of paper to Cathy. She looked it over, frowning.

"I don't understand," Cathy said.

"This will not help your cause," Almeida said.

"No, sorry, I don't understand Portuguese."

"Ah, of course, I will translate. Major Nhema says he has four illegal immigrants, one Australian and three Zimbabweans, and you are evading the Zimbabwean authorities. He asks for guidance as to whether you should be returned to Zimbabwe."

"Great," Michael said.

232

"This is not great."

"Sorry, I was being ironic. Where did you get this?"

"From Nhema's adjutant. Nhema wrote it longhand and asked the adjutant to send it."

Michael rubbed his chin. "If you got this, maybe you could get the adjutant to send a different message?"

"No I do not think so. Borrowing this is one thing, but to ask him to disobey his commander is something very different."

Michael pondered the piece of paper in Father Almeida's hands. "How would the adjutant send the message?" he asked.

"By telex."

"I know how to send telex," Cathy said.

Ah, brilliant, Michael thought. "So if you can get to the telex machine, you could send a different message for us."

Cathy nodded. "Except I can't read or write Portuguese."

"But you could do it phonetically?"

"Yes, but slowly. But what about this message?"

"They'll get two messages, but they'll also get the full story." Michael turned his head. "Father, if I draft a letter, can you write it for Cathy in Portuguese?"

"Yes. Wait, I will get some paper," Almeida said.

Father Almeida left the chapel.

"What's it like sharing with Peter?" Cathy asked.

Michael grimaced.

"Julie would be better with someone like you," Cathy said.

Father Almeida returned with a pad and pen.

"I think this," Michael said. "I have apprehended one Australian and three Zimbabwean illegal immigrants who escaped from the Zimbabwean Central Intelligence Organisation. There is clear evidence of rape and torture by the CIO. Therefore, I..."

"Please, more slow," Almeida asked.

"Sorry. Therefore I ask permission to treat the four detainees as lawful refugees."

"This is good," the Father said. "Your exercise time is running out, so we must act now."

"Why are you doing this?" Cathy asked.

"You have suffered and I am helping you."

"But you're putting yourself in danger for us, and we're just strangers. Illegal immigrants."

He looked at the floor. "I feel something," he said quietly.

Cathy stared at him.

"No, for both of you. I sense it."

"I see." Michael had his hands crossed in his lap, and Cathy gently put her hands on his. "Tell me Father," she said. "Why doesn't your Church let priests marry?"

"It is in the Bible, in the writings of Saint Paul. But it is more, we believe that a Priest marries the Church, and we cannot have two marriages at the same time."

"But you deny yourselves love."

"We have the love of God." He lifted his head and his eyes met Cathy's. "I know what you are trying to say, and at this moment I understand what you mean. This is why I will help you, even though it will be hard. How are we to do this?"

"Sick," Michael said. "I'll pretend to be sick, and you and the adjutant will help me."

"Yes, good. Good idea." The Father stood. "Michael come with me; Cathy, you wait by the door."

Michael followed the priest along the corridor to a small office full of files and books and a man at a desk with his back to the door. On one side was a timber desk with an electric typewriter keyboard set into it. Michael steeled himself; play-acting was contrary to his natural reserve. He took a breath like he was going to dive into cold water and jumped, crying out when he hit the timber floor.

"Ajude-me Corporal Chirinda!" Father Almeida shouted.

"Qual é o problema?" Michael heard in a deep voice, heavy and awkward-sounding.

"Tome-o for a."

Michael felt hands under his arms, and he was part-carried and part-dragged along the corridor. Pause, a faint squeal as the door opened, and then he was propelled outside into the warmth, noticing the bright sun despite keeping his eyes closed. He was laid onto the timber bench in front of the building.

"O que está errado?" a familiar voice asked, Sergeant Khumalo.

"Ele é doente," Almeida replied.

Michael kept his eyes closed and his eyelids relaxed, aware he was under very close scrutiny. And Cathy, how long would it take her to do what she had to do? Find the address, dial, and type a message in a strange language? Five minutes, ten minutes, more? Khumalo said something in chiShona and the corporal replied, and then Michael heard footsteps.

"Não em lá," the priest said, and the footsteps stopped. Lá was the French word for there, so not in there. In there, Cathy. Not enough time for her. What was going on; what was the sergeant going to do?

"Ele estará bem," Khumalo said.

What did that mean? Footsteps, boots crunching on gritty concrete. Where was Khumalo going now? Footsteps fainter, he was going away. But for how long?

"Vou me adquirir a água," the corporal said.

"Não," the Father replied.

"Por que?"

Another French-like word, why? And Michael was partly let go with only one man holding him. He heard the door open; the corporal was going inside the building. He glanced through a gap in his eyelids, but saw nothing but bright light. The door opened again, and he smelled the corporal on the bench, and water was splashed onto his face. He kept his eyes closed; minutes were passing but was it enough? The corporal shook him lightly but Michael resisted. The door opened again.

"How is he Father?" Cathy asked.

"I do not know."

She kissed him and Michael opened his eyes and sat up.

"Ela parece-se com princesa," the corporal said, and laughed.

"I will look after him now," Cathy said.

She put her arms around Michael.

"How is he?" Khumalo asked, frowning while he smoked a cigarette.

"Better," Cathy replied.

"Where were you?"

"Praying in the Chapel. I will look after him now."

Khumalo still frowned, and marched off smoking furiously.

"Did you do it?" Michael asked quietly.

Cathy nodded.

237

"I'll stand and you support my weight," Michael said.

He did and she did, and Sergeant Khumalo paced back and forwards while he smoked a cigarette.

"I found the address for the Australian ambassador and sent them a telex about you being tortured by the CIO and escaping here with three companions, and now being held by the FADM," Cathy said quietly.

Michael nodded. "Good," he said. The ambassador would contact the bank and his family. Maybe the ambassador could help through the Mozambican government.

They reached the cell block. Exercise over, and time to return to captivity.

Inside and separated, Michael wished for something to help him pass the time. But not a book, his mind was too fragmented to concentrate on reading. And talking to Peter? Cathy was right about that. Ah, it was hopeless.

Chapter Seventeen

Sunny but not yet bright, early morning, and Michael heard the front door slam. Moments later his cell door opened and it was Sergeant Khumalo.

"You two, Major Nhema wants to see you."

They went into the corridor while Khumalo fetched Julie and Cathy. Michael rubbed the sweat off his hands as he followed the sergeant to the main building. Major Nhema was behind his huge desk reading a sheet of paper. A few moments later he looked up.

"I have been ordered to send you to Beira where Australian authorities have arranged your accommodation and other requirements. Eat breakfast and get your things ready, and the Sergeant will escort you."

"Thank you Major," Michael said.

Nhema nodded. He looked at the sergeant. "Va kubisa," he said.

By the time they returned to the cell, food was waiting. Michael consumed his coffee and stale roll, and then he went to the bathroom and quickly showered and shaved. Feeling refreshed, he went outside and leaned against the car. Sergeant Khumalo and the young soldier who normally served them meals climbed into a nearby jeep, and the three Zimbabweans appeared a few moments later, Cathy and Julie talking quietly. Michael got into the car while the soldier started the jeep. Michael used the screwdriver on the stolen Nissan, some men opened the gate, and it was time to leave with the jeep leading the way.

They left the compound and headed to the main road. Before long, the convoy left Chimoio behind and sped across flat countryside on a well-maintained highway, the jeep setting their pace of 130. On either side pedestrians walked by, with many more pedestrians than in Zimbabwe. They flashed through a small town and picked up speed again. The jeep slowed, Michael braked, and they bounced onto a concrete bridge. And then Michael realised why the jeep slowed, because the bridge was about a metre above the road surface. Coming off the bridge they flew through the air before landing heavily, and Michael wondering what had happened. He glanced at Peter, and checked the girls in the back. And then another bridge and Michel slowed harder. Just as well, because that was the same deal. Either extremely poor bridge construction, or perhaps the road had sunk on what looked like fertile, sandy soil. They sped on, Michael watchful that the gap between the jeep and their car didn't suddenly narrow. From time to time they passed small towns and bounced over uneven bridges, all the while heading downhill to the coast. Michael rehearsed his priorities: contact the nearest Australian embassy, get in touch with work, talk with Cathy and help her with her future. And what was Cathy's future? Australia again, but more than a three-year work visa,

Australia for life. Marriage, when she recovered. He loved her; indeed she was the only woman he'd ever loved. It seemed strange that it took a twenty-four year-old from Africa, and at the same time it seemed natural. She was Manyika and she believed in Mwari, and she told stories from thousands of years ago. Perhaps those things were the core of his attraction.

More people beside the roads and a haze in the near distance. They'd been travelling for two hours so that must be Beira. A lot of cars on the road and they had to slow. Doing 100 they closed on the smog while passing decrepit houses like the outskirts of Chimoio. They entered the suburbs on a six lane arterial road lined by greenery; a centre median strip with timber light posts every 20 or more metres. They turned onto a narrower road and drove past apartment buildings in white-painted brick interspersed by tropical trees. Not so long ago Mozambique was a war zone, a conflict stoked by the white minority government in nearby South Africa. Now Beira was run-down, and although not bombed it had suffered from the war nonetheless. Michael imagined a time when rich Rhodesians drove the three hours from Mutare to Beira for a holiday, especially when he caught a glimpse of shimmering blue ocean in the distance. Yes, decades ago, Beira would have been a special place.

On the left was low-rise, on the right high-rise with many multi-storey apartment buildings. It was busier too, a paved square with palm trees and a fountain on the right, many pedestrians milling about, cars waiting to turn. They continued onwards past a mouldy white building, turning right then left and right again. The jeep slowed outside a four-story maroon-and-glass building with a big 'Comfort Inn' sign overhanging the street. The jeep turned and headed down a ramp and into an underground carpark. Journey over at a surprising destination; a comfortable tourist hotel.

Sergeant Khumalo climbed out of the jeep and lit a cigarette. Michael edged closer to Cathy and the sergeant led the way to a lift. They ascended one floor and stepped into a reception area that could have been any hotel anywhere in the world. Immaculate condition, speckled light-brown with maroon trim, a table with two chairs beneath a maroon and brown map of the world. Khumalo went to the young lady behind the reception counter and spoke to her in Portuguese. The girl typed on a computer while Khumalo talked, and then she bent down for a moment. She got up and placed four keys on the counter, and Khumalo took them and handed them around.

"Courtesy of the Australian ambassador," he said.

Michael nodded. "Excuse me sergeant, what happens now?" he asked.

"The immigration authorities will contact you. In the meantime you are to wait here. Your room and meals are paid for."

"Thank you sergeant."

Khumalo nodded and looked about, probably for an ashtray, but none were to be found. He pressed the button and the lift doors slid open. He stepped into the lift and turned around.

"Good luck, ubvumirgwe," he said, typically gruffly.

The doors closed and he was gone.

And Michael hadn't enough time alone with Cathy, and still they were surrounded. He glanced at Julie and she took Peter's arm.

"Let's find our rooms," she said.

Julie led her boyfriend towards the stairs.

"We need to talk," Michael said.

"I know, but not now."

"When?"

"I don't know."

"You should see a doctor."

She nodded.

"A medical doctor today," Michael said.

"I will ask the receptionist."

He touched her hand and she flinched.

"You know where I am," he said. "So when you're ready."

He checked his key for room 302. He pressed the button for the lift and the doors opened. He went inside, and was taken to the third floor to find room 302.

243

Chapter Eighteen

Michael strolled into the near-empty hotel restaurant and was pleased to see Julie sitting alone. It was time to talk. He dished out some cereal, poured a cup of coffee, and went to her table.

"Do you mind?" he asked.

"Of course not," she said.

Michael took a seat and started on his meal, but he had so many things he wanted to say and so many things he wanted to ask. But how? And then he knew.

"Have you spoken to Cathy?" he asked.

"A little bit at Chimoio, but she was very guarded. And you?"

"She's hurting and I want to help her."

"She mostly talked about Peter, said he caused us a lot of trouble. But I knew that already."

"She's got it in for him."

"And then she talked about you, how good you would be for me, how we should...."

"Me?" Michael asked, surprised.

Julie nodded, and ate some of her fruit. "I think she's trying to set us up together."

"What about Peter?"

"We broke up, and not because of Cathy. What she said was right, we weren't suited to each other. He's a nice guy but there's no future."

"I'm sorry for you."

"No, I'm good. What happened to Cathy made me realise that I've been letting things drift along." Julie looked him in the eyes. "Have you spoken to her?" she asked.

"I've knocked on her door but she tells me to go away."

"Same with me."

"What can we do? I'm worried for her. We've been here three days and I don't think she's left her room."

"We will go to her after this."

Michael finished his cereal, but his appetite had waned. Instead, he had another coffee. Julie finished her fruit and Michael drained his cup. He stood, she stood, and they went to the foyer. Lift to third floor and room 304.

"You knock," Michael said quietly.

Julie knocked. "Cathy, I'm here with Michael and we both want to see you."

Silence. And then a rattle of the security chain and the door opened. Cathy was in her jeans and black blouse from days ago, and it didn't look like she'd been shopping with the money that Michael cashed and slipped under her door. "Come in," she said.

Julie sat on the end of the bed and Michael sat beside her. Cathy sat on the red-covered chair next to the timber table.

"How are you?" Julie asked.

"I'm fine," Cathy said.

"I'm worried about you."

"Don't try to deal with this on your own," Michael said.

"I'm fine," Cathy repeated.

"Have you seen a doctor?" he asked.

She nodded. "She referred me to get x-rayed, and when I saw her again she said that the bruises from the torture will heal, and there are no broken bones. My vagina is bruised from the rape but okay, and I'm not pregnant but I knew that from my implant, but we won't know the results of the blood tests for a few more days."

"Okay."

"Do you want me to take you shopping?" Julie asked.

Cathy shook her head.

"I can buy you some clothes with Michael's money."

"It's on the table."

"Is there anything else I can do?"

"No, not really."

Julie looked at Michael and then Cathy. "I should go."

"Thanks for coming," Cathy said.

"Should I go?" Michael asked.

"Only if…. No, you don't have to."

Julie got up and took the envelope of cash. She left and closed the door quietly behind her.

"I'm worried about you because I love you," Michael said.

"Love?" Cathy asked incredulously. "I'm sorry but love hasn't a chance in this world."

"Where there's love, there is no darkness. The real problem is that many don't have love in their lives, and they become bitter in their despair. You and I are blessed; I love you and I know you love me."

"But how can you love me after what happened? How could you be with me after what you saw?"

"I love you and I want to help you. Together we can do this."

"But I can't do it. If you and I were to, you know, it'd bring those awful memories back. I just can't do it."

"Don't do this to us."

She stood. "I can't give you what you want. You're a good man and I will remember you forever, but I just can't. You should spend some time with Julie, she's a good person."

"But I don't love Julie, I love you."

"Go and see Julie, go now."

Michael went to Cathy and kissed her on the cheek. "I love you and you know where I am. If you change your mind?"

"I won't."

He left the room and Julie leaned against the wall of the corridor.

"How'd it go?" she asked.

"She ended it. She said you and I.... I like you Julie, but I love Cathy."

"I saw that when you came to my flat."

"Do you think it'll come back?"

"You had something very special with Cathy, so I hope so. Look, I should go shopping."

"I'll go and see that man about the passports. When you bring her the clothes, can you take her for a photo?"

Julie held his hand. "You've been too good to us."

"Nonsense. It's just a hundred US each, which is about a million of whatever the local currency is. A hundred's nothing for a brand new, genuine, forged, Mozambican passports."

"It's only been three days; you should give her more time."

* * *

Saturday morning and Michael debated whether to see Cathy again. But it was unfair to pressure her and it would take time for her to heal. After breakfast, he went outside and walked the streets until he reached the Punge River upstream of the overhead road complex. It was a lovely day and the river was beautiful. Wide, blue, calm; lined with trees on both sides, and with a delightful vista of colonial buildings stretching up the hill. He went to the water's edge and saw a family: a mother with her baby in a pram, and a father with his young son sailing a model yacht. Michael sat on a rock and watched them, fascinated. The father had so much patience while the mother beamed at her family. Africans had an affinity with children, while Westerners, for all their material gains, had lost something by comparison. Michael watched for a time, and then he headed upstream.

On the left was the Jardim Botanico, the botanical gardens. He went inside and a family strolled past, both young children fascinated by the trees and the garden beds. It was a peaceful scene with the children enjoying things as they were. Michael wandered through the gardens until he found a bench. He sat in the shade enjoying the peace as more families came by. Indeed, there were no single people and all the couples had children. Except him. He was the only single in the gardens. Feeling odd, he got up and headed towards the perimeter wall.

Out on the street and it was a tangle of narrow one-way streets surrounded by buildings on all sides: it was like a brick-lined canyon. Feeling hemmed-in, Michael searched for a way out, and eventually emerged into a street of shops near the university. Some singles, younger men and women, and couples who were older. There was order: the young people dated and got married in their twenties, and then they raised their children. And at twenty-nine he stood out and not because he was white, although being white was part of it. His feet were sore and it was hot, so he stopped at a cafe and had some coffee. It was smooth and strong, served with a jug of hot milk, and there was no doubt that Mozambicans knew how to make great coffee. Michael sipped his drink in the dark timber-lined cafe, one of only three patrons. He finished too quickly but didn't want a second cup. He gave the waitress thirty meticais for the delicious drink.

Outside was hotter, and Michael headed north in the general direction of the hotel. It was too hot and humid to spend all day on the street, and he was thirsty after the coffee. And yet the hotel was lonely. He didn't want more hours in his room. His feet were sore and his shirt stuck to his back. He needed a shower to freshen up. Michael turned onto Avenue Fernão Magalhães and the blue sign was on his right. He went inside and caught the lift to the third floor.

Half-twelve, showered and changed, now what? He drank some water, but it didn't satisfy his thirst. A beer would go down well; an ice-cold beer would be brilliant on a hot, humid day. He went downstairs to the bar, the first patron of the day.

"Deuce-M," he asked, and the bartender poured a glass. Michael downed it and it didn't begin to satisfy his thirst. He put the glass down and the bartender poured a second. Michael drank the second glass slower and it wasn't bad. He put it down and the bartender poured again. Michael paused, should he or shouldn't he? There wasn't anything else to do, but not on a stool at the bar. So he got up and suddenly felt dizzy; too much on an empty stomach. The feeling passed, and he took his glass to a table near the window, remembering times in the cafe with Cathy, coffee by the window. He sipped the beer slowly, remembering her peaceful and well-ordered city. Not rag-tag like Beira, Harare was pleasant and easy to live in. Pity Zimbabwe was falling to pieces. Cathy had her theories and they made sense, but it seemed impossible that the implosion of a nation could be attributed to three or four factors. And yet every African country disintegrated to a greater or lesser extent. He noticed his glass was empty and the clock showed almost two. It was time to stop drinking alone, a bad habit, so he caught the lift to floor three. There, across the corridor, room 304, Cathy's room. He unlocked room 302 and went inside.

Quiet room, so quiet. And tired, he felt tired. Michael kicked his shoes off and changed from trousers to a pair of shorts. That felt better. The bed with its red and gold cover dominated the room, and there wasn't much else to do.

He got onto the bed and lay on his back, and that felt much better. He closed his eyes for a moment.

* * *

The screech woke Mudiwa, there were birds nearby. Rudo was fast asleep with her arm draped across his chest. Mudiwa stretched to take the cramp out of his legs. The bird screeched again, and took off with a noisy flapping of wings. In the background something roared, lions maybe. Good, at least lions kept elephants and hippopotamus away. Another bird screeched, woken by the dawn light. Mudiwa stretched again and Rudo stirred. He brushed an insect from her cheek and she smiled at him, and she had a lovely smile.

"It's time to go," Mudiwa said. "We can wade downstream."

"So they won't see our tracks?"

Mudiwa nodded. "It's steep here, so I will go first and help you."

Mudiwa shoved Rudo's bundle under his left arm, and holding onto a sapling with his right hand he slid down the bank into knee-deep cold water. Aiwa it was icy! Mudiwa gasped with shock, and then he reached out for Rudo to take his hand, supporting her weight while she awkwardly descended. She splashed into the small river and screamed!

"Quiet!" Mudiwa snapped. "Sorry," he said quietly.

Rudo bit her lip and Mudiwa felt angry with himself.

Mudiwa put the bundle on the bank, and bent over to scoop some water to drink. He paused, and then scooped water over himself. Beside him, Rudo did likewise. Thirst sated and feeling clean, Mudiwa retrieved Rudo's belongings, took her hand, and they slowly headed along the river.

A small river, about five paces wide, and flowing steadily but not fast. A nearly smooth muddy bottom with a few rocks worn by the continual flow of water. But it was hard work walking in the water, and Mudiwa felt hungry too. No food, he was travelling lightly, all he had were iron tips sewn into his clothing. They would travel until the sun was half-way overhead, and then look for somewhere to build a hut. Mudiwa thought they should settle about one-day's walk from Ghanzi and from Mufakose. Far away to be safe, but close enough to return for help if they had to. They splashed onwards through the water.

In the distance Mudiwa heard water roaring, but he didn't know what it was as he'd never been that far downstream before. This was Rudo's tribe's land, but Mudiwa didn't think they ventured that far. Upstream, closer to his village, his people hunted along the banks of this river. This river had no name, but it fed into the bigger Odzi River a little way downstream. The Odzi marked the border between the tribe of Mufakose and the tribe of Nata. As long as they kept on this side of the Odzi, they would be safe.

The water roared loader and loader, maybe they were getting close to rapids. Mudiwa stayed in the river, if Munashe, Tinashi and the other men split up at the fallen tree and searched upstream and down.... But Mudiwa heard nothing except for rushing water and the sound of cicadas, and smelled nothing except the scent of the bush.

Just then they rounded a bend and the noise was a waterfall. Mudiwa stopped.

"We will eat here," he said. "At the bottom of this, the water should be wide and peaceful. It could be a good place to settle."

"Our home?" Rudo asked.

"Yes, our home. But first we should eat."

The bank was rocky and slippery; Mudiwa led the way, holding his arm out so Rudo could use him for support. They emerged out of the water and stood amongst a scattering of trees. Mudiwa went to a nearby baobab tree and picked some fruit, not quite ripe. Rudo dealt with a nearby avocado tree, and after a short time they were sitting in the shade of the biggest baobab eating fresh fruit.

"I feel like a young girl eating this," Rudo said, and laughed.

"I feel like a young boy."

"It's good though."

"Yes, it's good. Sometimes I long for my boyhood. Life was simple then."

"I sometimes feel the same way."

"But I would never go back, there's a part of adult life...," and Mudiwa didn't know what to say. Mere words could never describe the intensity of his love for Rudo.

Rudo rested her head on his shoulder. "I know what you mean."

Mudiwa put his arm around her and he felt peaceful with his lover by his side. This was a good place and nothing could spoil it. Mudiwa got onto his feet and went to the river to wash the juice of the fruit from his hands. Then they headed into the bush to descend a steep hill while tracking parallel to the river. On his right, Mudiwa watched the river cascading over the small waterfall, fascinated by the foamy white water and spray. Down the hill Mudiwa struggled for footing: holding onto branches of trees and bushes to stop from slipping. Behind, his partner wouldn't be used to this, she was a woman and her place was the village.

Down they went and emerged from scrubby bush onto a flat plain. The waterfall fed into a wide and lazy river lined by a grassy bank, with scatterings of trees twenty paces and more away. The river was calm for bathing and there were rocks to fish from. The trees meant wood to build a home, wood to make spears, and wood to burn in the cooking fire. Rudo got onto her knees and picked up a stick. Frowning, she scratched the ground, turning the grass over and exposing the damp, dark earth underneath. She picked up some soil and crumpled it in her fingers. She stood with her hands on her hips. "This is a good place for a home," she said. "Now we will make it ours."

Mudiwa laughed. Rudo ran her fingers lightly down his back. He shivered with her touch, and with the excitement of what was coming. Indeed, they *would* make this riverbank their home.

Chapter Nineteen

Michael woke with his heart beating fast and his hair matted in sweat. Where was he? Red bed cover, red curtains, it was the Comfort Inn in Beira. Mudiwa and Rudo had returned and he felt a pang of jealousy. But what were they were trying to tell him? What was the message? The end, christening their plot, they had a sensual relationship.

Michael got up and went to the bathroom to wash the sweat from his face. He felt better. He drank a glass of water and felt better still. And then he realised the message. He went to the chair beside the timber table and paused. He noticed his hands were shaking. He pulled the chair out and sat, this might be his last chance. He picked up the handset of the phone and dialled 304. The phone rang three times.

"Hello," Cathy said.

"It's me, Michael."

"Michael, what, why….?"

"Please, I understand how you feel and I don't want to pressure you. But there's something I must tell you."

"Tell me what?"

"This."

Chapter Twenty

Mudiwa descended the slope by the waterfall, burdened with carcasses of the two bat-eared foxes caught in his traps. Meat for dinner and Rudo could use the skins. It was dark amongst the bush and trees, and then the morning sunlight streamed across the path through a break in the scrub. Mudiwa stopped and surveyed their home below, a round mud hut built with the help of his friends Buru and Dakarai. They were good friends; it took many days to cut trees and erect the frame, and then to prepare and lay the mud walls. Rudo worked hard gathering the thatching, and later sealing the floor. Next to the hut and oblivious to him watching, Rudo worked the garden, uprooting weeds with a hoe. From a distance you would never know that she was pregnant; her child a miracle gift from the ancestors. Mudiwa knew that living together must be right and proper, or else the ancestors would never have blessed her that way. Mudiwa wondered how women came to have children. It was a miracle, one moment she was a girl, and now she was a woman with a child growing inside her. Rudo looked up and must have seen him admiring her. She waved and Mudiwa waved back. He smiled, despite the taboo of her pregnancy they couldn't help themselves. And her growing belly was just a minor inconvenience; almost nothing at all.

Mudiwa continued down the hill with his catch, perhaps Rudo could use the skins to make a blanket for her baby. He strode across the soft grass and she placed her hoe beside the hut and went to him.

"Darling, you're so clever," she said, hugging and kissing him.

"It's not me, it's this place."

"This place is paradise," she agreed, still holding him. "We have everything we need."

"Except for bringing new life into the world."

She frowned. "Yes, you're right. Soon I must go to my village and see my mother. I'm sure she will help when the time is near."

"I'm sure she will too."

"Are you thirsty?" she asked.

Mudiwa nodded.

"I made some mikaka wakakora; it's on the fire."

Rudo knelt beside the stones that made up their hearth and poured from their small pot into a cup. The pots, the cups, the plates and the hoe were all fetched from Ghanzi. She returned with his drink and Mudiwa relieved his thirst.

Suddenly, pelicans noisily took off and flew towards the waterfall, with wings flapping loudly as they screeched and squawked their way into the sky. Mudiwa looked around, but saw nothing out of the ordinary. He handed his empty cup to Rudo and continued to scan the boundaries of their home. And then, movement in the bushes, there was something out there, something big. Rudo picked up Mudiwa's catch and went to stand beside the hut, leaving Mudiwa to defend her and her child-to-be. Mudiwa picked up his spear and waited. He rolled his shoulders to ease the tension from his muscles; he had one chance and he had to make it count. Time dragged, moments taking an eternity to pass. Scrunching noises, a big animal and getting closer. Scraping, very close. Movement against a bush, closer still. And then a man, Tinashi! *Bechenura!* And whenever there was Tinashi, there were others. Mudiwa looked over his shoulder at Rudo staring wide-eyed. Mudiwa stood his ground with his spear at the ready, waiting for the others. Tinashi reached the plain and Mudiwa raised his weapon.

"No!" Rudo screamed. No, not screamed, much more than that. Mudiwa kept his aim at Tinashi.

"Put your spear down brother-of-Rudo," Mudiwa shouted.

"If you do the same," Tinashi shouted back.

Mudiwa lowered it, resting the tip against the ground. "See, I cannot throw. Now put yours down."

Tinashi jabbed his spear into the soft earth. Mudiwa let his spear go, and it lay on the ground next to his foot. He folded his arms while Tinashi closed to within talking range.

"Stop," Mudiwa ordered.

Tinashi kept walking.

"Stop Brother," Rudo said.

He stopped.

"Where are the others?" Mudiwa asked.

"They will be here soon," Tinashi said flatly.

"How did you find us?"

"Do you'd think I would stop searching?"

"I would stop searching?" Mudiwa echoed.

"Ah – I'm leading the search," Tinashi said.

Mudiwa crossed his arms. "No you're not; you're on your own. This is your obsession, isn't it?"

"The others...."

"There are no others; they've let us be. Maybe they had a skirmish between the two villages for what I did, maybe they threw spears without tips until Ghanzi lost, and then it was over."

"It will never be over."

"It's over. Look, proof, your sister is pregnant. The ancestors have given her a child."

"Mhata!" Tinashi yelled, and immediately ran towards Mudiwa.

"No, stop," Rudo shouted. "I order you to stop."

But he didn't and Mudiwa got ready.

"Tinashi stop," Rudo screamed

But Tinashi kept running with head down, eyes narrowed, and sweat glistening on his face and body. Mudiwa leaned forward. Tinashi closed the gap, reaching out and grabbing for Mudiwa at full sprint. But Mudiwa turned and swung at Tinashi, and momentum did the rest. Tinashi stumbled and fell, hitting the ground hard. Mudiwa stood ready, and Tinashi lashed out at his legs. Mudiwa jumped, and Tinashi wasted his energy flailing at nothing. Mudiwa dropped onto Tinashi and used his weight to advantage. Tinashi grabbed for Mudiwa's shoulders, but Mudiwa hit Tinashi's side in just the right place.

Tinashi groaned and curled his body despite Mudiwa being on top. Mudiwa pinned Tinashi's shoulders to the ground.

"Give up?" Mudiwa yelled.

Nothing.

Mudiwa pulled Tinashi's shoulders and banged his head into the earth.

"No!" Rudo screamed.

"Give up?" Mudiwa yelled again.

No response.

Mudiwa pulled Tinashi's shoulders again.

"You must give up!" Rudo ordered.

"Yes," Tinashi said, and Mudiwa let him go, sitting on his body with his heart beating fast.

Rudo came to them.

"Stupid fool!" she snapped. "Why did you come?"

"You bring shame...." Tinashi gasped.

263

"There's no shame you idiot. Mudiwa's right, the ancestors approve, they bless me. Do you know the minds of the ancestors? Are you that pretentious?"

"But...."

"But nothing! Leave us and never come back."

Mudiwa climbed to his feet. "I'm sorry," he said to Rudo.

"You did what had to be done. This is the fault of my stupid brother."

Rudo reached out and helped Tinashi get to his feet. Mudiwa watched Tinashi walk towards his spear, grab it, and head into the scrub. Rudo held Mudiwa's hand.

"Do you think he will come back?" she asked.

"Yes."

"With others?"

Mudiwa shook his head. "There would've been a skirmish until someone from Mufakose inflicted wounded pride on someone from Ghanzi. Then both villages would have been satisfied that justice was done for my wicked act."

Rudo giggled. "I will never understand the ways of men," she said, still spluttering.

"I was the most wonderful person in the world when I trapped those foxes. You can't have one without the other."

She kissed him, and whispered in his ear. "But there's one thing that's very special about men."

"Which is?"

She smiled brightly.

* * *

The rain ran from the roof and splashed on the ground outside. Inside, the hut was dry although dark and gloomy. Mudiwa had tied their gazelle-skin door back to let in as much light as possible. He looked through the opening at the grey skies and steady rain, they were trapped. Rudo stood beside him, and Mudiwa put his arm around her growing waist. It was lovely to be trapped. Rudo eased from his embrace and returned to their sleeping mat and lay on her back. Mudiwa went to kneel beside his darling. They kissed and his heart ran fast. She touched him and his heart ran faster still.

"I've come to get you!" and Mudiwa shuddered. Tinashi!

Mudiwa jumped to his feet and went to the doorway. Outside, alone in the rain, Tinashi. Rudo came to Mudiwa's side. Rudo had her hands on his arm, holding him tight. Mudiwa untangled his lover's fingers, grabbed a spear from beside the doorway, took a deep breath, and strode outside.

"You've come to get me?" Mudiwa shouted.

"No, I've come to get my sister," Tinashi bellowed in reply.

"Leave us!" Rudo shouted, emerging from the hut to stand beside her partner.

The rain beat hard, saturating Mudiwa's hair and running down his body.

"You heard her," Mudiwa shouted. "Just go."

"If I can't take her, I will kill her."

"Rudo...," Mudiwa tried to warn her, but the words wouldn't form.

Tinashi raised his spear.

"Run!" Mudiwa shouted, and Rudo turned but slipped and fell.

"Tinashi no!"

Tinashi's weapon was aimed at the figure lying on the slushy ground. Mudiwa threw and his spear buried into Tinashi's chest. Tinashi crumpled to the ground with the tip of Mudiwa's spear poking from his back, and his blood draining onto the sodden soil.

* * *

The door opened and there were soft footsteps on the timber floor. "He threw the spear and killed the brother, but he killed much more." Cathy said in a soft voice. "From then on it would be mother – daughter – husband. Husband would woo, daughter would choose, and mother would approve. And then the husband moved to his wife's village and they set up a house, and a new generation started. Woman – man – affection – respect. A man didn't own his wife, this was mutual. She chose him, but she could tell him to go too. But if it lasted, as it often did, it was special. She had the power in

266

the relationship, but because she was woman she didn't misuse it. Instead they were a couple: they shared their lives, raised their children, and respected their parents."

"So what's the lesson of the story?" Michael asked.

"True love is the most special thing in the world, and we must do everything we can to hold onto it. Sometimes, we must make terrible sacrifices for love."

"Do you love me?"

Cathy put her head down.

"Do you love me?"

She nodded.

"This story is about love and the first ever marriage. But there's another lesson for us, isn't there?" Michael asked.

"Men and women are different but equal, and the ideal marriage is that of two equals."

"Love and marriage and equality?"

"Yes," she said quietly.

"I love you Cathy and I want to marry you, and I want our marriage to be like Mudiwa and Rudo."

Cathy sat on the bed. "I will marry you, but I have suffered. It will take time for me to heal, but one day we will be like Mudiwa and Rudo."

"I want to help you heal."

"I want you to help me."

"This is the lesson of the story. We're going to spend the rest of our lives together, and we're going to do it as two equals in love."

She kissed him.

Chapter Twenty One

Michael rubbed his chest and winced. "I think Rudo's returned," he said.

"For today she has," Cathy said. "Oh, did I do that?"

He nodded, and she bent down and kissed his scratches. Her moist lips were soothing. "I'm sorry," she said.

"Don't worry, you're getting better."

"It's been hard."

"I know."

"I couldn't have done it on my own."

"Jane?"

"Yes, my therapist and her support group. You Australians have so much to help people like me. But the one thing that's healed me is love, and where there's love, there is no darkness."

"Do you think it's time for the next step?" Michael asked.

"I don't know, I'm still thinking." Cathy climbed off and lay on the bad. She lightly ran her fingers over Michael's chest.

"I can get a better job at the bank," he said. "And you'll have an opportunity to change your country from the outside. You know they need chiShona speakers."

"I know and soon I will be better." She suddenly moved, sitting cross-legged. "Hey, let's go for a holiday."

"Geneva?"

"Of course, and we can visit Beira on the way. We can see how Julie's Portuguese is going."

"I would guess that it's better than your French."

She playfully punched his shoulder. "It will be good to see Julie again; I feel so lonely sometimes. I miss my family, I miss my home, I miss my mitupo. It must seem selfish to love you and to have all these people help me, and still need more."

"But it's you, the result of five thousand years."

"Yes, five thousand years."

PART TWO

Chapter Twenty Two

Michael woke. The room was quiet with the only sound being Cathy's gentle breathing. He stretched and then moved to get close to his wife. Her breathing changed, she waked. Michael pressed against her body and draped his arm over her arm. She took his hand and placed it on her breast. He held her loosely, feeling the steady rise and fall of her chest. It was peaceful to be holding his darling like this.

Cathy was wonderful, more wonderful than when they met, especially the last year and a half. Geneva did her good; it made her complete. She stirred and Michael gave her room. She was facing him now and Michael kissed her. Cathy brushed the quilt away and leaned over Michael. She kissed him deeply, a lover's kiss. She moved astride Michael, still kissing him while he held her hips. They made love while they kissed: intimate, connected. They kissed until Cathy was ready for more. She sat up, looking down on her husband, eyes joined from a distance. He held her lightly, and she closed her eyes and went to another place. She returned for a moment but disappeared again. He knew where she was going; that was her way. She tilted her head back, as she always did. She made love to him, as she often did, and then he heard her and felt her. So quiet, so gentle, so real. Michael wondered what he had done to deserve not just that moment, but all the wonderful moments of their life together.

He dug his fingers into her fleshy bottom and she returned to him. Cathy looked down and smiled brightly, enjoying her partner's pleasure. She bent down and kissed him, and that's all it took. And then she rested her head on his chest.

"What's your past?" she asked quietly.

Michael looked into his lover's eyes and he put his hand on her cheek.

"What's your past?" Cathy repeated.

"You know my past. School, university, a job, a career, a relationship that went bad but taught me a lot."

"What's your present?"

"Love, our home together, work."

"And your future?"

"Forever in love with the most wonderful woman in the world. And you, what's your past?"

"Home, family, education, a good job, and never the right man."

"And your present?"

"Loving the most wonderful man in the world, and making a difference for my country."

"And your future?"

"One day soon our family, and one day I will return to my home and my parents." Cathy kissed him and then she looked up, glancing at the clock.

"Are you making a difference?" Michael asked.

"Yes," she said softly. "The regime can't be stopped for now, so here in Geneva we're planning for when it's over. Because of our work, the world will be ready to rescue those poor souls." Cathy kissed him again and sat up in the bed. "Now it's time for work." She wrinkled her nose. "I have to interpret a meeting, although only one claims not to speak English."

Cathy slid out of bed and Michael watched her disappear into the bathroom. He sighed. She was saving the world, and all he was doing was increasing shareholder value for a multi-national bank. At least he had a life full of love, and soon a family. The water stopped, and a few minutes later Cathy returned. Michael immediately felt aroused despite seeing his wife naked hundreds of times before. Love did strange things to a man. Only when Cathy began to dress did he make an effort to go to the bathroom. He showered and shaved, and by the time he straightened his tie he smelled coffee. He loved everything she did, he truly did, she was precious.

Coffee and baguette for two, and they ate a meal with the sun shining through the window; and with a glimpse of Lake Geneva between trees and buildings. They were lucky; the bank looked after them well. A house of their own, ten Rue de la Marie in the delightful village of Cologny. A two-storey house: spacious and modern.

"Looks like a nice day," Cathy said.

Michael nodded.

"Soon it will be winter." she said.

"I know, but we'll cope better with the cold second time around."

"I'm not looking forward to today; I hate interpreting."

"Who are you meeting?"

"A delegation from Zanu protesting our imperialistic lies."

"Do they ever learn? If it's not the British, it's the UN or someone else."

"I know."

"I can't believe they won't let aid into the country."

"The people must be punished for voting for the MDC."

"It's like genocide on your own people."

"That's true, although food shortages help Mugabe with his militia. For food and shelter, kids join Zanu to be brainwashed. Everything's the fault of the Whites and the British, and the MDC are part of that racist conspiracy. And then those kids are set loose to rape and torture supporters of the MDC."

"That's terrible."

"It's tragic, especially the girls. They're starving and they join Zanu to survive, but then they're taken to indoctrination camps to be just – used. Young men turned into thugs and young women abused by those thugs in vile ways. They're called the green bombers and the world does nothing."

"If Zimbabwe had oil...."

Cathy smiled. "You're too cynical," she said.

"How can you deal with these people face-to-face?"

"I know that one day we will help those who have suffered, so...," and Cathy shrugged her shoulders.

Michael finished his coffee while Cathy stacked the dishwasher. A few minutes later they were in the sun, and it felt like winter was getting close. Thursday the eighteenth of August with autumn half-over. A short walk to the bus stop, and a wait for the number two bus through Geneva Plage. Cathy led the way onboard and grabbed a seat for two. Michael sat beside her, and the bus wound its way down the hill, with the Jet d'Eau in the distance while they headed to the older part of town. Passing three-storey stone and stucco buildings hundreds of years old; ancient and beautiful. But Geneva was a living city, and those old buildings were apartments and shops. They reached Rue du Rhône and Cathy pressed the buzzer. The bus slowed and Cathy kissed Michael's cheek.

"Bye darling, see you tonight."

"Bye."

She left the bus and Michael watched her go to the number eight for her journey to the Palais des Nations.

Michael continued towards Morgines and the Centre Commercial Lancy-Onex, to the concrete and glass building that would be his prison for the day.

* * *

The door slammed and hard-soled shoes echoed on the timber staircase. Cathy burst into the family room, breathing heavily like she'd been running. Michael turned the stove down.

"I saw him," she gasped. "That man, Mandipaka."

Michael dropped the spoon he'd been holding, and it hit the tiled floor with a loud 'clang'. "From Rusape?" he asked.

Cathy nodded while bent over and held her hips. Michael raced to her, and she straightened so he could hug her.

"How did you feel?" he asked.

"It was like a dream at first, but then... Then he started, taunting me in 'Shona. Awful things, Ndi u bhaudha, I will fuck you." She put her head against Michael's shoulder, and sobbed quietly. He held her while she cried, and then she pulled free from his grasp. Standing straight, while holding her hips once more and frowning. "It's terrible. He did awful things to us, to poor Mr Chipateni, and to how many others? I hate him and I hate my country!"

"Ssh, don't fill your heart with anger."

"But what he did was wrong. Torture, rape and murder: they're crimes and he should be punished. Instead, in my country...."

Michael hugged Cathy again, and she relaxed in his arms.

"After the meeting, I spoke to Guillaume and he was very sorry," Cathy said. "Poor man, I don't think he's ever been near such a thing."

"What'd he say?" Michael asked.

"He was very flustered, but he said I should see the police."

"Will you?"

"Yes, tomorrow. I couldn't do it today; I need to be under control."

"Okay. Do you want me to come?"

"I will see them first, and I will find out what they want from you."

"Okay. You hungry?"

She kissed him. "You're a good husband."

"I know."

She punched his shoulder.

"You Africans....," Michael said.

"What?"

He kissed her. "You Africans are the most amazing people on this planet."

"I will take that as a compliment."

"For you it is. Dinner's almost ready."

"Good, I'm quite hungry," Cathy said. "I was with Guillaume and I cried a lot, and I didn't each lunch."

"My poor darling."

"But I'm better now."

"That's what I mean."

Chapter Twenty Three

The security door was locked but not deadbolted; Cathy must be home. Michael climbed the stairs while wondering how her visit with the police went. The stove was bubbling with the exhaust fan rumbling. Michael went to his wife and kissed the side of her neck. She rolled her head and he kissed her again, nibbling her. They made love, fully clothed, in the kitchen. In a moment, he could have picked her up and carried her to the bedroom, but he was curious.

"How'd it go?" he murmured.

"Terrible," she said.

"How so?"

She eased away and Michael leaned against the bench.

"They said they can't do anything. It's more than six years ago, it's another country, and there's no evidence other than you, my husband. And he's here as a guest of the United Nations, which means he's a guest of the Swiss government."

"You don't seem upset."

"I expected as much. Yesterday I was angry, today I'm resigned. He's Zanu. He's gotten away with murder, and he will get away with more."

"But still...."

"But still nothing. My work with Monsieur Dupont is more important than one murdering rapist, more or less."

"You Africans...."

"You keep saying that."

"Some Africans can be so cruel, and you're all so stoic about it."

"That's the way we are."

"I love your calmness."

She laughed. "You just love me."

"I love a lot about you, especially your calmness. It's soothing."

She turned away and stirred the rice, and Michael loosened his tie and put on his 'Back to Bedlam' CD. Then he went to the bedroom and changed his suit for some tracksuit trousers. Just as he was tying the cord at his waist, the doorbell rang. "I'll get it," he shouted to no response.

Michael went down the stairs two at a time and used his key on the deadlock. He released the second lock and opened the heavy wooden door. And, fuck, it was Mandipaka! There, in front of him, on the other side of the security door. Michael didn't know what to say.

"Mr Page," David Mandipaka said.

"What're you doing here?"

"Who is it?" Cathy asked, lightly treading on the staircase. "No!" she squealed.

"Fuck off you bastard," Michael snapped.

"Not very welcoming," Mandipaka said.

"Just fuck off and don't come back."

"I know where you live."

"That's obvious. Now you know, just go."

"It is not that simple."

"Yes it is."

"You will see me again."

Michael slammed the door, and even though Mandipaka was still there, he felt safer.

Cathy grabbed his arm. "He knows where we live," she said.

"It's okay, he won't do anything."

"How do you know?"

"He's got no reason to."

"You know him, he doesn't need a reason." She squeezed Michael's arm tight. "I've got to do something to stop him."

"You should talk to your boss; he should be able to help. Either get Mandipaka out of the country or give us protection because of your job."

"I will do that first thing Monday."

Michael put his arm around her. "You talk to Guillaume Dupont; he seems a good man."

"He is, although he's very Swiss. Still, if anyone can help, he can."

"In the meantime, be careful, okay?"

"Yes darling, I will be very, very careful."

* * *

Michael and Cathy were the only people waiting for the Saturday morning bus to the city centre. Holding hands and waiting on a cloudy and chilly morning.

"What's this CD you're after?" Cathy asked.

"'Et si le Monde...,'" by Sandrine Françoise."

"And if the world what?"

"Can you guess?"

"Peace and harmony."

"Yep. I've heard a couple of tracks and it's good, but there's a very strange story about it. She came fourth in Eurovision three years ago with one of the songs, and she's got an amazing voice. Then the CD was released and sank without a trace. Jacques ordered it in for me, which is why I'm going to his father's shop."

"Eurovision; that's not like you."

"But it's French, substance over superficiality."

"So you say."

The bus arrived and they took the seats behind the driver, sitting side-on. There were only a few on board, Michael would have preferred to drive their car but parking was always a challenge. The bus made more sense, even if it seemed like going to work six days in a row. Cathy wanted a new pair of jeans; maybe once their shopping was over they should make the most of the journey. Perhaps a picnic at La Perle du Lac. The bus stopped and a woman with two children got on. Michael looked up and his eyes followed the young mother as she passed. Soon Cathy might be a mother. The woman took a seat and then Michael spotted him in the rear section of the articulated bus, just metres away.

"It's Mandipaka," Michael said quietly.

"Where?" Cathy asked.

"Don't look, but he's on the bus."

"He's following us."

"He didn't get on with us, unless he sneaked in through the rear door."

The bus reached Rue du Rhône and Cathy pressed the buzzer. Michael got off with Cathy, as did Mandipaka, and they waited for a bus to the other side of the river. Michael and Cathy got onto the number eight with three or four others, including their shadow. Michael led Cathy to the rear seat where they could keep an eye on him.

Michael wondered what to do, and there wasn't much they could do. Mandipaka was going to follow them all day if necessary. Michael was frustrated, and then he remembered the CD shop. That was a place where he could confront their nemeses in privacy, but close enough to a major street so there wasn't any risk. Well, not much risk.

"We'll get off near the Nôtre Dame and walk along Rue de Berne," Michael said.

"There will be lots of people around," Cathy replied. "So he can't do anything."

"I know a place near the CD shop."

"What have you got planned?"

"You'll see."

The bus turned left onto Rue de Chantrepoulet, and the buzzer was pressed by another passenger. Michael and Cathy got off just before the ancient cathedral. Without looking behind him, Michael headed northwards towards Les Pâquis along narrow footpaths hemmed by tall buildings; swept along by the crowd while wondering how events would unfold. He strode onwards and glanced over his shoulder, Mandipaka was about thirty metres behind them. Right onto Rue Sismonde, and then he guided Cathy into a lane on the left. Her shoes echoed on the cobblestones, amplified by the tall buildings on either side. There was a narrower lane on the right which led to the next street.

"Go down there and wait," he whispered.

Cathy went around the corner while Michael waited for Mandipaka. Moments later the smell of a cigarette was clear and distinct. Michael stood with his arms crossed and Mandipaka came to him.

"What do you want?" Michael asked.

Mandipaka said nothing.

"I'm here, so now's your chance," Michael said.

"You and your whore caused me a lot of trouble," Mandipaka said.

"By escaping?"

"Yes."

"That was years ago."

"I don't forget."

"What about us you bastard? You raped her."

"She had it coming, helping a traitorous criminal like you. But you are worse than her; you are free when you should be in jail."

"Me?"

"You confessed to a serious crime." Mandipaka tossed his butt onto the ground and stubbed it.

"I only confessed to stop you."

"You confessed."

"Okay, you've made your point, now you can fuck off."

Mandipaka came right up close and Michael caught his foul breath. "I have just started," he said. "I am like a lion. First I play with my prey, and then I kill it."

Michael stepped to one side and fresh air. "This is Geneva, not Zimbabwe."

"I am like a diplomat here."

"Not even diplomats...."

"I am here for a long time, remember that." Mandipaka moved away and stopped. "Remember, a long time." Mandipaka edged away, creeping closer to the street like he expected Michael to attack; until he disappeared out of sight.

Michael sighed and went along the narrow alcove to where Cathy waited.

"What happened?" she asked.

"Says he's angry about us escaping."

Cathy frowned. "You burned his house down and you made him look like an idiot."

"He is an idiot."

"That's not what he's thinking. But he's dangerous and I must do something about him."

Michael took her hand. "We'll not let him spoil our day. First some shopping; then lunch by the lake."

"Ah, beautiful."

"Baguette et fromage, et du café?"

"Parfait."

"Bon. I'll get my CD, you get your jeans, and we'll meet by the Musée."

Cathy nodded and they headed out of the narrow walkway and returned to Rue de Berne.

* * *

La Perle du Lac was beautiful. Grass sloped gently to a path running along the water's edge, with a pretty steel fence separating the park from Lake Geneva. All around, trees had leaves turning brown, autumn turning to winter. In the background, Jet d'Eau in the lake sprayed water 140 metres into the air. Behind the fountain, gracious stone buildings stretched towards mountains in the distance. Despite the

cloud it was a clear day and the lake looked a treat. Michael
sat on a white steel bench near the museum, and guessed it
would take Cathy longer to buy clothes than for he to buy his
CD. He waited for about an hour while watching people pass
by. And then Cathy arrived, looking beautiful. Michael stood
and she kissed him, and he led the way to the museum kiosk.
A few minutes later they had a baguette with cheese and a
café crème each, and they strolled across the grass to a bench
near the lake. Switzerland was quite bland, but Geneva was
pleasant and pretty, and it had many of the good things of the
French. Even simple things like bread and cheese were
delicacies. A middle-aged couple strolled past, walking their
dog. A younger woman in a tracksuit jogged by, Swiss
women worked hard to keep slim. Michael finished his
baguette and he sipped more of the smooth coffee.

"You will like these," Cathy said, patting the parcel on
the seat beside her. "They're really tight. I've set myself a
target to wear them three months after giving birth."

"You don't know how much I'm looking forward to
being a father," Michael said.

"You will be a good dad."

Michael never had anything to do with children, ever.
He wondered. "But I'm scared, you know," he said quietly.

"Just be yourself; no-one expects any more than that."

"It's easy for you."

"No it's not."

"And us…?" Michael asked, thinking about what happened to so many couples, and also feeling guilty and selfish for such thoughts.

Cathy smiled brightly. "There will always be time for us. No matter what, I will always find time for us. I promise."

"You're a special woman."

"No I'm not."

"To me you are."

Michael took a last sip to finish his coffee, and when he turned to put the cup into a bin, he noticed Mandipaka. Leaning against the steel fence, barely two metres away, watching. He must have followed them from the laneway.

Cathy put her cup down and went to him. "What is it with you?" she snapped.

"Did your husband not tell you?"

"He did. You're here representing Zanu, the elected government of Zimbabwe, are you not?"

"Yes I am."

"Well why don't you and the rest of the Zanu delegation go home and fix up the mess you've created. You've ruined my country, and yet you're more worried about my husband and me. Look at what you've done."

"But this is not…."

"It is!" Cathy interrupted. "You and all of Zanu, you support a tyrant who's ruined things. What happened? It

289

started in the Congo, didn't it? Kabila gave Mugabe and his cronies timber and diamonds to fight a war there. And you went to war with money the country didn't have; printing notes to pay the bills. And then what, inflation hit fifty percent? And if that wasn't enough, you kicked the white farmers out of the country, and suddenly exports dried up. More money got printed, and what's inflation now?"

"One hundred thousand percent."

"Rubbish! Four hundred thousand percent, or more. And eighty percent living in poverty, and ninety-five percent unemployment!"

"But...."

"But nothing, this is tragic! What's eighty percent living in poverty, what does that mean? And inflation, for those few who have jobs, prices doubling every few hours, the currency next to worthless. How can we measure such suffering in percentages?"

"You are saying very dangerous things."

"I work for the United Nations and I can say what I like."

"You are Zimbabwean."

"Not any more."

"You were born there; it is your home, your mitupo."

"And one day I will go back, but only when it's safe, only when people like you are brought to justice, if that'll ever happen. Mugabe's cunning, he's bought the army and the police. He looks after you, doesn't he David Mandipaka? Despite the suffering around you, you want for nothing."

Mandipaka waved his finger in Cathy's face. "You watch yourself Catherine Shoko, you are saying treasonous things."

"Not here it isn't."

"For your family it is."

"You leave my family out of this."

"But your family is in Mutare, is that not so? It could be dangerous for them there."

"I said to leave my family out of this. Here at the UN we monitor and report, and we prepare for the future. I just happen to know more than the people in my country."

Michael was worried. Cathy was justifiably angry, but arguing with that thug wasn't a good idea. He went to them.

"You've both had your say," Michael said. "You, Mandipaka, go before I call the police."

"What for the police?" Mandipaka asked, genuinely confused.

"Stalking and harassment."

"That would be a dangerous thing for you to do."

"Just go."

Mandipaka glared at Michael, and then reached into his shirt pocket for a pack of cigarettes. He lit one with the smoke pungent in the clear Geneva air. He held it between his fingers.

"I will go," he said. "But do not think it is over because it is not. Soon you will understand what I am saying."

Mandipaka drew on the cigarette and Michael took one step back to give him room. A few moments later he was gone.

"I said too much," Cathy said.

Michael put his arm around her. "It's a wonder you haven't said more."

"But still...."

"But still nothing. We've finished lunch; let's go home.

Chapter Twenty Four

Michael unlocked the security door and then the deadlock. He opened the front door and an envelope was slid under. The top was unsealed and inside were A4-sized pictures. It took a moment, and then he recognised the scene. Cathy's parent's home in Mutare. A second page, close-ups of her mother and father. A third page, a car reversing along the driveway and heading along the street. He handed them to Cathy.

"Oh no, Mum and Dad!" she exclaimed. "I went too far."

"It's too soon." Michael looked over Cathy's shoulder. "Look at the date: nineteen zero-eight zero-five. That's yesterday."

"Yes, you're right. But this is bad. There's no choice; they will have to leave now."

Michael rubbed his forehead.

"The phone might be bugged," Cathy said. "I know; I will pass a message through Julie. I will ring her."

"What sort of message?"

"Listen." She went into the study and sat at the desk, grabbed the phone and used one of the speed-dial keys. "Hi Julie, it's me." Pause. "Sorry, but it's so hectic here sometimes. How's Ntokoto?" Pause. "Good. And your pregnancy?" Pause. "Great. Look, there's been some trouble here, David Mandipaka's in town." Pause. "You know, you and Michael burned his house down. Well, he's threatened us, and he sent us photos of Mum and Dad." Pause. "That's right. Look, what I want you to do is ring Mum and tell her you're in trouble with the pregnancy, and ask for Dad to drive her to you, but don't mention Beira in case the phone is bugged. But when they get to you, they're not to go home, but don't tell them that on the phone." Pause. "I know, but they must stay in Mozambique. It's a good idea anyway, Zimbabwe's really bad and it's going to get even worse. They will have to leave sooner or later." Pause. "I know, they will have to go over the mountains, but how do we tell them? I know, tell Mum they should, no, they must go past Auntie Francis's place and keep going that way." Cathy stopped for a long time. "I know but it's better than starving. We're both sending them money, but there's no food anymore. As soon as we can, we will come and visit. Michael can see the man with the birth certificates and passports, and we will make them Mozambican like you. Remember, their phone's probably bugged, so be very careful of what you say." She waited a moment. "Thanks Julie, and we will see you as soon as we can. Love to your partner. Bye."

And Cathy hung up.

"I hope that works," she said.

"It'll be hard for your parents to start over with next to nothing. And they'll have to learn Portuguese too."

"Auntie Francis can rent their house out, and we can work out a way to get the money out of the country."

"It's worthless."

"I know," Cathy said glumly.

"Is there any future for Zimbabwe?"

"Only if they have foreign exchange. If they can pay their debts and import essentials, they can dig the country out of the hole."

"How do they get foreign exchange? Gold? Diamonds?"

"If they were lucky. Cecil Rhodes crossed the Limpopo searching for diamonds but he never found any. But that doesn't mean they aren't there."

"That's interesting."

"But knowing Zanu, finding diamonds would create a whole new set of problems. They would seize the lot, and if the diamonds were on the land of another clan, can you imagine what would happen?" Cathy got up. "You know, it's funny saying 'love to your partner' to Julie. Of all people, I never thought my sister would give up her beliefs and end up living with a guy."

"Something happened to someone very close to her and she got enlightened. They're very happy together, and I can't wait to be an uncle for the second time."

"Being a dad's much better."

Michael nodded in agreement.

"Let's go upstairs then," Cathy suggested

She took Michael's hand and led him to the staircase.

* * *

Cathy was home and Michael head chiShona from the top of the stairs. He put his bag in the study and went to the family room where Cathy and two guests were sitting at the table. The man and the woman stood and Cathy handled the introductions.

"My husband Michael Page, this is Joe Dube and Rufaro Banya."

Michael shook hands. They both looked fresh off the plane: tall Joe Dube was wearing a thin white cotton shirt and cheap black trousers, and was underdressed for autumn in Geneva. Stocky Rufaro Banya was dressed colourfully in a blue and green dress that went to her knees, which contrasted sharply with severe-looking, black plastic-framed glasses. Both were middle-aged.

"Sit darling," Cathy said. "Do you want a drink?"

"I'll get changed first; just be a moment."

Michael went to the bedroom and changed his suit for jeans and a fresh shirt. Then he went to the bathroom and splashed water to freshen himself. He returned to find out what was going on.

"Want a drink darling?" Cathy asked.

"A beer please."

Michael sat at the table and Cathy had something cooking on the stove. It smelled like nothing, so it must be sadza and rape. Silence until Cathy returned with his beer and another bottle of lemonade.

"Joe and Rufaro are here representing the MDC," Cathy told him.

"I see," Michael said.

"They met with Monsieur Dupont and myself, and I invited them home."

"How did it go with Monsieur Dupont?"

"We went to the police and they're going to talk to Mandipaka."

"That'll scare him."

"I know, but it's the best he can do for now."

"Catherine told us of your trouble," Rufaro Banya said. "And this is why we came to your home."

"We think we can help you," Joe Dube added.

"In what way?" Michael asked.

"All of us will go to the Zanu people and make it clear that this behaviour is not acceptable."

"Do you think that will make a difference?"

"Maybe not with the man who is causing you trouble, but it should with the other men in the delegation."

"Misbehaving while guests of the United Nations is a serious thing, even for Zanu," Rufaro Banya said. "I am sure the other members of Zanu will realise this and make Mandipaka behave himself."

"It's worth a try," Cathy said.

"And if Monsieur Dupont gets the Swiss police to turn up as well...," Michael said.

"That will make things seem more serious," Cathy finished his sentence.

"What've you got cooking?" Michael asked.

"Sadza and rape. I can make something else for you."

"No, sadza's fine."

* * *

Michael reversed their blue Peugeot 206 out of the garage and Cathy climbed in the front. Their two guests climbed in back, although space in the compact four-door was somewhat tight. Michael headed past the Parc La Grange before turning left towards Route de Malagnou. Along the busy road, and then right to Route de Florissant and the apartment building where the Zimbabweans were staying. Number twelve was on the right and Michael found parking about fifty metres away.

An impromptu conference on the pavement with Michael unsure about how to approach things. Because he was the oldest male, Joe Dube offered to knock on the door and speak to the Zanu people. A typically African way of solving the problem. They walked along the quiet street in the suburbs of Geneva towards a small apartment building amongst many others. Apartment two, ground floor, Dube pressed the button. From the speaker a disjointed voice, but African-sounding. "Who is it?"

"I am Joe Dube and with me is Rufaro Banya, Catherine Shoko and Michael Page. We wish to talk with you."

"Why is it you want to talk?" the voice asked.

"Can we come inside?"

"What is this about?"

"Mr David Mandipaka is causing problems."

A buzz and click, and the timber-and-glass door was released. Joe Dube led the way inside, Michael next, with the women following. Cream-coloured corridor, gloss-white doors, a black number two. Joe knocked and the door opened, and the face was hostile.

"What is this about David Mandipaka?" he asked.

"Please, can we introduce ourselves?" Joe Dube asked.

A grimace. "I know Mrs Shoko and I know of her husband. You two are traitors."

"We're from the MDC."

"Traitors, like I said."

"He's Ron Chamisa," Cathy said. "Inside I see Nelson Mutasa. Where is Simon Muchemwa?

"I am here Mrs Shoko," a voice came from another room.

"You do not speak English Mr Muchemwa, or so I was told," Cathy said.

"Can we speak to you about David Mandipaka?" Joe Dube asked.

"Speak."

"He is harassing this man and his wife."

"They are escaped criminals; is that not so?"

"So you know."

Chamisa nodded.

"It does not matter what you believe or not," Dube said. "Such things are not allowed here in Geneva."

"So go to the police, or will they not do anything about us?"

"We would prefer not to take things that far."

Michael became aware of an odour in the corridor: stale sweat and cigarettes. He turned his head and Mandipaka was there with a gun. A hand gun: automatic, dark grey. Aimed at them.

"I can take things this far," Mandipaka said.

Michael edged away but Dube took a step closer to Mandipaka. "Please put the gun down so we can talk," Dube said.

Mandipaka suddenly lashed out and struck Dube hard on the forehead with the handle of his gun. Dube grunted, and reached for the wall while blood ran from his wound. Mandipaka pressed the gun against Dube's forehead.

Michael was stunned at such a brutal display of violence. That was going too far, even for Zanu. "Chamisa…," Michael said while looking over his shoulder, and then he was looking at the barrel of another gun. And this didn't seem like a good idea anymore.

"What do we do with them?" Mandipaka asked.

"We take them to the chalet, and then we get them out of the country."

"Kwete!" Cathy shouted and Chamisa grinned. He was enjoying this. Michael caught his wife's eye and slowly shook his head. She nodded.

"Both cars now," Chamisa snapped. "You two with me," he said, motioning at Michael and Dube. "You two with him."

Two more men emerged from inside the apartment, and with two guns and four men it was impossible to get away. One of the men grabbed Cathy and Rufaro Banya's arms, and the two girls were guided towards the front door. Mandipaka held the door, and then he followed the girls onto the pavement. Michael and Dube followed with a gun pressed into Dube's back. Joe Dube's forehead was bleeding and it looked quite bad. He was unsteady on his feet, like he was concussed. By the time they reached the pavement, the girls were climbing into the back of a two-door Toyota Starlet. Chamisa unlocked the door of a red Peugeot 106, and folded the passenger's seat forward for Michael and Dube.

An engine started and the silver Toyota pulled out and roared down the street. Two men were pushed in the back of the 106, and there they were trapped when the front seat was dropped into place. Chamisa took the passenger seat while man number four got behind the wheel. Chamisa turned around and pointed his gun while the driver pulled out and away, with the Toyota well gone.

They were passing very close to parked cars, like the driver wasn't used to driving on the right. And his gearchanges were slow, like he wasn't used to changing gear with his right hand. Heading south-east away from Geneva and towards the mountains, probably to the chalet they mentioned. Michael wondered just how to get out of this.

They reached a 'T' intersection and stopped with the driver checking for traffic. They turned right, but onto the wrong side of the road.

"Idiot!" Chamisa shouted while grabbing the wheel and forcing the car to the right again.

"Pfidza," the driver said, sorry, and Chamisa grimaced at the apology.

They continued along a tree-lined boulevard through a wealthy suburb, climbing steadily. On and on with Michael quite sure they wouldn't end up in Zimbabwe but worried that something else might happen. Something bad, rough justice. Mandipaka was a dangerous man, a lion he said. Stalk his prey and kill it. It wouldn't surprise Michael if that was going to happen. Mandipaka killed Chipateni by accident, and almost certainly he'd killed others. Cathy and he would just be two more. At the chalet they'd realise that getting Page and Shoko to Zimbabwe would be difficult, but there were other forms of justice.

Engine note changed, the driver slowed, and ahead was an intersection. Stop, left turn and again the idiot ended up on the wrong side of the road.

"Boorangoma!" Chamisa snapped, and then the siren screamed.

The driver swerved to the right and accelerated hard, trying to outrun the police, not likely in an overloaded 106. He revved the engine hard but lost momentum on his awkward gearchanges. The siren wailed with blue lights bathing the interior of the car, while the driver flogged the engine for little effect. It brought back memories of an overloaded Nissan Sunny over steep mountains. But that was different; the jeep didn't suit high speed. This time the Africans stood no chance.

But still they pressed on, pursued by the police. The road veered left, and suddenly blue lights ahead. A second police car parked was across the road with blue lights flashing. Michael was thrown against his seatbelt and Dube's head lolled forward. And only then did Michael realise that Dube was unconscious. The Peugeot slowed hard, coming to a halt just short of the parked car. The siren behind stopped but the lights continued to flash. Two unformed men approached from behind, and there was no hope for the Africans. The policemen stood on either side of the car.

"Montrez-moi votre permis," the policeman on the left asked.

No response, the driver didn't understand French.

"L'homme a un fusil!" Michael yelled.

The policeman pulled his gun. "Quel homme?" he shouted.

"L'homme devant à droit," Michael shouted back.

"Ouvrez la porte et mettez votre fusil sur la terre. Open the door and put your gun on the ground."

Chamisa squirmed.

"Maintenant, now!" the policeman bellowed.

Chamisa opened the door and placed his gun carefully on the ground. The policeman on the right kicked the gun to one side without taking his gaze from the two Africans.

"Get out of the car and put your hands on the bonnet," the policeman on the left ordered.

Chamisa opened the door further and climbed out, as did the driver. Moments later, handcuffs on wrists and arms running down bodies searching for more weapons. Two men subdued, the policeman on the left, name tag Vioget, bent down and looked through the door opening.

"Monsieurs, please get out of the car," he said.

"This man is unconscious," Michael replied.

"Who is he?"

"An acquaintance."

"And those two men?"

"They're from the Zimbabwean government. They kidnapped us. Two other Zimbabweans have taken my wife and another woman."

"Slow down Monsieur, I don't understand."

"I'll get out."

"Slowly please."

Michael released the driver's seat and climbed from the rear of the car. The policeman held his gun ready but not aimed at Michael.

"What is going on?" Voiget asked.

"My wife is Zimbabwean and she works for the United Nations. Those men are part of a delegation from the Zimbabwean government and they kidnapped us. My wife and another women in one car, and this man and I in this car."

"And why did they do this?"

"They want to send us to Zimbabwe."

"Why?"

"Six years ago in Zimbabwe, one of the men from Zanu tortured us. We escaped and now we're here, and he's here too."

Voiget grimaced.

"I'm sorry Monsieur," Michael said. "I know this is confusing."

"I can't do anything here. I will call an ambulance, and then we will take you and those men to my station."

Voiget turned his collar up and spoke into a microphone to ask for an ambulance and gave the address. A woman squawked that the ambulance was on its way and would take a few minutes. Voiget asked Michael to wait, and he went to the policeman, name tag Pilat, who was guarding Chamisa and the driver. They conversed quietly for a moment and Voiget returned.

"My colleagues from the other car will take those two now, and you can wait here with me."

Michael nodded and then he leaned against the red car.

"Monsieur, is there anyone who can corroborate your story?" Voiget asked.

"My wife's manager."

"What is his name?"

"Guillaume Dupont at the United Nations. But I don't know where he lives."

Voiget pressed a button on his microphone. "Trouvez monsieur Guillaume Dupont des Nations Unies, s'il vous plaît," he said.

"Oiu," came the scratchy reply.

306

"We will look for your Monsieur Dupont, but we may not find him until tomorrow," Voiget said, shrugging his shoulders.

"You'll get him at work."

"Probably. But this story of your wife and the other woman...."

"I know. They said a chalet, but it could be anywhere."

And a siren in the distance, the tone rising and falling, the ambulance approaching. Louder and louder, closer and closer. Red lights flashing, the ambulance pulled up, and the siren was shut down. Red lights contrasting against the blue lights of the police car still flashing. One man opened the rear doors of the white ambulance, while the other came to Voiget and Michael.

"Un homme unconscious derrière la voiture," Voiget said.

"Qu'est-ce qui l'a provoqué?" the white-uniformed ambulance officer asked.

"Lui a été frappé par la poignée d'un fusil," Michael said.

The ambulance officer nodded and folded the passenger seat forward. He felt the side of Dube's neck for a moment and then he went to his vehicle. The two men returned with a stretcher which was placed on the road. It was awkward lifting the prone body out of the small car, but eventually they had Joe Dube strapped on the white bed. They lifted and the legs locked into place.

"Nous le prendrons à l'hôpital."

And a couple of moments later, Joe Dube was in the back and the ambulance left, siren shattering the night-time quiet of this upper-class Geneva suburb.

"Monsieur...."

"Page," Michael interrupted.

"Monsieur Page, you can come with us now."

Pilat opened the back door of the police car, a white Citroen, and Michael climbed in. Everything rested on finding Guillaume Dupont and hoping he knew about the chalet. And if he didn't, Cathy was in big trouble.

Chapter Twenty Five

Michael was aware of someone. He rolled over on his makeshift bed and saw a man in a dark blue suit. Tall and slim with black hair, neatly groomed. Expensive clothes: a made to measure suit with a white silk shirt and a blue silk tie. Michael's age, more or less, and obviously well-off.

"Monsieur Page?" the man asked.

Michael sat up on the pair of seats that he pushed together the previous evening. "Yes," he said in a husky voice, "I'm Michael Page."

"Guillaume Dupont," he said, extending his hand. "Your wife works for me."

Michael stood and shook hands; aware of how dishevelled he must look after a night of lying in the waiting room. Not sleeping because his mind was too busy for that.

"This is tragic," Guillaume Dupont said. "I'm sorry; I should've done more."

"You weren't to know the Zimbabweans would go this far."

"But Cathy knew, is that not so?"

"We both knew it could get dangerous." Michael rubbed his chin. "Excuse me Monsieur Dupont; I should wash first."

"Certainly."

Michael pushed against the brown door to the gents, and inside it was sparkling and clean like everything in Geneva was sparkling and clean. With soap, water and paper towels, he felt much better. He returned to the waiting area and Dupont was on one of the two seats. Michael went to the vending machine and dropped a pair of two-franc coins in the slot and pressed the button for café crème. The machine whined and whirred for a moment, and he had a plastic cup of hot coffee. He sipped some, and then he sat on the second seat. He sipped again.

"The men from Zanu said they were taking Cathy and Rufaro Banya to a chalet," Michael said. "Do you know where it is?"

"No Monsieur, I do not."

"Do you know how we can find out?"

"The police asked me and I do not know."

"The men in custody?"

"Apparently they won't talk. They think themselves diplomats, but have asked for a lawyer to make certain."

"Their apartment?"

"The police are there as we speak."

Michael drank more of the coffee. "Let's hope they find something."

"Yes."

"Do you know of Joe Dube, the man in the car with me?" Michael asked.

"He's in hospital," Monsieur Dupont said. "They've done a CT scan as a precaution, and now they're keeping him in observation."

"So he's okay?"

"Yes, he's okay."

Michael finished his coffee and tossed the plastic cup into a bin. He looked up, the clock showed a quarter-to-nine. He sighed. He felt restless; he wanted to do something, but what? The police had the matter in hand and Guillaume Dupont was very calm about it all. Michael stretched, hoping that the location of the chalet would be discovered soon, and that he and Dupont would be kept informed. He wondered if they would wait for hours and hours. Last time was better; with Julie and Peter he really got stuck-in. He looked at the clock again and it barely moved. He sighed and he felt hungry. Breakfast to soak-up some time; breakfast to prepare him for what was to come.

"Have you eaten Monsieur Dupont?" Michael asked.

"Guillaume, and yes I have."

"I'll get something if you don't mind. If you hear anything, call me straight away." Michael pulled out his wallet and handed over a business card. "Please call my mobile."

"Certainly Monsieur Page."

"Michael."

* * *

Michael returned a half-hour later after baguette and coffee, and there was a man in a cheap, black suit talking to Dupont. Older, wavy brown hair, grey at the edges, top button loose and a blue tie hanging low. The man looked up as Michael closed.

"Bonjour Monsieur, Je m'appelle Detective Lisle."

Michael shook hands. "Bonjour, Je m'appelle Michael Page."

"Detective Lisle said they found nothing at the apartment," Guillaume said.

Michael rubbed his forehead wondering what to do. "Someone must know; the kidnappers are representing the Zimbabwean government, so perhaps the embassy might know something."

"They have a mission to the United Nations, but even if they know why should they tell us?"

"Diplomatic immunity?"

"Yes."

"It's worth asking though. Detective Lisle, do you mind coming with us?"

"If you want, but you know I cannot act without clear evidence of a crime."

"I know; it's a psychological thing."

"I will get constables Brun and Morel."

"Good."

"So we go?" Dupont asked.

"Yes, we go."

* * *

The Mission was near the lake, just north of the botanical gardens, a long drive from the police station. Dupont parked his Ford out front with the police behind in their white Citroen. It was an unimposing structure, a brown-painted brick wall with a pair of black, steel security gates. Dupont went to a speaker set into the wall and pressed a button.

"Who is it?" the dismembered voice asked.

"Guillaume Dupont from the United Nations. I called about half-an-hour ago."

"Wait a moment."

The right-hand gate swung partly open, revealing a stout African in a dark blue uniform with ribbons on his chest and a fancy golden rope from his left epaulette.

"I am Major Chihuri," he said, shaking hands with Dupont. "I see you've brought a delegation."

"This is Michael Page, husband of one of my workers."

The major nodded.

"And Detective Lisle, and Constables Brun and Morel," Dupont continued.

"I must protest about the police."

"I'm here to see the ambassador about a serious matter."

"I cannot let the police in."

313

"This is a serious matter," Michael repeated while pleased that the police presence had created a fuss.

"Mr Dupont and Mr Page," Chihuri said, "you can come with me." Chihuri frowned at the Geneva police force. "You must stay here," he said.

The major led the way across a small paved yard, with a couple of lonely-looking trees losing their leaves. Ahead was a modern two-storey house in copper-coloured brick, with a protruding balcony fronting a pair of ornately-shaped white wooden doors. White American-colonial style windows made the house look like it had been transplanted from the US. Michael and Guillaume Dupont were led into a hallway finished in rich burgundy and gold wallpaper.

"Please wait here," the major said, before going into a room on the left, with his shoes echoing on the timber floor.

Michael looked around; there was a brass hatstand on the left and a brass-framed mirror opposite. The brass was brilliantly polished, reflecting the light from a brass chandelier. It was hard to imagine such opulence from the poorest country in the world. Footsteps on timber and a man in a blue suit emerged from the left. He was a fat man with his suit stretched over his belly, and a single button straining. Sweat glistening on his forehead despite the moderate temperature.

"I am Ambassador Mahlangu," he said. "What is this about a worker for the United Nations?"

"Ambassador, I am Guillaume Dupont and this is Michael Page. Cathy Shoko was kidnapped by the delegation from Zanu-PF and...."

"Absurd!" the ambassador bellowed. "What proof do you have that the government of Zimbabwe was involved?"

"Michael Page is Cathy Shoko's husband, and he was abducted by the delegation as well."

Mahlangu pulled out a handkerchief and wiped his forehead. "Come with me," he said. "This way," and he went into the room on the left. It was a study, with a large antique desk, a modern timber and leather chair, and a couple of antique straight-backed, wood and red velvet chairs. Mahlangu took one of these chairs. "Please sit," he offered.

The two men sat.

"So you accuse the delegation of doing this thing," Mahlangu said. "And you, the husband, are the proof."

"There are police outside who rescued me," Michael said.

"The police cannot do anything, surely you know this. Legally this is a piece of Zimbabwe."

"The police are involved because this is a serious crime, and we would like you to help us before this incident gets worse."

"Help in what way?"

"The men from Zanu took my wife and another woman to a chateau; do you know where their chateau is?"

315

"I am afraid I cannot help you."

"Do you know where their chateau is?"

"I am – no, I do not know."

That pricked Michael's interest. "What do you know?" he asked.

"You cannot come here and make accusations to me, the ambassador." Mahlangu squirmed on the chair while he extracted his handkerchief, and then he wiped his forehead again.

"We don't want this to become a diplomatic incident," Michael said.

"This had nothing to do with me."

"What had nothing to do with you?"

"The…," Mahlangu wiped the palms of his hands together. "The, the, your kidnapping."

"Monsieur," Dupont said. "A woman's life is in danger."

"I cannot help you in any way; surely you understand this?" Mahlangu squirmed in his chair. "You should go now, I will call…."

Things were slipping away. And then Michael realised it would take more than diplomacy to rescue Cathy. Threats. Zanu didn't know any language beyond threats and intimidation. "Excuse me Ambassador," Michael interrupted. "Before we leave, I would like to discuss something with my colleague."

316

Mahlangu frowned.

"This will only take a moment," Michael continued. He gathered his thoughts. "She's an Australian citizen, she works for the United Nations, and she was kidnapped by representatives of the Zimbabwean government. This could get serious."

"If you insist Mr Page. There is a meeting room through there."

"Thanks."

Michael steered Dupont into a small room with bookcases on three sides, and he closed the door behind them. He paced back and forwards while trying to work out a threat. "We're going nowhere," he said, frowning. "I'm wondering how much we could threaten."

"Monsieur....!"

"She's my wife!"

It was Guillaume Dupont's turn to frown. "There's no link between the mission and the delegation; there's nothing we can do."

"I think he knows something. We need to pressure him, but something unofficial."

Dupont nodded.

And then Michael realised he shared the room with someone important. "I have an idea," Michael said. "And it's do-able with the right connections."

"We must be careful about such things."

"He's Zimbabwean, so we have to do what it takes."

"I'm uncomfortable about this."

"What do you think of Cathy?"

"She's a fine lady and I'm lucky to have her working for me."

"We can wait for diplomats to be expelled, but by then it will be too late. If you want to rescue Cathy it has to be now, and you'll have to trust me. I know these people and they're a peculiar mix of aggression and passivity. They protest, but in the end they do nothing."

"Are you sure?"

"Perpetual lack of inertia is their greatest weakness."

"Okay, we will do it your way."

Michael opened the door to the study and went to the chair. Only he didn't sit.

"When I was in school, we knew how to handle bullies. We didn't take them on face-to-face, we ostracised them instead. Do you know what that means, Mr Ambassador?"

"Of course I do."

"So what we're going to do is ostracise you. As from today, every person you contact will be unavailable, every message you leave will be unanswered, every communication will be disregarded."

"You cannot do this!" Mahlangu snapped, jumping to his feet.

"He's the United Nations," Michael replied calmly.

"But even the United Nations...."

"We have contacts, so we can and we will," Michael interrupted. "And more. Life here can be difficult without power or water."

"But you cannot do that!"

"It's all about contacts. If the power were to fail in this street, it might take a long time for it to be repaired. And the water, who knows how long that would take to fix. And gas, with winter coming...."

"No-one can do such things."

"With the right contacts, Ambassador Mahlangu, we can."

"These are nothing but empty threats."

"Try us out then. You know that if you want something, he's the man you call. So try us, and maybe you'll be lucky."

"I protest."

"Protest all you like, because it'll fall on deaf ears."

"But I am the ambassador."

"And you're a guest of this country. You rely on people like us more than we rely on you."

Mahlangu flopped into his chair.

"Is Cathy Shoko worth such inconvenience?" Michael asked.

Mahlangu wiped his forehead again. "You must understand that I have no involvement in anything to do with your wife, but in the interests of cooperation I may be able to help you. Please wait here and I will make a phone call."

Michael nodded, and the ambassador left the room. Michael took a seat and noticed that his heart was running fast.

"Are you a card player Michael Page?" Guillaume Dupont asked.

Michael shrugged his shoulders. "This is from my job," he said.

Footsteps in the corridor followed by Mahlangu striding to his desk. He sat in the leather chair and leaned forward.

"I have located the women and I am assured that they are in good health. The men involved have told me that this is all a misunderstanding, do you understand what this means?"

Dupont nodded. "Yes I do."

But Michael was confused.

Dupont looked at Michael. "I think," he said. "That it would be better for all if Mr Mandipaka went home. I don't want any more misunderstandings."

The ambassador nodded and he gave Dupont a piece of paper.

"You will find them there," Mahlangu said,

"Thank you."

Mahlangu pressed a button on the cumbersome-looking telephone console on his desk. "Major Chihuri will show you out." He shook hands with the two of them. "Good-bye gentlemen."

The major appeared at the doorway and led the way to the front gate. The gate swung open to reveal a detective and two constables sitting on the kerb.

"We've got the address, but we're not to touch the Zimbabweans," Dupont said.

"A deal?" Detective Lisle asked.

"We get the girls and the ringleader goes home."

Detective Lisle frowned, or worse. Michael was ambivalent.

"Can you come with us?" Michael asked. "Just in case."

The detective nodded. "Where is it?"

"Saint George."

Lisle opened the passenger door of the police car and pulled out a map directory. He flicked through pages, and nodded. "Not far, near Rolle."

"Let's go," Michael said.

Dupont shrugged his shoulders and climbed into his car. Michael joined him the front, and the police got into their car with Constable Morel behind the wheel.

* * *

It took about forty-five minutes to reach the small village of Saint George, hugging the side of the mountains with the barren snowline in the near distance. Houses, a small hotel and a general store all huddled together. Michael traced their route on the map and the chalet was north of the town and off the main road. Mahlangu's handwriting was hard to follow, but it looked like 'bridge'. They continued north, climbing, and Michael spotted a road on the left.

"I think there," he said.

Dupont slowed, indicating to turn onto a narrow road that thread its way through rolling pastures. Horses grazed in an unfenced paddock on the left, and cattle grazed on the right. Dupont drove slowly while they passed a farm with white buildings topped with dark shingle rooves. And into the open again, winding left and right.

"We're close," Michael said, and he looked over his shoulder to see the white Citroen still following.

They rounded a curve and the road ended at a pasture of long grass speckled with bright, yellow daisies. Nothing around, except a gravel car park on the right, next to a walking trail. Michael saw deep tyre marks on in the soft gravel.

"Over there," he said, and Dupont parked his Ford, with the police parking alongside.

Michael got out and went to the tracks; Detective Lisle joined him.

"What do you think?" Michael asked.

"These are fresh," Lisle replied.

"Where's the bridge?"

"Some chalets are like this," Dupont said. "Too steep for cars to get close."

"Okay," Michael said. "We'll try this place out."

The walking trail passed between two boulders and wound between trees, out of sight. Michael headed off with his shoes crunching on the gravel. It was clear and crisp, fresh and cool, and Michael continued onwards in the shade of the trees, the track curving to the left. No bird or wildlife noises. Silence, except for a muted roar somewhere ahead. He was steadily climbing with the noise getting louder. Ten minutes, almost a kilometre from the carpark, and the noise was clearer: surging and splashing. Michael passed over a crest of a hill and the land dropped away. Ahead, a varnished timber bridge about twenty metres long, spanning a narrow but swiftly-flowing creek, or brook in Switzerland. Beyond the bridge was an undulating field. To the rear of the field was a modern building: granite for the lower storey and a varnished timber second story with a balcony. A dark roof with an attic nestling beneath, the attic in varnished timber as well. No movement, no noise beyond the rushing of the brook. No animals, no birds, nothing. Dupont and the police caught up, and Michael led the way across the uneven field, marching briskly to the front door. Up three steps and he knocked on the door. No response. Michael tried the handle; it was unlocked. He opened the door and went inside to semi-darkness, and all was silent. He sighed and the detective and two constables separated, Lisle went through a doorway to the rear of the ground floor while the uniformed officers went upstairs. Dupont joined Michael who surveyed the big living room, a cliche if ever he'd seen one. A large stone fireplace on one side, a heavy timber mantle above, a dark brown leather lounge suite facing the hearth, a dark timber chair and desk on the left. Michael went to the desk and sat in the chair: a telephone, a fluorescent desk lamp, and a pad and pen spread before him. Untidy writing on the pad, impossible to read, Michael fumbled around the base of the lamp until he found the switch. The light flickered on and Michael held the pad diagonally, and the writing was clearer. Mostly codes: LX2807, 10.15, LX332, 12.05, UM275. 18.30. LX was the code for Swissair. Michael checked his watch; just a few minutes before twelve. Almost too late, he grabbed the pad and ran through the open doorway to find Lisle in the kitchen. The sink and table were piled high with unwashed dishes.

"Detective Lisle, these are their flight details. They've gone and we haven't much time."

Lisle grabbed the pad and frowned before checking his own watch. He unclipped a bulky, old-fashioned mobile phone from his belt and punched the keys. Michael listened and Lisle greeted the party on the other end with bonjour, as the French and French-speaking Swiss always do. He quickly and precisely explained the situation, two Zimbabwean men and two Zimbabwean women were leaving the country, and then he read out the details from the pad. Silence, it took ages. Michael leant against the table, waiting. Eventually Lisle said "merci, au revoir." He pushed a button on his phone and looked across at Michael. "Monsieur, two men on Zimbabwean passports travelling under the names Sam Ncube and Victor Kunonga along with two women, also on Zimbabwean passports, caught flight LX2807 from Geneva to Zurich, transferring to LX332 to Heathrow. The women were travelling under the names Alice Moyo and Janet Mnandi. UM275 is the regular Air Zimbabwe service from Gatwick to Harare."

"What can you do?" Michael asked.

"If we caught them in Switzerland.... Unfortunately, it's going to be hard. You and I can guess they have changed identities, but the police in the UK will need more than our guesswork to detain these people."

"What can we do?"

"We will go to your home now, and we will email a picture of your wife to Britain. We can ask them to check for her at passport control and maybe we will be lucky. But Monsieur, you must be prepared for the worst."

"That's okay," Michael said, feeling anything but okay. They had missed the girls, but by hours. They would have been on their way when Mahlangu made that call, probably to someone's mobile.

Guillaume Dupont entered the room.

"They've gone," Michael told him.

Chapter Twenty Six

It was the last place Michael ever expected to see again. He was on the last leg of a long journey: Geneva to Heathrow, Gatwick to Beira for a few days, Beira to Johannesburg, and finally Johannesburg to Harare. Harare International Airport had changed much since 1999; ahead was a massive white terminal building with an integrated control tower. Extravagant for a country in dire straits. In the adjacent seat, Joe Dube peered past Michael and through the window. Michael contemplated his colleague with a disguise not effective enough. Michael's six-day growth of beard coupled with black-framed, low-strength reading glasses was transforming, but Dube's beard was scrappy and didn't do anything to hide his facial features.

The aircraft drifted to a halt and soon they were on the aerobridge. A whiff of local air; still that strange musky smell laden with diesel fumes. To immigration; Michael presented his newly acquired Mozambican passport at the counter. The African official turned to the photo, glanced at Michael, and stamped a visa. First obstacle out of the way: Michael Prince was officially in Zimbabwe. Dube was next, and after a moment he entered under the name Adam Gorova.

Following the signs to luggage while mingling with fellow passengers and the army. Michael's red-tagged case rumbled past, and he grabbed it and placed it at his feet. Dube watched and waited and Michael was aware of someone behind. He glanced over his shoulder to see a neatly-dressed couple standing close, Gonda and Matutu perhaps. Dube retrieved his large, soft and battered bag before turning around and breaking into a big smile. He went to the young man and they shook hands vigorously, greeting one-another in the standard Zimbabwean 'how's your day, my day's fine if your day's fine' sequence. Michael knew enough chiShona but wasn't in the mood. Less in the mood when, towards the end, he heard Dube say the name 'Michael Page'.

At the end of the long greeting, the young man turned to Michael and introduced himself as Mitchell Gonda, the two shaking hands while Michael replied as Michael Prince. The young lady, Alison Matutu, also shook hands with Michael. She went to grab Michael's bag, as a Zimbabwean would, but he beat her to it. Their hosts led the way out of the terminal building, through one of many automatic doors, heading towards the carpark.

"When were you last here Mr Prince?" Gonda asked. Mitchell Gonda was early to mid-twenties, tall and wiry, and dressed in black cotton trousers with a white cotton shirt. He could have been any Zimbabwean in the street, except that he risked much to support the MDC.

"Michael please, and it was March 1999."

"Much has changed," Gonda said. "Inflation, unemployment, Operation Murambatsvina...."

"I know. How do people get by?"

"We are suffering; the world knows this."

"But how much can a country suffer?"

"As much as you are going to see over the next days."

They reached a 1980s vintage Peugeot in sun-faded green, and Gonda unlocked the boot. Luggage stowed, Gonda and Matutu in front, Dube struggling to fit into the rear, and Michael felt rather squashed himself.

"What do you wish to do, Mr Prince?" young Alison Matutu asked. Mid-twenties, wearing jeans and a blue cotton top. She reminded Michael of Julie Shoko, which meant that she was an attractive, young lady.

"Michael please, and I would like to see where they're holding Cathy and Rufaro."

"Harare Remand Prison."

Gonda turned the key and the engine eventually struggled into life. Soon they were on their way and heading north towards the city of suffering.

Much had changed: formerly cared-for houses were in disrepair: paint peeling, roof gutters sagging, gardens overgrown. The previously well maintained multi-lane road was littered with potholes and badly-filled excavations. Many walked along the road, ambled along the road, with just a few cars and thousands on foot. A shopping centre of boarded windows hosting a small crowd nonetheless. Closed, but somewhere to hang out. Decrepit cars lay abandoned; broken-down and discarded where they stopped. And then a line of vehicles in the left lane, car after car for at least a kilometre, while drivers leaned on part-opened doors and conversed with one another. The Peugeot passed the head of the queue and Michael saw that it was a petrol station with hundreds waiting to fill tanks and plastic drums from fuel in short supply. The army passed heading south, six jeeps in immaculate condition, bristling with soldiers and machine guns. And still the pedestrians ambled past, heading to who knew where? Not one bus so far, but Michael doubted they'd be able to afford a ticket in any case. When one cannot afford to eat, a bus fare is a luxury. How had prosperity been transformed into devastation in just five years? Physically, socially and economically devastated.

"How do people survive?" Michael asked.

"Mrs Shoko has relatives here, is that not so?" Mitchell Gonda replied

"She has her parents and we send them money."

"That is how people survive."

"Surely not the whole country?"

"Money from abroad, a bit of barter, black markets, but mostly money from abroad."

"From Zimbabweans in South Africa?"

"There are millions of illegal immigrants in all of our neighbouring countries, but mostly in South Africa."

Michael went silent; on the right was the township of Mbare. Part of old Salisbury, a low-cost, high-density township-within-a-city for the African working-class. Only it was ruined. Michael had driven past Mbare dozens of times, he heard the stories, but nothing prepared him for how it looked. Huge swathes of mangled landscape, with piles of rubble the only evidence that hundreds of homes had once stood there. Basic homes for sure, but homes for many. Now there were shanty structures, made out of loose bricks and cardboard boxes, as shelter for the few who stayed on. In the near distance were several run-down, multi-storey apartment blocks; the only buildings spared from demolition. The destruction of Mbare was the price paid for living in an area that overwhelmingly voted for the MDC. It was almost beyond comprehension, and more incomprehensible that the rest of the world did nothing. Operation Murambatsvina was over and many had been forced out of the cities and into rural areas, like Cambodia in the seventies. If nothing else Mugabe knew his history. He knew how to terrorise a nation into submission.

They left Mbare behind and passed into the city centre, heading towards the former regional head office of the CBAC bank. The city looked healthier than the suburbs: there were more cars on the road, and some shops and department stores were open. And not: many abandoned buildings: boarded shops and closed offices, including Michael's former work place relocated to Johannesburg. They turned right at the still lovely Harare Gardens and headed out of town on Samora Machel, veering left after a kilometre or so. Michael saw the unmistakeable silhouette of a prison on the right. Gonda pulled into the carpark and stopped. Michael got out and contemplated the prison while he leaned against the car with his arms crossed. Dark grey walls, razor wire, guardhouses at regular intervals, rows of cyclone fences. It was impregnable. Gonda and Matutu came to him.

"It's hopeless," Michael said.

"It is," Alison Matutu replied. "What are your plans?"

"I don't know. Do you have any ideas?"

"Hope for an honest judge and a decent trial. We have a good lawyer for them."

"What's the charge?"

"Accomplice to treason for Cathy, and aiding a fugitive for Rufaro."

"How can it be treason?"

"Your confession."

Michael nodded. "It was my confession; not hers."

"We know, but she left the country with you. Some may say she helped you escape."

Michael nodded slowly.

"We want you to speak to our lawyer," Alison Matutu said.

"When?" Michael asked.

"Now. She is at the safe house in Waterfalls."

Michael sighed. "Let's go then." He climbed into the cramped back seat and their MDC hosts got in front. Soon they were on their way through the city and south along Simon Mazorodze Road, turning left at Derbyshire Road. Waterfalls was untouched by the horror, and it seemed bizarre that the suburb was more-or-less the same. Waterfalls was clearly a Zanu enclave, which was even stranger.

"Why do you have a house here?" Michael asked from the back seat.

"This is the last place Zanu would look," Alison Matutu replied. "It's safe, as long as we are discreet."

Hiding in plain sight. "Is it really safe?" Michael asked.

"I am worried about Mr Dube, sorry Mr Gorova, as he is well-known. Perhaps he should stay with our lawyer."

They pulled up at a cream-painted brick wall, where Alison Matutu got out to open the white steel gate. Mitchell Gonda drove along the well-maintained gravel driveway, and pulled up in front of a cream-painted brick house that was very typical of that area. Large, solidly constructed and surrounded by a couple of hectares of yard. Their hosts opened the door and led the way inside, and Michael found himself in a home that was eerily similar to his once home. Michael followed Alison Matutu along the corridor and into a spacious kitchen, and at the table was a plump woman surrounded by sheets of paper and lever arch files. Older, perhaps as old as he, and dressed formally in a black skirt and white top. She stood and Michael shook hands.

"Barbara Tembo," she said.

"Michael Prince and Adam Gorova."

"I am the lawyer for your wife and Mrs Banya. Please sit."

Michael took one of the wooden chairs and Dube sat as well. Matutu sat at the end of the table.

"So Mr Prince, you have heard of the charges?" Tembo said.

"You can call me Michael; and yes I have. Look, my confession had nothing to do with Cathy; she never said a word, never admitted anything."

"Did you do it?"

"Of course not! We'd been tortured for days, and in the end I confessed to stop Cathy from being raped. But that didn't help. We both escaped because of the torture and abuse."

"I see. Unfortunately, torture and rape are often used by Zanu against its enemies."

"I know that now. What do judges think of such behaviour?"

"It depends on the judge. Some are Zanu members and only too keen to follow the party line, and some are appointed by Zanu and then take their responsibilities seriously."

"And juries?"

"The jury could be stacked against us; this is true."

Michael scratched his beard while trying to frame the situation with logic. "It's too random," he said.

"It is very unpredictable."

"What if I testified?"

"You would be arrested, charged and convicted, and your testimony wouldn't mean that Mrs Shoko would be acquitted either. A judge could instruct the jury that you are fabricating stories of abuse to get your wife acquitted, and you are using these stories to be acquitted yourself."

"But it could help."

"That's unlikely." Barbara Tembo leaned forward and looked at Michael. "My advice is for you to assist us here and now, and if she is convicted you can assist us with the appeal."

"Are you sure?"

"Yes."

"You know there really isn't anyone we can call as a witness, other than Cathy herself. The only ones involved were me, her sister Julie who now lives in Mozambique, and Julie's ex-boyfriend who also lives in Mozambique, but it'd be too dangerous for them to come here and testify." And then it hit Michael. "Cathy saw a doctor in Beira and she would have records of Cathy's injuries, and of the rape too."

"This is good, if we can find this doctor. We have time, the committal is this Thursday, but I don't expect the trial to start before early next year."

"There's also her counsellor in Australia, and witnesses from our work."

"Such testimonies will help, but not as much as the doctor who saw her injuries."

"Can we get Cathy free on bail?"

"Not for treason and not for this case. The ruling party has made much publicity on television and in the newspapers."

"So she's going to be stuck in that place for months?"

Barbara Tembo nodded and shuffled papers while Michael felt empty, hollow and strangely restless.

* * *

Michael was feeling almost satisfied after his dinner of sadza with meat and rape. In the background, the television. Then he heard the theme music, such that it was, for 'The Main News'. Well, it would pass the time, and it might be interesting to see how the ruling party explained away the never-ending catastrophe that was life in what was once the most prosperous country in sub-Saharan Africa. Michael went to the doorway and stopped with a start. In the living room, Mitchell Gonda and Alison Matutu in an embrace, hugging and kissing with enthusiasm. Michael backed away, but Alison Matutu must have sensed something because she pulled away from her partner and looked past Mitchell Gonda's arm, being too short to see over his shoulder. She jumped and almost pushed poor Gonda away.

"I'm so sorry," she said.

Michael smiled. "It's okay; this is your house and I'm the guest."

"No, this is not our house and what we did was wrong."

"It was nothing," Michael said, actually feeling warm and fuzzy at the display of young love.

"Do you wish to watch the television?"

Michael nodded and Alison Matutu went to the sofa. Mitchell Gonda also sat on the sofa, but as far away from his companion as he could get. Michael took one of the armchairs and got comfortable for the half-hour propaganda event.

'The Main News' didn't disappoint: disaster trivialised, and much made of a few modest successes. And always the British: the British this and the British that. Nation-wide brainwashing, but Michael's two young companions showed that tactic didn't always work.

"I do not want you to get the wrong idea about us," Alison Matutu said after the broadcast finished.

"Relax," Michael said. "Although I'm a married man, I'm young enough to remember."

"That's what I mean."

"What?"

"You're married."

"Not always. You see, I met Cathy when she was working in Australia and we moved in together. Then we came to Zimbabwe and shared a house not far from here. Later we got married because we loved each other."

"Um...." Alison Matutu said.

"True love is very precious," Michael said. "Too precious to be bound by rules and conventions. I can see that you love each other, so enjoy this gift you have. We're sharing this house for however long it takes; so feel free to enjoy each other's company."

"Are you sure, Mr Page?" Mitchell Gonda asked.

"Absolutely," Michael replied.

Chapter Twenty Seven

Michael was frisked by the uniformed guard with two equally stern-looking colleagues looking on. Without saying a word, the guard gestured towards a black steel door covered in scratches and graffiti. Michael turned a chrome steel handle and entered the room.

He found himself in a large open space, brightly lit by many fluorescent lights without covers. A big room in white-painted brick with plain concrete flooring. There were several simple laminated tables, and dozens of old-fashioned steel and plastic chairs scattered about at random. Hushed and quiet. Standing against the far wall was a line of female prisoners, eleven in all, and she stood out. Michael went to a table in the far corner of the room and a female guard said something to Cathy. She left the line and strolled casually to Michael with her hands in the pockets of her baggy, green overalls. Cathy stood beside Michael and he kissed her on her cheek. The kiss made no difference to her frown, however. Michael grabbed a blue plastic chair and sat at the table, and Cathy sat opposite him.

"What are you doing here?" she snapped.

"Visiting," Michael said.

"It's too dangerous."

Michael put his index finger in front of his lips and her face changed. He leaned forward. "Did you recognise me?" he asked quietly.

"Not at first."

"That's right. So here I am."

"But why are you here?"

"Because I love you and I had to see you."

Cathy leaned closer. "I knew you would come," she said. "It's your style."

"There are more important things than this visit, and you know what they are."

"But what can you do?"

"Your best defence is proof of the abuse we suffered. If we can get testimony from the doctor you saw in Beira; that might make a difference."

"She was just around the corner from the hotel. White, Doctor Cordova. Maria Cordova."

"I hope we can find her."

"I hope you can find her too." Cathy reached across the table and Michael took her hand. "I've missed you," she said. "I have news for you my husband, I think I'm pregnant."

"That's great."

"Is it?"

"It will be when we get you out of here."

"Can you?"

"We will do everything we can."

"But will it be enough?"

Michael leaned even closer, talking barely above a whisper. "I don't trust these people and we may have to do things differently. You remember what I did in Rusape?"

Cathy nodded.

"We may have to do something the same," he said.

"What will you do?" Cathy asked.

"I don't know, but we can't just wait for fate to take its course."

One of the bulky female guards came to the table and tapped Cathy on her shoulder. Cathy looked across and glared, but the message was clear enough. Visiting over. Cathy stood, still holding Michael's hand. He stood and they parted. Cathy was led to the rear of the room and into a corridor, passing out of sight. Michael stood at the table, staring at the doorway. He turned towards the black door covered in scratches and graffiti. The guards led him through long corridors of painted brick walls and concrete floors, with their footsteps echoing in the confined space. Through long corridors and passing steel doors until, eventually, he was outside. Bright sunshine uncomfortably glaring on the concrete surrounding the prison. Beyond the forecourt was the carpark, and the faded green Peugeot with his guide patiently waiting.

"How was your wife?" Mitchell Gonda asked.

"Good," Michael replied. "I have the name of the doctor she saw in Beira. It may be of help."

"Anything will be of help."

"Let's go."

Michael climbed into the passenger seat and Gonda got behind the wheel. Gonda turned the key, and after a while the engine fired up. They left the Harare Remand Prison behind, headed along a near-deserted Pauling Road, and at the end they turned right into Enterprise Road, which was busier. Michael stared out of the window, watching the landscape passing by. He was going to be a father but his darling wife was locked in jail. What a catastrophe. He had to do something like at Rusape, but what? No matter how hard he thought, nothing came to him. He felt frustrated. He had to do something really important and creativity had left him. All he had were threads: a court case, a doctor named Maria Cordova, a counsellor who heard a story from Cathy, and the notion that such things weren't enough.

They approached the city centre and there was activity on the road. Army jeeps passed, followed by police cars with lights flashing but no sirens. A personnel carrier also overtook and it was clear something was happening. Mitchell Gonda looked all around, and clearly he was uncomfortable. But Michael was curious to find out what it was. The future was hopeless and almost beyond redemption, and perhaps the only solution to the randomness of Cathy's fate was something random. Something random like whatever this was. More jeeps passed and Gonda had enough, slowing and indicating to turn left into Fourth Street.

"We should see what's going on," Michael said.

"But why, Mr Prince?" Mitchell Gonda asked.

"I'm interested."

"This could be dangerous."

"Not if we're careful."

Pedestrians finished crossing and Gonda was able to make his turn.

"Pull over and let me continue on foot," Michael said.

"I cannot let you go on your own," Mitchell Gonda said.

"Park the car and come with me then."

There was space just ahead on the left, and Gonda sort-of slotted his Peugeot into two parking bays, untidily at an angle. Michael was out of the car in a moment and Mitchell Gonda had to rush to lock the doors, catching Michael while he crossed the road and walked west along Union Avenue. There was a low-down, rumbling noise not far away. Some shouting and a dull thud, like a muffled explosion. More shouting and Michael knew what it was. The Zimbabweans were generally peaceful and law-abiding, but there were limits.

"What's down there?" Michael asked, looking towards the noise.

"Parliament House," Mitchell Gonda replied.

"Do you know of any demonstrations?"

"No, not at all. But this could be impromptu."

Third Street was a teeming mass of humanity; the entire road filled with men, women and teenagers. Peaceful demonstrators, not even chanting political slogans. Very Zimbabwean: an understated display by thousands who were tired of suffering. Michael got close to the fringe of the demonstration, but kept a buffer zone in case the police or army moved in. Mitchell Gonda stood behind him.

"Have you seen enough?" Mr Prince.

"Not yet, I want to see what happens next."

"Water canon, tear gas and rubber bullets."

"For this?"

"Yes."

That demonstration wasn't going to change anything, and Zanu would be ready to denounce those involved as traitors manipulated by the Whites and the British. Michael imagined the dry coverage on the 'Main News' that evening. And yet, at that moment, the city centre had stopped. If parliament was sitting, and he hoped it was, then Zanu would be trapped inside. It was a message, and surely any message was better than none. It was chaotic to a degree, and that was interesting.

"Cathy's remand trial...." Michael said.

"What of it?" Mitchell Gonda asked.

"Where will it be?"

'The Magistrate's Court."

"Near here?"

"No, on the other side of the city."

"Okay, let's go to the other side of the city."

"Mr Prince…."

"I think we can rescue the girls."

Mitchell Gonda looked at Michael blankly, clearly unable to comprehend the idea of breaking two women out of custody and taking them away.

"Let's go to the Magistrate's Court," Michael said, and he backtracked to Fourth Street where the car was parked. They climbed in and headed south to Robert Mugabe Road. Gonda turned right, and drove beyond the Indian shops. He turned left on Rotten Row, and drove slowly while looking for parking. He pulled into a space on the left and switched off the engine.

"Mitchell, where's the courthouse?" Michael asked.

"Over there," Mitchell Gonda replied, pointing across the road towards a building surrounded by grasslands dotted with a few trees. Dead grass, suffering from the drought. Michael took in all that was around him: commercial buildings on his left, mostly closed and barricaded, the open space on his right, and the size of the courthouse. The route from the jail would be south along Rotten Row, which meant that it could happen from the buildings on Michael's left. From the buildings and across the road towards the court.

Michael got out of the car and crossed the parkland of dead grass; striding towards the large green building with Mitchell Gonda following. Prominent was a large steel door, too solidly constructed to be a loading bay door. All around were 'keep clear' and 'no parking' signs. There was no doubt that door was for prisoners in custody. Further along was a rear entrance, more hospitable-looking in timber and glass. Michael walked around the building to the main entrance doors of glass panels in wooden frames, typical for a 1960's building. There were three guards in blue uniforms with holsters and handguns at their waists. Michael went inside and one of the guards strolled towards him.

"Can I help you sir?" the guard asked.

"My companion and I are studying law at the university, and we wish to view one of the hearings."

"There is a hearing in courtroom one. Just down there," the guard said, pointing along a corridor that seemed to divide the building into two halves.

Michael went along the corridor to the door marked 'one'. He opened the door carefully and went inside to take a seat at the rear. The courtroom was beautifully finished in varnished timber which reflected the ceiling lights in a thousand different ways. At the far end of the room, sitting behind a large varnished timber desk on a raised platform, was the magistrate, a stern-looking man in a black robe. A man with a deep and almost hypnotic voice that suited the authority of his position. On the right was the dock for the prisoners, formed out of hip-high walls in varnished timber. In front of the magistrate were two tables, each with two chairs, again in varnished timber. The only other furniture were the rows of varnished timber seats, very much like pews in a church. To the left of the magistrate was a timber door, and to the right of the room, near the dock, was a second timber door. The courtroom was not terribly large, about fifteen metres by fifteen metres, with seating for, maybe, about fifty.

Michael waited while the case proceeded; it was a traffic case so the accused was in the body of the court, not in the dock, and his lawyer and the prosecuting policeman were at the tables in front of the magistrate. It didn't take too long for the accused to be fined one-thousand dollars, and for he and his lawyer to depart the courtroom. Michael got up and followed the two men outside, but instead of going right towards the entrance he went left. He followed the corridor towards the rear entrance of the court, and there was a branch on the left that ended at a solid timber door. Michael carefully opened that door, and found himself in a corridor of unpainted concrete blocks. Michael surveyed that corridor, lit by glaring fluorescent lights without covers. On his right, the reverse side of the large steel door. On his left were a

347

number of doorways at regular intervals. So that was it. Michael closed the timber door carefully and faced his colleague.

"I think we can do this," Michael said.

"What is it you want to do?" Mitchell asked.

Michael knew just the man, if he was available. "I need to contact someone in Rusape."

"We have telephone books at the house."

"If he has a mobile and not a landline?"

"I can ring a contact in Rusape to find this man."

Michael was pleased. "Let's go Mitchell," he said. "We've got much to arrange."

Chapter Twenty Eight

Michael checked his watch and it was ten to ten. From his vantage point he had a good view of the Magistrate's Court about a hundred metres away. He leaned against the wall and looked towards their get-away car: an old, white Nissan Sunny that brought back memories. He checked his watch and the minute hand crept slowly forward. The hearing was scheduled for ten, which meant the police had to get Cathy and Rufaro Banya into the building about ten minutes before. About now. He scanned the street but nothing moved in a country of perpetual petrol shortages. Michael crossed his arms and frowned; if there were any delays they would fail. The crowd would move too soon and their one chance would fail.

"How is it?" Mitchell Gonda asked.

"It's good," Michael replied; feeling anything but good.

"Everyone is ready."

"All we need are the prisoners."

"Yes."

They were cutting it fine, it had to be about five to ten but Michael didn't want to check the time yet again. He sighed; it wasn't looking good. He turned towards the buildings opposite, where timber and steel barriers had been removed to enable the crowd to wait out of sight. They were three hundred or maybe more, and Michael wondered if that would be enough. It was a big task to get that many, but on a large open space a few hundred demonstrators would look anything but threatening.

"Look Mr Prince," Mitchell Gonda exclaimed, pointing, and Michael followed the outstretched finger. A white van approached ever so slowly. Michael checked his watch, five to; they were cutting it fine. The van had a blue light on the cab roof with a large, box-shaped rear. It was no wonder they were delayed given the van was speeding along at barely forty.

Indicators flashed, the van slowed even more, and then turned right onto the access road to the court. Michael tensed, his heart beating fast, echoing in his ears. He touched the bulge under his pullover and felt the cold, grey Glock automatic jammed behind his belt. He hoped he wouldn't have to use it. He wondered if he could. Two guards opened the rear of the van and led two figures, obscured by the van, towards the steel door. The guards opened the door and disappeared out of sight.

Movement on the right and the demonstrators emerged right on time. Michael watched the crowd advancing, many, many demonstrators, at least a thousand; numbers had swelled during the night. A mass of humanity crossed the open ground. Zimbabweans of all ages: from teenagers to the grey-haired. A magnificent display, so many grouped up tight, a thousand pairs of feet raising dust from the dry ground, all in MDC red. It was a stirring sight as the enormous crowd crossed the parkland, and even more emerged from the abandoned buildings. For sure, many more than a thousand; a sea of red. They closed on the complex: quiet and peaceful as was their way, some holding banners demanding justice for those wrongly accused. Not only Cathy Shoko and Rufaro Banya, but justice for all those imprisoned on confessions gained from beatings, torture and rapes. The demonstrators spread out to surround the building, and as Michael hoped, security staff went outside to deal with the situation. He gestured to Mitchell Gonda, Albert Nyathi, and Albert's friend Obert Ayanda, all armed like he, and they crossed through the crowd of demonstrators to the timber and glass rear door. They paused and pulled on their balaclavas, before Albert used a tyre iron to wedge the door around its lock and break it free from the frame. They went into the courthouse which was eerily quiet. Doors were flung open one after the other, until they reached courtroom two which was packed. It was identical to courtroom one of the previous day except for the two prisoners at the dock: Cathy in a white blouse and black trousers alongside Rufaro Banya wearing white with a black skirt, guarded by a policeman more or less standing to attention. Barbara Tembo talked while the stern-looking magistrate from

Tuesday frowned at her. His body language wasn't good, not that it mattered.

Suddenly an ear-splitting explosion as Albert Nyathi fired his pistol into the air. Barbara Tembo's mouth fell open when she looked at the intruders and probably recognised Michael. The policeman fumbled for his gun, but Albert ran across the courtroom with his pistol aimed.

"You're outnumbered," he said calmly.

The policeman looked towards Michael, Mitchell and Obert, and back to Albert.

"Give me your gun and put out your hands," Albert ordered.

The policeman did, and Albert bound his wrists with an electrical tie pulled tight. While that was happening, Michael advanced on Magistrate Kumbula with his Glock aimed like he'd seen in movies and on television.

"What do you mean by this?" Magistrate Kumbula calmly asked in his deep and sonorous voice.

"Quiet!" Michael bellowed, "I've seen enough of Zimbabwean justice, and now it's time for justice of my own!" Michael strode along the aisle between the two banks of seats, still pointing his gun at Magistrate Kumbula. "If anyone in this room moves or even breathes, they get it from my friends!"

"You!" Michael shouted at Kumbula. "Open the door." The magistrate turned towards the door on his right.

"The other one!" The magistrate stepped from the platform and went to the timber door behind the dock, opened it, and stood to one side. "No," Michael said. "You lead the way."

"Lead the way where?"

"Along the corridor and outside."

"I must protest."

Michael pressed the cold, hard barrel of his gun against Magistrate Kumbula's forehead. "Lead the way outside," he said in a steady voice.

Kumbula eased himself towards the doorway. Michael turned to the Cathy and Rufaro. "Follow him," he said.

They filed out of the dock, through the doorway and into the concrete-lined corridor. Michael and Mitchell Gonda trailed, leaving Albert and Obert to cover from the rear, and prevent anyone from using their mobiles or leaving the courtroom. They went to the dark grey steel door where Michael grabbed the lock and tried to turn it, but nothing happened! Fuck! The door was deadlocked. Michael paused and there was another way. He back-tracked to the nearest door and eased it open to a semi-darkened courtroom, illuminated by light spilling past a part-open door to the main corridor.

"Through there," Michael growled to Kumbula, and followed him through the room. "Stop!" Michael said before easing the door to the corridor a few more centimetres and peering past the gap. Nobody around, so all was good. "Follow me."

Michael led the way to the broken back door while expecting to be stopped or at least to hear a shout, but heard nothing except for the rumble of the demonstration. He removed his balaclava and tossed it aside, as did Mitchell Gonda.

"You lead the way," Michael said to Kumbula.

Kumbula went outside to the chaos of demonstrators surrounding the building. The dusty field was in a state of anarchy, with three security guards and a few police totally overwhelmed. The girls followed Kumbula, with Michael and Mitchell bringing up the rear.

"Over there; that white car," Michael ordered.

Magistrate Kumbula headed into the crowd while Mitchell Gonda fell in beside Michael.

"We did it," he said.

"So far," Michael replied.

"Stop! Who are you?" a voice shouted.

The group stopped. Michael looked all about, and then he spotted a policeman holding a truncheon while he approached through the crowd. "Who are you?" the policeman shouted.

Michael grabbed Kumbula and poked the barrel of the gun at the back of his hostage's head. "Stop right there!"

Michael shouted, and the policeman did. "Let us go and he'll be safe."

Michael shoved Kumbula, who stumbled before regaining his stride.

"Michael, no!" Mitchell Gonda yelled; Michael looked up and the policeman was closing while tugging at his holster. In a flash, Gonda raced through the demonstration and smashed into the policeman at full speed, with the two men hitting the ground hard. They wrestled in the dirt with Gonda grabbing for the policeman's gun but unable to get it free. Michael raced to them and dropped to his knees, and used the barrel of his Glock to hit the policeman as hard as he could. Gonda kept wrestling but the policeman showed no response.

"Stop Mitchell," Michael said.

Gonda stopped his struggle. "He is unconscious," he said.

"No, but he's dazed. Let's go before he recovers."

Magistrate Kumbula had fled, taking advantage of the distraction, probably getting help. "Go to the car over there," Michael ordered. The girls ran as best they could, Banya struggling in her heels, with Michael and Mitchell Gonda following. At any moment Michael expected more shouts or worse, but the demonstration was holding everyone's interest. Michael looked over his shoulder at the magistrate's court well and truly surrounded. They reached the cars parked in

Rotten Row with Alison Matutu behind the wheel of the Peugeot, but she climbed out.

"Where's Dube, sorry, Gorova?" Michael asked her.

"He decided not to leave," Alison said. "He wishes to continue the struggle."

"I will stay too," Rufaro Banya said.

"Are you sure?" Michael asked.

"It will be dangerous, but there is always danger in supporting the MDC."

"That'll be too dangerous," Michael said.

"We will look after her," Matutu said. "But you two must go."

Michael looked to Cathy who he half-expected to stay as well.

"Mrs Shoko is doing great things for us in Geneva," Alison said. "And now it's time for her to continue her good work."

"Cathy?" Michael asked.

She looked strange.

"You must go, Mrs Shoko," Alison said. "You will do more good in your job than anything you can do here."

"And your baby…," Rufaro said.

"Yes, of course," Cathy mumbled.

Michael climbed into the white Nissan while Cathy went to the passenger side. She stopped and looked over the roof of the car. "That man, Mandipaka, he got away with it.

Torture, rape, murder and now kidnapping. There's no justice in my country."

"Maybe one day."

She got into the car. "If we ever live long enough to see it."

Michael started the engine.

"Where are we going?" Cathy asked.

"Gaborone in Botswana."

She nodded, and Michael indicated to pull away from the kerb. He headed along the street while in the distance, at the front of the courthouse, the army had arrived with tear gas, water cannon and rubber bullets. In the mirror he saw one man and two women climbing into a faded green Peugeot. He wondered if he would ever see them again.

Epilogue

The first blow to the Zimbabwean economy came in 1991 with the end of apartheid in South Africa. Until then, sanctions against South Africa meant that many multi-national corporations located their southern African regional head offices in Harare. After sanctions were lifted, many corporations moved to the larger and more prosperous city of Johannesburg in South Africa. By the late 1990s, Zimbabwean soldiers were fighting 'rebels' in the Democratic Republic of Congo, and in return, Congo president Laurent Kabila gave timber and diamonds to senior members of Zanu-PF. To pay for this war, Zanu resorted to printing money, which fuelled hyperinflation. The GDP of Zimbabwe shrank by more than 50%, shortages became an everyday part of life, poverty became endemic, unemployment skyrocketed, and many left the country.

Trade union leader Morgan Tsvangirai was originally a supporter of Zanu-PF, but by 1999 he was despairing of the economic collapse of his country. He formed a new political party: The Movement for Democratic Change (MDC). He was arrested a number of times where he was tortured and beaten, but he was too well-known to be made to disappear. In 2005 the MDC split into two factions, with the larger faction ruled by Morgan Tsvangirai and a smaller faction ruled by Albert Mutambara. At the 2008 Presidential and

Parliamentary elections, the two factions of the MDC won a large minority of seats, while Tsvangirai forced the presidential election to a run-off, even though the MDC were convinced he had won an absolute majority. Tsvangirai was further harassed, and amidst terrible political violence he withdrew from the presidential election.

In 2008 the Southern African Development Community appointed South African President, Thabo Mbeki, to arrange power-sharing between Tsvangirai, Mutambara and Mugabe. It was supposed to be a unity government with Mugabe remaining as president, while Tsvangirai became prime minister with Mutambara as his deputy. However, Zanu-PF held a majority in parliament backed by Mugabe as president, and they continued to act unilaterally. Land seizures, which had already destroyed the economy of Zimbabwe, continued, despite protests by Tsvangirai.

This power sharing agreement came to an end at the 2013 elections where Tsvangirai once again ran against Mugabe for the office of president. Amidst allegations of electoral fraud, Mugabe was returned as president while Zanu-PF increased their majority in parliament. A motion supported by Zanu-PF to amend the constitution to abolish the office of prime minister was passed.

In 2009, foreign currency transactions were allowed within the domestic economy of Zimbabwe, which meant the

US dollar, the South African Rand and even the Chinese Yaun, took over from the Zimbabwean dollar. This simple change brought an end to hyperinflation. By that stage much of the population was living in poverty and there were few jobs. GDP began to grow slowly, but this economic growth has been insufficient to improve the standard of living, which remains at 80% of the population living below the poverty line, and 95% unemployment; the highest in the world. The economy now runs on money sent by Zimbabweans working overseas to their relatives still living in Zimbabwe. These Zimbabweans are usually illegal immigrants and are often exploited. Prior to forced land seizures by so-called 'war veterans', Zimbabwe was an exporter of beef and tobacco in particular. Now, much Zimbabwean farmland is unproductive, and the country can't produce sufficient food for domestic consumption. The Zimbabwean government owes much debt, but there are insufficient export earnings to pay these debts when they fall due.

The USA, European Union, Australia and a number of other OECD nations have imposed travel and financial sanctions against individuals involved with the situation in Zimbabwe, including Robert Mugabe and Grace Mugabe. A number of other nations, particularly China, have taken advantage of the vacuum this has created.